BENEATH THE VEIL

BENEATH THE VEIL
Copyright © 2021 by Martin Kearns
All rights reserved.

ISBN-13: 978-1-7373996-1-2
Library of Congress Control Number: 2021917963
First Paperback Edition

Cover art by Maurice Mosqua
Logo design by Amanda Baker
Edited by Angela Traficante & Erin Al-Mehairi
Cover & interior design by Dullington Design Co.

Martin Kearns
New York, USA
www.readkearns.com

BENEATH THE VEIL

BOOK ONE: THE VALOR OF VALHALLA

MARTIN KEARNS

NEW YORK, USA

Dedicated to my wife Kimberly, the light of my world, and my two sons Daniel and Charles, without whom the spirit of this story would have been lost.

Fallen Cherub, to be weak is miserable
Doing or suffering: but of this be sure,
To do ought good never will be our task

— PARADISE LOST, BOOK I

Beneath the Veil

PART ONE

THE VALKYRIE

CHAPTER ONE
CROSSING THE SPAN

David lurched awake to find icy tendrils groping his legs. Water crept in through the closed doors of his sedan and the eerie sensation pulled his mind from a fog. Time moved slowly for the young man as he gained his bearings and the moment of solace allowed him space to appreciate the beauty of the river water at night before his thoughts came into focus and panic pushed away all but his baser instincts for survival.

His hand crept to the center console for his cell phone, only to find it soaked through to the circuits. Not the first casualty of the seasonably cold water, either, he'd bet. David's rapid heartbeat reverberated in his ears as the weight of the engine pulled the front end of his sedan down further into the depths. As the water left any pretense of cordiality behind and began to maraud around him, he reached for the door handle and found it stuck.

I can get through that, David thought, sizing up the window. Pulling his knees up to the wheel in an awkward motion, he propped his feet on the seat and thanked his mother for his skinny ass as he pushed himself into the frigid liquid.

David strained and arched his back as he contorted through the window to freedom. The water beneath should have been black as the night outside of a well-lit window, but instead, the horrors normally hidden by the veiled depths were illuminated by headlights. Scores of cars were in the water. The whole damned section of bridge he'd been on, every soul that had been around him, was sinking to the riverbed.

His young legs managed to kick him free of the car, but he had already been pulled down to a depth of thirty feet or more. Pressure compressed his inner ears to an ache as he swam toward the kind light of a waxing moon.

A dark outline nearby in the abyss stole David's attention. It was a hatchback. It was *the* hatchback. A memory returned to David. *A cigarette jettisoned from ahead and erupted into an elegant ballet of carcinogens, jarring him from a daze. Light beaconed off from a reflective green sign reading Bridge 1 Mile.*

Excitable waving coming from the backseat of a baby-blue hatchback caught David's eye, and he waved back to the reward of a mischievous grin reserved for young boys lost in adventure, however small.

Some time passed as he sat in queue, and David was happy to see the crossover was again beside him. The boy had black hair contrasted by spectral ivory skin. As he flared his nose, his top lip curled to transform him into a little glowing goblin. David flipped his eyelids back and touched his tongue to the tip of his nose in reply.

Slides of memories turned to times when he'd enjoyed playing with little cousins at the smattering of gatherings his family had had over the years. He'd take the role of some load-bearing beast as various tikes took turns using his lumbar as a trampoline. His love, Rose, would watch on with her wry smile, and his mother would tell him to stay young forever. He wished he could. He was thinking all of this, lost in a cloud of pleasant memory, when the bridge let out its first groan.

Conscious thought played no role in acting to save the kid. The boy might not be alive, but David was destined to try. He swam to the right of where his car had been swallowed by the inky depths and reached the hatchback, trying the door closest to the unconscious boy. Luck had flashed its brilliance once already in allowing David to free himself, but it was absent here. The door was jammed.

Time was not on David's side. Even for a guy who had never smoked and ran as often as he could, he still needed air. His view of the boy was blocked by the hatchback as the car sank deeper. *The hatch!* David swam to the rear door, pulled on the handle, and the door yawned open. A push helped it along, and he squeezed his torso inside. The boy's arms floated above his head in an unnerving imitation of an unstrung puppet.

David wrapped his arms under the boy's and used his knees for leverage as he pulled the kid in close. He felt some resistance, then a sudden lurch, and they were free from the tether.

He was thankful to see the escape hadn't caused them to sink much further, and he used the roof to propel himself and his precious cargo to the surface.

His fevered lungs ached, but he resisted the urge to empty spent oxygen in anticipation of fresh air. Eyes pressed tightly together, he pulled the kid close to his chest to reduce drag and kicked. Lights danced against the backs of his eyelids, beckoning him to explore their nature. They were bright, yet soft. Unlike anything he had ever seen before. He thought he knew their purpose as they attempted to steal him away to a place where lungs didn't burn. Where the horrors of being crushed by crags of metal weren't a factor. Where little boys weren't separated from their families by cruel twists of fate.

David looked at the lights as though with wide-open eyes. He bore them no ill will, these jesters ushering him to the unconscious void, but he made his intentions known to them somehow.

I'm not ready.

The surface of the river fragmented into shards of moonlight, and David inhaled a lungful of air rivaling the first he'd taken entering this world. The wind stung as his chest billowed the sputtering flame within him.

He leaned back to pull the kid atop his own chest after the primal urge to fill his cells with oxygen had ceased and began to administer

CPR, by pulling in and up on the small diaphragm. *Kind of like a modified Heimlich*, he thought. Fingers danced about and explored for a moment as he adjusted his grip on the boy and hoisted him until his arms were around the small ribcage. He was gentle at first, careful to avoid causing more harm than preventing, but David had no luck. The piston motion was awkward, and David felt how absurd his actions were with no leverage; he began to compress the small ribs to the breaking point.

The boy gasped as his head listed forward and to the side allowing him to expel river water. David wished he could aid him, but keeping them afloat was all he could manage. The boy's raspy breaths pervaded the evening as the sounds of chaos at the bridge slowly ceased.

Ω

Two hundred feet above the murky surface of the Hudson River, an ethereal presence stirred. Asmodeus flexed against the cool night atop his perch on the bridge's cantilever. Beside him, little Nirah slithered between steel columns. The serpent stared unblinking at the witless victims who moved below as Asmodeus thought over his clear directive. *The boy must die.* Though, the act of focusing on one soul lacked something he craved.

"You will draw eyes by extinguishing so many," Nirah said.

"I hadn't considered that you might deliver an opinion." Ruinous eyes drifted to the serpent. "Do you have any more insights?" Asmodeus asked.

Nirah moved away and said, "I fear the focus of light will fall upon us."

"Your fears are those of a bottom dweller. They tether you to the menial, little worm, and there at the bottom you will stay," Asmodeus said. He removed his hand from the column to reveal a clawed impression. "I won't let fear cast me down beside you."

Nirah stared at his cohort and said nothing. Glass eyes at one with the night lent no notion of the small demon's thoughts, though Asmodeus knew he would balk to their mother. A forked tongue flicked to the passing seconds, and Asmodeus looked toward the ordeal he'd set in motion. In truth, he wished to expand the devastation preordained by the Jacob's Ladder of circumstances leading to this night. Misery, pain, sorrow-all were sweet nectar to be savored by the centuries-old entity.

"You're sure the boy is among them?" Nirah asked.

The presence of the boy felt close. A newly familiar sensation he had felt few and far between over his long existence had ground its way through Asmodeus's bravado as the boy approached. He had abhorred vulnerability since the days of Solomon, yet as of late, he and Lilith had chosen to dwell where this feeling was ever present. She had told him it radiated from the presence of a variable in the world which must not persist. This boy, one who reeked of divinity and filthy fire bearing the weight of ideals and edicts.

"He is there," Asmodeus said.

The people below had grasped something was amiss shortly before the center span fell from the bridge. The taste of their fear was sour, not yet ripe, so unlike lambs catching the scent of a wolf, they looked incredulous of the danger before them. Humankind, made soft and supple by their lack of perception. *I will make them know fear tonight*, Asmodeus thought. Excitement surged within the warden of lust before becoming tempered by a sudden assault on his senses.

Nirah reacted first by throwing his small wings out to catch the night air and fled without uttering a word. Asmodeus kept his eyes on the horizon. Something was racing toward the span. Something too fast to be ignored. Something burning bright and hot.

The internal switch from predator to prey flipped, and he followed Nirah toward the succor of the forests, glancing longingly behind him as he went before being swallowed by the opaque night. The sound of Nirah being torn apart soon pierced the calm, but it too was consumed by the notes of boundless sorrow broadcast by the victims on the Hudson.

Ω

The current carried David and the boy downriver from the bridge. He saw emergency lights where the toll booths were situated on the east side of the span and wondered how long he and the boy had been in the water. Five minutes? Thirty?

"What's your name?" David asked.

"Timmy," the boy said, "but I like Tim too."

David noted the quick response which was a good sign.

Tim was looking to the bridge. "It looks like Christmas lights."

David said, "Oh yeah? Now that you mention it, it does." He spoke in measured doses, struggling with their weight.

"They look far. We've gone away so far," said Tim, his voice becoming smaller and more distant with each utterance.

David tugged Tim in closer. "Don't worry, they're not too far away to find us. We just have to make it to shore." David wished he was as sure as he tried to sound.

"My mom and dad—" Tim said.

"I'm sorry. I didn't have time to get you all. I didn't see your parents. They may have made it out of the car." David was never a good liar and Timmy demonstrated his opinion of David's feigned optimism with an elongated silence.

David's legs fought the water, and they drifted on down the river amidst glints of refracted light.

"Are we going to die?" Tim asked.

"Well," David said, "I think it'd be a pretty cruel joke to have us get this far and then not make it. Plus, I don't think I want to die just yet. I haven't even eaten dinner."

Tim stifled a small laugh. "What's your name?"

"David," he said, "Nice to meet you." He reached down to feel at the leg that had to be broken. "Does that hurt?" David asked.

"Just feels numb, but if I try to bend it, something doesn't work right," Tim said. "It's like up is down and left is right. Hard to explain."

David worried over the leg, but he worried more about the boy's shivering and speech. Tim had begun to slur. "Hey, what's your favorite subject in school?" he asked. *If I can keep this kid speaking, I can keep him awake.*

"I don't really like school. I like reading though."

"Oh yeah? Me too. What do you read?" David asked.

"I like *The Boxcar Children*, but my favorite book is *Where the Red Fern Grows*," Tim said.

David smiled. "I like that one too. My girlfriend really loves it even though she cries every time she reads it. She named her hamsters after Old Dan and Little Ann when she was a kid."

"The dogs are the best part, because they love the boy and want to stay together forever," Tim said. "I always thought it would be nice to have a friend stay forever." Tim heaved a sigh. "My parents won't let me get a dog."

David thought he could use a forever friend or two to help him out right about now. Numb to the bones, his legs labored beneath jeans of lead. He looked over his shoulder; the shore seemed miles away.

"Are we getting closer?" Tim asked.

"Almost there. You hang on, okay? We'll be wrapped in warm blankets and sipping cocoa in a few minutes," he said, rubbing the side of Tim's head.

"You have to leave me. You won't make it," Tim said.

David gave him a little squeeze. "You think I'd risk drowning to get you, and then just leave you here afterward? That's not a great return on investment, kiddo."

The pauses between words and phrases grew loud with silence. Tim was right. If a boat didn't come upon them soon, they'd be found somewhere down by Rye in the morning. He could have made it alone, sure, but David knew himself. Abandoning the kid would have cleaved from him a portion of his humanity his subconscious refused to lose. He might have survived this ordeal, but he wouldn't be able to live another day as the person he was before.

"You seem pretty interested in those stars, Tim. Do you know a lot about them?" David asked.

"I like how pretty they are up there," he said. "They always seem brighter when the leaves are changing color."

David risked lifting his arm to point at the sky. "You see the one that looks like a warped Q-tip? That's Aquarius." He outlined the stars with his finger as best he could for the kid.

"I like it. It's big," Tim said. His teeth chattered. "I see some more near it too. Are they constellations?" The word sounded more like "consolations."

"There are some more near it, sure," David said. "There's Cetus there, and Pisces, and that one is Eridanus."

"I wish I knew their names," Tim whispered. His thin voice was stolen by the cold night air. "How do you know so much about them?"

"My mom is a pretty big enthusiast. She used to take out a blanket and we'd lay in the yard together. She'd point them out to me while we were looking for shooting stars," David said. "Eridanus is a river. So it's like we're looking up at a river while we are floating in one."

The thinness of his own voice escaped his notice. They watched the stars as they drifted, bodies intertwined but fates diverging. The stars stood vigil from above as David eventually stopped kicking. Time moved forward, and the winks of light, many older than the earth itself, blurred and scattered.

CHAPTER TWO
THE VEILED WORLD

Light poured onto Chelsea as she pushed through the glass doors of the Jericho Hospital emergency room. She was overcome with bustling nurses and orderlies in scrubs whose pajama-like attire seemed at odds with their feverish pace. Well-occupied by citizens as well as hospital staff, the lobby was a scene of organized mayhem. People actively paced and discussed matters with staff. One section denser with the concerned showcased a woman who appeared to be fairly upset with what she was hearing if arm waving and yelling were any indication.

The controlled chaos was a muted charade to Chelsea as she trod over the ornate tile floor. "Excuse me," she said to an unencumbered hospital employee. "I received a call about an accident. I'm here looking for my son."

"One moment, miss," responded the middle-aged woman. "We are a little overwhelmed. If you're here about someone involved in the bridge collapse, please see the man at the end of the counter."

Chelsea followed the woman's gesture and saw she was being

directed to the man on the receiving end of the hostile hand gestures and incredulous expressions she'd noticed when she arrived. "A bridge collapse—" Chelsea said. "What happened?"

The woman's expression softened. "The eastern span of the Newburgh-Beacon Bridge collapsed at about eight o'clock. There have been many casualties, and the injured are being taken here and over to Hudson Valley Hospital Center. Nobody knows the cause yet, but the police haven't ruled out terrorism. It's insane, I know. I wish they'd tell people what is actually happening," she said. Chelsea's expression reminded the receptionist who she was venting to. "Let me check your name and see if it's related."

Chelsea stood motionless as she gave her information. *A bridge collapse?* She didn't much care for the news, especially the nightly news—drab and bleak stories at the center of local news broadcasts were not how she enjoyed spending her evenings. Even if she needed background noise while she worked, Chelsea usually preferred to play a podcast or music instead of panic-inducing rhetoric. She simply had no way of knowing about the bridge collapse. The gravity of the statement crept into one part of her mind as another desperately tried to assure her that this was impossible.

"Ms. Dolan, you will have to see the gentleman at the end of the counter. I can give you no further information. I'm sorry," said the receptionist, after reading her monitor and leaving Chelsea to deduce that the news was bad.

I'm sorry. This is what beleaguered and underpaid professionals say to the widowed wives of war veterans or grieving mothers of motionless children on sonogram machines. *I'm sorry...*

"Can you please tell me if David is alive?" Chelsea asked. The employee's eyes did not waver, her lips pursed, but she nodded slowly as she pointed to the man at the end of the counter. A mercy. Chelsea could only thank her with a small nod. She left the poor woman to gather her mettle for the next confused person inquiring after a loved one.

The atmosphere was heavier just twenty feet away. A gentleman standing amidst an anxious crowd attempted to answer questions and seemed to be more responsive than the front desk employee. Maybe he was even trained for this—majored in reassurance with a minor in doublespeak. Armored in a charcoal fitted suit and a flat-blue tie just wrinkled enough to indicate he'd probably worked all day and was called upon for extra innings, he fielded questions and patted shoulders.

Chelsea waited for an opening to form and slid to the front of the pack. "Hello, my name is Chelsea Dolan, and I received a call saying my son was involved in an accident. I was told to come here by the front desk."

The man paused, and his eyes briefly flashed recognition. "Dolan? You are the mother of David Dolan?"

"Yes," Chelsea breathed.

"My name is Patrick Barge, ma'am," he said. "Please call me Pat. I am part of the hospital's public relations department."

Nailed it, Chelsea thought.

"Your son is here with us. His doctors would like to speak with you as soon as possible. Will you please come with me?" he asked.

Once again, Chelsea felt as though she was in a dream. Escorted through hallways flooded by fluorescence and adorned with surrealist art in cheap frames, she might as well have been floating three miles above the hospital. Labyrinthine hallways turned her left and left and right and straight and then through metallic elevator doors to be whisked up to the seventh floor. Chelsea peppered Pat with questions, but he must have practiced withholding information with more diligence than the front desk employee because he didn't leak a detail worth a damn to her.

When they arrived at the terminal double doors, he buzzed in and led her to a small side room with a couch, two leather chairs, and a meager assortment of peace lilies. Chelsea took a seat on the large couch, seemingly designed to make her feel insignificant. She looked at Pat and willed him to speak.

"Ms. Dolan, your son's situation, as far as we know, is that he was found unconscious on the eastern bank of the Hudson River," Pat began. "Specifically, he was found north of the span of bridge that collapsed this evening. The extent of his injuries is unknown to me at this time, but I have been informed he is not currently in a life-threatening situation."

Chelsea exhaled for the first time in what felt like years. "And the doctor will explain his injuries to me?"

"Yes," Pat said, "but I believe representatives from law enforcement will wish to speak with you as well. The location where your son was found is unusual. They haven't disclosed much information to me directly, however I do know they are confused about how your son ended up north of the span of the bridge."

Chelsea ruminated on this for a moment. It was very strange that David would wash ashore north of the bridge when the river flowed south toward New York City and the Atlantic Ocean. "Who saw David on the shore?" she asked.

Leather groaned as Pat crossed his legs and shifted his weight to the side of his chair. "Many people took part in the rescue effort after the bridge collapsed. I am not sure if your son was found by authorities or civilians, Ms. Dolan. Unfortunately, when the Department of Homeland Security becomes involved, full disclosure tends to stop."

A triple rap vibrated on the door, and a slender woman in a white coat and glasses entered.

"Hello, I'm Dr. Sall." Wasting no time as Chelsea and Patrick greeted her, Dr. Sall took up residence in the remaining armchair. She placed her hands on her knees and turned toward Chelsea. "Have you caught Mrs. Dolan up on the details, Patrick?"

"Yes, up to the site where David was found," Barge said.

"Very good. Mrs. Dolan, as you've been told, David was found on the shores north of Beacon and is believed to have washed up there about two hours ago." Dr. Sall rustled her notes. "That was approximately eleven o'clock. Paramedics responded immediately and found him to be breathing but unresponsive. David did not have a lowered body temperature despite being in water cold enough to cause hypothermia and he did not show many signs of physical trauma except a small laceration on the back of his head." Sall looked up from her notes and made eye contact with the mother of her patient.

"Mrs. Dolan, David's condition is difficult for us to understand. He is in a coma—"

"A coma?" Chelsea asked.

"Yes. It may have been brought on by the trauma at the back of David's head. We are putting him through a battery of tests to see if an MRI shows swelling in David's brain, but as of now, we have no reason to believe swelling exists. Although there is an absence of hypothermia, the comatose state will keep David in the ICU for now."

Pat's cell phone began to vibrate, and he quickly excused himself to take the call. Chelsea tried to make sense of what was happening as she stared at the white lilies, unable to discern what was off about them before discovering they were plastic.

"Mrs. Dolan—" Dr. Sall began.

"It's Miss," Chelsea interjected. "I'm a single parent, and David is my only son. I don't know what to do with all of this. I don't know what to do if he is hurt." Chelsea had not been able to speak her mind for the entire time she had been inside the hospital, having been whisked around since she entered the building like some bemused tourist. *How could I not have noticed hours had gone by since he called me and said he was a half hour away?* This was a thought that berated her as she traveled to the hospital. She felt the guilt waver after having spoken her feelings to Dr. Sall. She could grasp the situation more now than before, as though she could wrap her hands around a small part of it and feel out its nature.

"Ms. Dolan, I'll be frank with you," Dr. Sall said as she glanced at the door where the public relations rep had vanished. "I have no reason to believe your son's life is in danger at this time. His vital signs are clear—strong, actually—and his only visible bodily harm is from what could have been sustained by either one of us bumping him on the head. His coma gives us some pause because we can't explain the cause as of now, but I assure you I will be attending to David very closely until the specialists arrive to see him."

Chelsea unclasped her hands and allowed more tension to release from her shoulders. The room took on a less ominous quality to her as she looked at a woman roughly her age, late forties, who said she would do all she could for her son. Chelsea believed her.

"It's just so odd to me. Today was normal, like any other day. I didn't even know David was late in coming home. Even if I had, I'd have thought he might have been trying to surprise his girlfriend by showing up where she works." Chelsea's voice caught in her throat.

If Rose had seen the news, she'd be beside herself with worry. Even if David wasn't supposed to be coming home until tomorrow night, you never could rely on that. David was spontaneous. Always had been. Rose may have even texted to warn him about taking another route home. "Can you believe the Newburgh-Beacon Bridge collapsed?" she might have said and never received word back.

"I have to make a phone call, is that okay?" Chelsea asked. As she stood, she heard hard-soled shoes beat the tile floor to the rhythm of an approach. Pat entered along with two other men.

"Chelsea, here are Officer Dodd and Officer Ramirez from the Federal Protective Service of Homeland Security. They would like to speak with you," Pat said.

Chelsea noted that she wasn't asked if she'd like to speak to the men. Officer Dodd regarded Chelsea with a large smile that matched his jovial features. The man was a colossus, especially next to Ramirez. Chelsea was glad he chose to sit in the open armchair and not crowd her couch.

The more reasonably molded Ramirez sat at the opposite end of the couch as Chelsea scooched to make room. Dark hair and long eyelashes. Her grandmother would have loved him. "Men always have the best eyelashes," Nana Dolan would say. She also had a deep distrust for authority, a trait that Chelsea had not inherited.

"Mrs. Dolan, as Mr. Barge said, Officer Ramirez and I work with a local branch of Homeland Security. Particularly, we head a unit that focuses heavily on terrorism and threats to infrastructure. I know the circumstances of tonight's tragedy were explained to you prior—"

Chelsea couldn't help but interrupt Dodd. "Yes, I know about the collapse and that my son is in a coma. What I'm not sure of is how I may be of any assistance to Homeland Security."

Dodd's smile didn't falter as he leaned his elbows onto his knees. "Well, there are some interesting details involved here. David was found upstream of the scene of the bridge collapse, Mrs. Dolan, and that's an odd circumstance. Ramirez and I have been in communication with engineers from the state and contracting companies that have worked on the bridge, and they've assured us that the bridge could not have possibly fallen due to being in a state of dilapidation. Although it's well aged, it shouldn't have fallen on its own."

Chelsea heaved a sigh. "Maybe David found his way to shore and then walked until he collapsed from his injuries."

"His hospital chart doesn't indicate any serious injuries, Mrs. Dolan," Dodd said as he glanced at Dr. Sall.

Dr. Sall nodded solemnly before correcting him on one point. "It's *Miss* Dolan."

"Exhaustion, then," Chelsea said, brushing this aside.

Dodd nodded and looked to Ramirez who was turned toward her on the couch. "What do you do for a living, Ms. Dolan?" Ramirez asked.

"I'm a professor of historiography at SUNY," Chelsea said.

"That's interesting," Ramirez chirped. "So you teach history. What are your areas of focus?"

Chelsea folded her hands and crossed her legs. "I teach a few broad courses, but the university has me on for my work with the archeology, history, and religious artifacts found in and around ancient Israel and Syria. From these finds, I, and a few others in my department, work to fill any gaps there may be within the historical record of Israel and correct any mistakes. For example, we've made corrections based on which religious settlers may have had an effect on the Israelites and their depictions of false gods and prophets within the Old Testament."

Ramirez weighed this for a moment. "This would call for you to travel to the Middle East pretty often?" he asked.

Chelsea shook her head, seeing where the conversation was going. "Not for more than fifteen years. But, if it'll help you to believe that my son and I aren't ISIS insurgents, I'll happily disclose my email communications with colleagues overseas."

"That won't be necessary," Dodd said. "Just trying to get a lay of the land here. We are aware that there aren't legions of Irish Americans signing up to join ISIS, but we have to cover some bases."

Ramirez once again picked up the prior conversation about the bridge. "When odd circumstances pop up at a crime scene or a tragedy, they tend to point to some form of foul play, so we felt compelled—"

"Were ordered," Dodd said. "Let's be honest."

"—were ordered to check you out as soon as possible," Ramirez finished. "Occam's Razor and all."

Chelsea looked to Ramirez. "Well, I'm afraid your Occam's Razor is probably going to wind up being Murphy's Law for you gentlemen."

Dodd laughed. "You're probably right. We still have to look through maintenance reports and vet all of the travelers who were on or around the bridge during the tragedy. Plus, the FBI will likely be on this if it doesn't find a quick explanation, so there's that."

Ramirez began to stand, reaching into his coat pocket for a card. "We appreciate you taking the time to speak with us, Ms. Dolan. If anything comes up that seems compelling or odd, please give us a call. We may be in touch in the future."

Ω

"She's legit," Ramirez said as the two officers entered the elevator bank.

"Sure," said Dodd, "but there's too much back story here to ignore. You remember that kid on 9/11, right?"

"The one who flew the Cessna?" Ramirez asked.

Dodd thumbed the L button into illumination and turned back to his partner. "The kid flew a Cessna 172 light aircraft into the Bank of America building to copycat the planes that hit the towers." The overhead lights flickered as the elevator descended floors. "A kid being idealistic and getting the idea in his head to blow up a bridge isn't out of the question here. It's just not what my gut is telling me on this one."

The doors slid open, and the two men briskly walked toward the lobby. "That kid, Dolan, he can't fake a coma, right?" Ramirez asked.

Dodd chanced a quizzical look at Ramirez, taking measure of him in an instant. "You know, every once in a while, I wonder if they lowered their standards for entrance into the state troopers after the eighties."

"I've heard of weird shit, man," Ramirez said. "There's people who fake their deaths by taking drugs, guys who've lifted computer chips and flash drives from government buildings by swallowing 'em, and a woman who smuggled her tiny little husband out of prison by hiding him under her dress."

Dodd stopped just after rounding the corner. "She must have been a very large woman," he said.

"She was, and she faked a limp walking in to sell the ruse to cameras and security. I'd hate to be the guard in charge of count that day," he said.

"I'd hate to be the guard who had to watch the trailer swaying during conjugal visits," Dodd shot back as he started walking again.

The two officers entered the lobby and waited by the door as Ramirez made a phone call to touch base on findings from the site of the collapse. As he spoke on the phone, Dodd did what most semi-retired detectives do—he watched people. He imagined a hospital waiting room was not dissimilar to the line at the pearly gates. There were a lot of people here who didn't really seem to know where to go or who to talk to, and they definitely didn't want much to do with one another. Maybe it was more like the line to hell.

Ramirez ended his call. "No signs of explosives on any parts of the structure still standing. Won't know much about what's underwater for a while. The divers still working on clearing cars for bodies say it could be days. They're bringing in outside help."

Dodd nodded. "Did the trooper who was monitoring the tolls get wind of anything?" Ever since the 9/11 attacks that rocked the collective conscience of the nation, cops had been stationed at the ends of bridges. They are said to be charged with protecting the scene should something nefarious occur, but they were mostly just a costly and visible way to make the general population feel better about the state of things. In reality, they were the law enforcement equivalent of only allowing three-ounce containers of liquid in a carry-on bag at the airport.

"Guy's name is Fricks. He said he didn't see anything. Made the brass proud, though. Ran out on the bridge and started traffic moving through the tolls. Got a good fifty cars off the middle of the span before the thing fell. He probably saved a hundred people, all told," Ramirez said.

Dodd nodded as he stared into the waiting area of the lobby. "There's a commendation and a fast promotion for Fricks, and piddly for us on what the hell happened last night. No way the bridge fell on its own, no explosions heard and no residue on the metal beams and columns, and this kid's lifeless body floats against the current to deposit him on the shore nearly a quarter mile north of the bridge," he said. "Full stop, the answer to most of our questions has to do with this kid. Let's go see the people who found him."

"Off we go then. It's not too far." Ramirez clucked his tongue. "Hey, there a nice set of legs in there or something? You haven't taken your eyes off that waiting room since we walked up."

Dodd snapped his attention to his partner. "No, sorry, there's just a guy in there blowing bubbles when everyone else is whistlin'. The one with the crossed legs."

Ramirez looked into the waiting room and picked up on the guy Dodd was talking about the way most people can spot something out of place in their house. A man of slight build and wearing business casual attire sat in a chair with rouge fabric. A khaki jacket was the cherry on top. He looked more like he was enjoying a day off from work on his front porch than sitting in a hospital emergency room lobby. Mister Pert and Perfect was reading a book laid upon his crossed legs, the ghost of a smile on his lips.

Ramirez couldn't place it, but the dude was odd. Eager to change the topic, he said, "Speaking of legs, that *Miss* Dolan sure wasn't ugly."

Dodd gave a wry grin as he gestured to the door. "That there is a classy woman, Ramirez. She's got looks and brains and you know what else?"

Ramirez shrugged.

"I'll just bet she's got secrets."

CHAPTER THREE
BENEATH THE VEIL

David didn't experience waking so much as he realized consciousness. His mind loosened its grip on resonant memories where he soared through prismatic shapes and wonders. Eyes open, he firmed an understanding of where he was laying. Water. He remembered water, and there was water here, but this felt different. David looked a few feet down an embankment to see glistening granite specks twinkle through lapping waves. This was not the Hudson. For one, there was no grass. David was laying on and surrounded by, firm well-shaped rock. A cave, yes. It felt like a cave, but there weren't caves like this on the banks of the Hudson. For another, the water itself was darker—a pervasive inky quality dominated its movements and gave the impression that to touch it meant to be permanently stained.

Where is the light coming from? The place should be black as night.

Turning his head to look for a fissure or opening above him didn't reveal any source. Sparkling glints drew his gaze from above to below and unwrapped the mystery of light emanating from the spots in the rock he'd thought were granite. This place was surreal. David forced himself to his feet, careful to avoid any slippery spots, and took in his full surroundings. This was indeed a cavernous space. One where a river ran through the center. The breadth of it was immense compared to David's original guess, and it became clear that he couldn't see the far bank. Water simply met darkness, and after their embrace, there was nothing.

The shore was steady and devoid of obstacles, making the decision to begin walking an easy one. More difficult, though, was the choice of which direction. From what he could see in the low light he had at his disposal, both ways seemed identical, but which would be the path to salvation?

"Flip for it," he said, reaching into his pocket for a coin. His wallet was missing, but he felt the familiar smooth surface of what he believed to be quarters against his knuckles. He raked them out. Three heavy coins revealed themselves as he checked his palms. The first was gold in color, the second black as obsidian, and the third silver. All had been inscribed with images. He traced his thumb over a wolf on the black coin. A lion and a leopard on the others. Each contradicted with a cub on one side and a mature predator on the other. The coins held David's attention for a moment as he tried to ascertain where they'd come from before his brain circled back to where he might be in the first place. The truth of his predicament remained cloaked in a similar darkness as that which covered the water.

"Left for lion and right for cub," he said. The coin spun in the air and the sound of the slap that trapped it to his wrist echoed around him. He lifted his hand to reveal the pathway dictated by chance. "Cub."

He set out walking in what he hoped was the right direction.

Ω

Rose dragged a worn rag across the table of her recently departed party of four. The clock ticked off the seconds to the end of her shift, but she didn't make a habit of checking it like some of the other servers. She liked what she did for a living, and the time passed quickly enough. Interacting with people was something she had come to cherish, even if it was in the capacity of slinging wings to patrons. She might choose to do something that required people skills for her future career if she ever got around to really thinking about that step.

For now, she was happy to wait tables at The Bone Yard, a local chicken and waffles place that took its shtick from both Hooters and The Waffle House. Tips came frequently, especially for girls in a work uniform comprised of a skimpy pair of spandex shorts and a form fitting T-shirt with the word BONE emblazoned on the front, and Rose didn't mind at all. Patrons tended to be respectful with their comments if not their gaze, and Rose knew how to keep the atmosphere light, and she charmed her way around the restaurant enough to keep herself well paid. David was secure enough to not bat an eye at this aspect of her job, a circumstance that would certainly show the jealous side of some boys. Perhaps most.

She placed a five-dollar tip in her pocket, reached into the booth to straighten the slightly askew painting of a rancher leaning on a fence, and assigned fresh silverware before returning to the kitchen. Her eyes landed on the news bulletin playing on the flat-screen TV reserved for sports events during the dinner rush.

Horror on the Hudson: Bridge Collapse Kills At Least 22...

Before her brain could process what she was reading, her phone began to vibrate in her pocket. Her ears pounded with the jackhammering of her heart as she read the name on the caller ID. Chelsea Dolan.

Ω

David walked for what could have been hours or a matter of minutes. He couldn't rightfully gauge time in the karst; there was no sun to go by. No chirping birds, no rush hour traffic horns, nor anything else. The silence was only interrupted by his shuffling footsteps and the soft sound of water. What kept David's mind occupied were the memories beginning to flood his brain. He remembered who he was, his mother, Rose... But he didn't know how he'd gotten here. One frame of his mind had him playing with his radio and then nothing. He sifted through possibilities and was left without a golden nugget of truth. The best he could guess, he was in some sort of cave off the shore of the Hudson River. Maybe he'd stopped to empty his bladder and fallen through a long-forgotten hole from when glaciers carved through the crust of this area like a chisel through soft clay.

His thoughts quickly shifted back when he noticed a difference in the light ahead. The soft glow around him emanated uncontested, but up ahead, it was being pushed aside by a more familiar glow. Fire light. David marched on for a few dozen paces and spied what looked to be a lantern sitting atop a hooked pole on a dock. He ventured nearer to the only man-made feature the cave had offered up to him, and something else struck him as odd. Situated on the dock rested a small bell the size of a basketball and darker in color than the brass fittings that affixed it to its place. His soles beat as a metronome as he stepped across the dock.

David remembered the wooden docks from the lake he summered at with his friend Aaron as a kid. Aaron's uncle would take them down to the waterside and attempt to expertly tie hooks on fishing lines as David and Aaron squished fake worms between their fingers and threw them at one another. The wood comprising the docks there had the weather-worn look that treated wood does as it cycles through four seasons over a span of many years.

The dock David stood upon now had seen no weather sealing agent. The first thought that flashed through his mind was of driftwood, but the appearance was not one of dilapidation. It looked as strong and dry as the day it had been constructed. The structure caused him unease, though. There was something off about the grain as soft light from the flame flickered across it, and David could swear the dock had its own effervescent quality which met the light from both the lantern and the rocks.

He knelt and inspected the bell. Odd symbols adorned the bottom, and there was no lever to ring it. David slid his fingers along the cool surface and a deep chime resonated throughout the cavernous space. The sound echoed off the walls and vibrated the wood beneath his feet. He worried it might shake apart beneath him before it finally retreated like a wave departing; having crashed onto shore, its only choice now was to be cast back to the great expanse of the sea.

"What the hell is happening?" David uttered as he marveled at the bell.

"There'll be no hell here, boy," a voice carried through darkness.

David had not known what to expect when he woke here. Certainly not the loud disembodied chime jarring the cavern, or a voice from out in the river. He did what he felt he needed to do in that moment to keep from losing his mind completely: He sat down to feel grounded.

Ω

Rose raced to the cab idling out front of the dingy eatery. The news still didn't feel real, as though the world, *her* world, had tilted on its axis upon hearing the phrase *unresponsive coma*. David was her first love, and he was a part of the life she had dreamed up as her future. It had broken her heart into a thousand pieces when he left for school, but she never doubted that they'd endure as a couple. They fit in a way that was alien to some, both pieces shaped in odder contours and cutouts than most but joining in a way that completely removed the seam. One piece.

The driver was one who drove with purpose. For that Rose was thankful. She wanted nothing more than to rush through the lobby and see David, but she had to go through the motions, and it took time. Whirling through the checkpoints at the direction of hospital staff, it was impossible to miss the surrounding chaos. Panic-stricken people found themselves being directed over and over in a perverse version of *Pong*. Rose's attention fell upon two men seated across from one another in lobby chairs—the waiting room for the waiting room.

One gentleman, with his back oriented to the entrance doors, was clad in acid washed jeans and a leather jacket, the salt-dried animal flesh was struggling to contain his arms and shoulders. Two vapid eyes remained at attention and deviated from the hallway leading to the elevator banks and to the other man. This gentleman was slighter in stature and dressed in casual attire with a seasonable khaki jacket. Soft-rimmed glasses hung low, giving the impression that his attention was on the novel he held open in his lap, *Temptation* by Vaclav Havel.

Rose could tell that the soft-blue eyes of Khaki Jacket weren't being guided by the spectacles, though, and he was looking squarely at his counterpart across the seating area with an expression both intense and casual. The men exuded an aura of extreme conflict that Rose could not place. Perhaps it was akin to feeling a storm approach. Rose gasped as a voice jarred her from the snapshot of potential energy before impact.

"Ma'am, take the second elevator to the seventh floor and follow the signs for ICU," said a man wearing almost as many wrinkles under his eyes as on the jacket of his suit.

Rose nodded and briskly made her way to the seventh floor. She thought of David's poor mother being there alone, waiting for her. *How was this all possible?* This morning, the world had been affixed with endless possibilities, and this night, the dice rolled to reveal snake eyes.

Rushing through the usual roadblocks along the way, she finally entered David's room and was quickly met by his mother.

"He's here, Rose, and he's alive," Chelsea said as she collapsed into Rose with a hug to both give and receive comfort.

Rose could see she had been crying. She simply uttered, "What happened to him?"

"He was on the bridge when it fell. It looks like he was clear of the car when it hit the water, or he swam out, but he took a hit to his head. He was on the shore when they found him and the police..." She paused for a moment, studying the arrangement of flowers in the picture on the wall beside them. "They don't know how he got there yet. Everyone is a bit on edge about that point, but I'll tell you about that later. For now, the doctors aren't worried that he is in mortal danger, but they can't really explain why he is in a coma either. I'm just so happy he's alive."

Rose nodded as she absorbed the information. "Can I see him now?" she asked. Chelsea turned and led her to the bed.

David lay in a hospital gown covered by a light white blanket. "He won't respond when I talk to him, but his hands are warm, and his face is so peaceful. He looks like he is taking a nap on a weekend afternoon."

Rose ran her palm down the length of his cheek before sitting and taking his hand into her own. Her emotion, boiling over minutes before, eased as his energy coursed through his hand and to her own. She studied his face for a few moments before speaking to Chelsea. "Do you remember when he brought me on tour of New York City for my birthday a few years ago?" Rose asked.

Chelsea thought for a moment and smiled. "I do. It was to see that street art stuff, right?"

Rose nodded. "Banksy. He's a kind of anonymous street art activist. His works are spread all over the world, but a lot of them are in New York. I was interested in them at the time, and this charmer knew that." Chelsea nodded as she took the adjacent chair. Rose continued, "He made a map and charted all the spots where we could see a real Banksy in the city. He planned our trip, made a schedule, everything. It was amazing. We went to Hell's Kitchen, Bowery Park, all over to the other boroughs. It was exciting, like we were searching for treasure." Tears welled and rolled down Rose's cheeks like morning dew that has outgrown its place on the leaf of a flower. "We can't lose him, Ms. Dolan."

Chelsea watched tears fall onto Rose's hand, which held David's, and she forced a smile. "He's coming back, Rose." Despite Chelsea's reassurances, Rose's tears continued to fall. "Can you imagine a man who would do something like turning your world into a fairy-tale adventure for a day not finding his way back to you?"

Ω

Two men sat in the lobby, one's eyes locking onto the other. The slighter fellow, with his back facing the way into the hospital proper, gently placed a black feather in his book and closed the cover. He leveled his gaze across the semi-ornate tile floor onto that of his leather-clad counterpart, who was no longer able to glance away. Eyes locked, and in those seconds, the friction between them rose.

Patrons in the lobby wouldn't know why, but the atmosphere became heavy, as though an electrical current was rising to a dangerous level. Flickering began in the lights, and the gentleman wearing leather finally tore his eyes from the standoff the way a mongrel dog relinquishes a ball. He made no move to leave, however. The book opened once more. An unremarkable-looking man lifted out the feather, and tension fled from the room.

The sentinels carried on.

Ω

The bow of a small boat emerged from the murk. It didn't surprise David to see the wood held the same visual quality as the boards of the dock where he sat. The boat was not wide, per se, but it did not sway at all as the man standing atop it raised his arm in salute.

"Hello, young man. You've tolled the bell, and the bell told me. Twould be proper to ask a toll be paid, but your fare has been covered for this ride, you see, so there's no bartering to be made," the ferryman said.

The boat eased forward at a steady pace, despite David being unable to identify how it was being propelled. As it drew near, the ferryman became easier to discern. David's eyes explored the curious figure, and he was confronted with an unexpected sight. Standing upright, wearing an amicable expression, was a middle-aged man clad in jeans, a brown belt, and a tucked in plaid shirt. He had a round helmet of brown hair and matching beard. David was positive he couldn't be shocked by anything at this point in his journey through wherever the hell he was. This development rearranged that idea very quickly.

The man lowered his arm and said, "I'll take you across now, unless you'd like to stay here and tend the bell. Be warned though, the bell tolls for you now but may not toll again for some time, and you won't be hitching a ride with any other. Every soul rides alone."

The man's speech did not match his features, that was certain. He spoke in a way seemingly both backward and forward. There was the nagging feeling of familiarity, and David stood and squared his shoulders.

"I guess I'll take my ride now, considering the alternative, but I've got to say I'm more than a little confused about where I am, why I'm here, and what I should do," David replied.

The man nodded. "Yes, that's common—common enough, anyway. You will find some solace in knowing answers await on the other side of the expanse, but less solace in the knowledge that I myself have few in the way of them. Now, will you step onto my boat with steady legs and ride 'cross the way the water flows, or will you go back to making my far dock your seat?"

David stood and asked, "Just out of curiosity, what would happen if I stayed on this side?"

"Some do, yes, they do. It's not a fine tale to tell, dear boy. Souls may stay and try to reach across the barrier from this world to the other of the living. To bend the barrier enough to affect small change over there isn't unheard of, but it's for naught. Torture thrives in not moving on," said the ferryman.

David's foot moved with hesitation toward the end of the dock. The ferryman nodded his approval as the dock met the boat at its bow. "Walk right on and stay true to your balance," said the ferryman. "This is not water you'll be wanting to dip in."

"Why is that?" David asked as he stepped sure-footed onto the middle of the boat, happy to find it as steady as it had looked.

"This water has an effect on most any who touch it, and to the degree to which they touch it will vary that effect, you see. Some have found great power and might from being dipped, and some have become lost altogether in the water itself. It flows deep, you see. Deeper than a fathom or two and deeper than fathom can you."

David took this in as he stared at the black surface. He saw the glowing from the rocks did not extend to beneath where the surface of the water touched.

The boat cast off without the ferryman moving to push it in the way you might use your boot to push a boat off before pointing it to sea. They turned in a similar fashion before slowly gliding away from the shore into the murk that lay ahead. Darkness embraced them, concealing the dock, but it did not crush David and the ferryman. It was held at bay by soft illumination from the wooden boat.

"What's your name?" David asked.

The ferryman smiled. "I've been given more than a few of those in my time, but I'll ask you to call me River for now. Seems fitting, since it's a river that brought you to me and on the river we're met."

"Fair enough," said David. "I'm David. David Dolan."

He reached a hand toward River out of habit, and the ferryman looked at him with an expression of wonder, appearing to David to be enshrouded in a small dollop of fear. Young skin met sandpaper as they shook, River wrapping his long fingers around David's own.

He met the boy's eyes. "That's what you call yourself... David, then?" he asked as he released the hand but retained his gaze. "I wonder if you've more than one name yourself, David." River looked on ahead of them into the endless nothingness. "David, I see you're blind down here. I can see it in how your eyes hold me like a child holds its mother. I would like to show you something. Look out ahead of you into the murk beyond us."

David did as he was instructed, more out of habit than obedience, and his eyes drank heavily from the void. "I see nothing but black out there."

"One needs to know dark to see the light," River said, and as his words hit home in David's mind's eye, he began to make out images in the murkiness beyond the boat.

David saw flashes of a bridge collapse, two figures struggling with the current in the water, the paramedics tending to the one who made it to the shoreline, a woman talking to official looking men in a small room... He saw a small figure holding the hand of another who was in a bed. The fleeting images held a thin quality, making them distinct enough so one could understand the broad concept of what they entailed, but lacking in the detail the mind weaves into context.

"Be so very light," said River. "Be a gentle whisper. Use absolutely no pressure. Be like an angel's wing."

David was transfixed by the impressions behind his eyes, like the negatives of sunlight that appear upon closed eyelids when pointed skyward at noon.

Images continued to roll forward, and David saw more. There was a powerful-looking man squatting inside what appeared to be a sandstone cavern wholly unlike the place David found himself when he woke. He saw a dark fog that was departing from another river and into the dark trees of the forest beyond. He saw a brief glimpse of warriors gathering with a cacophonous clash of violence.

Just as the amount of information flooding David's mind felt as though it would overcome his ability to process it, the volume ebbed to a slow stop. David found himself stunned and panting.

"What did you just do to me?" he asked.

"You looked through the murk for the first time, boy, and it marks the last time you will ever be called such because no *boy* has seen what you have. It takes time and wisdom to glean past the murk, and a boy's seen too little time for much wisdom to have yet come." River reached out a hand to steady David.

"I'm not alive, am I?" asked David.

"Oh, I wouldn't say that," said River. "You're more than you say or more than you know, which is to say you know yourself not. This is a truth of which I am most certain. Steady now—we've not much longer to go. Answers await on the other side."

CHAPTER FOUR
ANTIPHON

D odd and Ramirez broke off from one another before heading to see the couple who found the kid by the river. The sun was up when they pulled into the parking lot of their motel, and Dodd wanted to shower and get on a fresh set of clothes. It was too easy to end up in the same duds for days at a time when you were chasing leads, and Dodd didn't like the idea of starting his twenty-fifth hour in the same boxer briefs. He'd spent more three-day stints in the same underwear as a young detective than he'd like to admit.

The corroded handle turned his shower to scalding hot, and he washed as luxuriously as one could with a bar of soap that looked like a Chiclet in his big hands. At six foot eight and pushing two hundred and seventy, he was used to feeling like a Kodiak bear in a cage when he entered a shower stall. After the hot water was spent, he hopped out and walked through the steam into his room. The full-sized bed was still untouched and he plucked up his clothes from the floral bedspread. The bed seemed comically small to him. He would sleep diagonally on a queen bed, if they had one, but he more often than not had to push two full-sized ones together to be able to sleep without hanging his feet off the edge like a sideshow.

He dressed, ran a comb through his wet hair, and went outside to wait for Ramirez, who always took a good ten minutes longer than Dodd. Work wife stuff. You get to know each other's idiosyncrasies after a while when you're partners. Even before they both landed their Homeland Security designations, which really was a fancy payout for upping your jurisdiction without the necessity of becoming a full-on Fed, he and Ramirez orbited similar areas as detectives.

Ramirez was about a decade younger than he was, but Dodd appreciated the way he looked at things from a slicker angle. Dodd tended to do things by sweeping cards from the deck over time and trimming enough fat so the truth couldn't help but be caught with its ass out in the open. Ramirez liked to find the shortcuts and latch onto a collar faster. Even though both men had worked in different precincts, they were both New York, and talent has a way of growing a mouth and wings. Word gets around when there's a cop who sees past smoke screens, and both Ramirez and Dodd had had that kind of reputation. The two being paired up for the past few years was more than dumb luck, too. With their superiors calculating they could catch better headlines having two older bloodhounds tracking down domestics together, their partnership was all but foretold.

Ramirez sauntered out of the hotel room with his usual swagger and gave a few familiar hunger tells which led Dodd to say, "We can eat breakfast after we talk to the witnesses." Ramirez pouted. "You're not going to buy all of the pancakes at Denny's and get sluggish on me."

Ramirez blinked wildly in feigned shock. "How can a man be expected to bring his A game to the table on an empty stomach?"

"You'll manage," Dodd said in his de facto no bullshit tone.

"C'mon, man, I hadn't even eaten yet when we got the call to come out last night," Ramirez said. "I don't have a Martha Stewart type gene for at-home cooking like you do. You were probably on your second drumstick after polishing off mashed potatoes when we were called in."

It was true in a sense. Even though the call about the bridge came in late, both men tended to have long hours and that meant later dinners. Ramirez was also right about Dodd's dinner being interrupted by the call, but he had been eating shepherd's pie at the time. It was good, too.

"After," Dodd said with understanding, yet unwavering resolve.

Ramirez sighed deeply and used the key fob in his pocket to unlock their car. Both men piled in, and they began to drive toward the river again, this time vectoring off to the right a few miles from where they'd usually turn onto the interstate to cross.

"The place is in Fishkill, just north of the bridge. The couple is older, retired. They say they were out walking their dog," Ramirez said.

"Any particular reason they gave for why he was out over the train tracks?" Dodd asked.

"Nothing in the brief about that. Apparently, the guys who questioned them didn't care about trespassing on Amtrak property. We should probably start with that," Ramirez said.

The two drove on and swung the car onto Hudson View Drive. Dodd had the luxury of being the passenger, so he surveyed the neighborhood. It was nice here, the houses kept in a way to indicate middle to high-middle income, the streets well maintained and curbed. He could see this being the ideal spot to plant roots for raising a family.

They turned onto Lamplight Road and slowed as Ramirez looked for the house numbers on the mailboxes and front doors. When they'd spotted the number twenty-one, Ramirez angled the sedan into a newly sealed driveway and the men exited. "You going to be the barber on this one, or am I?" Ramirez asked.

"You took the wheel, so I'll do the talking," Dodd said as they stepped up to the door and rang the bell.

The two men waited a few beats, listening for activity inside. "Maybe we came by too early," Ramirez ventured quietly. Then the telltale sound of nails excitedly clicking on hardwood floors came to the door, quickly followed by hushed but firm words ushering the dog back.

The door opened and a man in his late sixties wearing a pair of slacks with a tucked-in white undershirt stood before the threshold. Dodd smiled at the baby boomer generation's uniform for loafing around the house, as opposed to the mesh shorts and hoodies millennials had adopted.

"Can I help you gentlemen?" asked George Stuart, as he swung the door open a bit, revealing his foyer.

Dodd stooped a touch to appear less intimidating. "Yes, sir, we hope so. I'm Detective Brendan Dodd and this is my partner Detective Saul Ramirez, Homeland Security. We were hoping you could answer some questions for us about the boy you found out by the river last night."

"Sure, sure. I'd had a feeling I'd not left that out to dry just yet," Stuart said as he gestured the men inside.

Ramirez and Dodd said good morning to Mrs. Stuart, who delivered two mugs of weak coffee bolstered with strong sweetener. They sat at the table while Dodd pet the lab-pointer mix who was eager to be fast friends.

"Is this little beauty the reason you were out that way last night, Mr. Stuart?" Dodd asked.

"Yup, she needs a walking late at night or she gets us up as soon as the sun cracks light. We usually take a walk down Sterling Road. That's what Lamplight turns into if you keep going toward the condos there." He gestured his hand at the bay window showcasing tall condominiums peeking at them over treetops. "Bella usually doesn't pull me out farther than the pool they have there, but last night she had a bee in her bonnet about getting on down further. Took me up over the tracks for the first time in a few years."

"We were curious about you being out over the train tracks. Those trains come in fast. It's dangerous," Ramirez said, keeping the word "illegal" in his pocket.

George pushed his glasses up the bridge of his sun-marked nose. "Yeah. Meredith isn't too big a fan of that little trick. S'why we don't do it as much as we used to, but the fast ones are the Amtrack passenger trains. They stop running southbound at 'round six p.m., and the CSX freighters are the primaries from then until twelve hours later. Those, you can hear coming clearly out by the water. Especially at night." He clicked his cheek a few times to call Bella over to him so Dodd could take a break and enjoy his fast track to diabetes in a mug.

"So, you used to go over there often?" Dodd asked. "What was the allure?"

"Ah, there's a mossy little spot on the other side that runs up to the water," George said. "It's low, and the ground is soft... I mean, firm as it needs to be so you won't lose a shoe in it, but soft on the dog's feet. She likes it. She also likes to grab some of the driftwood that piles up over there and wrestle 'em around for a bit."

"Sounds nice," Ramirez said.

Dodd picked up the pace. "So, you hopped over the two sets of tracks..."

"Three sets. There's an old siding there too. Lackawanna steel, if I remember right. Real old, the good stuff. Means it'll probably hold up longer than me and maybe longer than you or him," George said, gesturing with his hand.

"Used to work for the railroad, Mr. Stuart?" Dodd asked.

"Yessir," George replied. "Spent quite a few years out there as a roadmaster, but up farther north a ways. Commute was hell, but the pay was good enough to keep us planted here."

"So, what happened after you and Bella crossed over the tracks?" Dodd asked.

"We climbed down the ballast there, then over some bigger rocks they've piled up in case of flooding. Can't under-engineer after Sandy," George said.

Dodd and Ramirez nodded knowingly. Upstate New York took a big hit from the outer bands of the hurricane.

George continued, "I took Bella off the leash to let her run around a little even though it was so late. She bolted right for the water so fast that I thought she was aiming to jump in. I hustled after her quick as these knees would let me and found her pointing at the boy... don't remember what they said his name was. Well, she was pointing at him lying on his back on the shore there."

Dodd gave it a moment before he said anything. He knew the old man was telling the truth the same way a honeybee knew the soda on top of the can is sweet, but he didn't yet know if George was giving him all the honey.

"Was there anything strange about the way the boy was lying there? Anything around him, or maybe signs of a boat landing nearby recently?" Dodd asked.

"Not a boat, no. Those leave an impression on the soft mud by the water. You can tell when kayaks come ashore 'cause they leave those shallow Vs in the mud. A fishing boat or a motorboat would have been deeper, plus a motorboat would have run the risk of getting its outboard engine caught up in the shallows or sucking up god knows what into it if it was inboard. No, I'd say the chances of there being a boat out there last night are damn near zero, but there was something—" he said as he gestured his mug to his wife. "Merry, honey, can you top me off?" Meredith, who'd been hovering by the counter cleaning up the same spot since they'd arrived, dutifully collected the percolator coffee pot and poured more caramel colored speed into George's mug. "Good, that's good. Thank you." He took a long sip. "But there was something strange out there, fellas."

Dodd relaxed his expression and glanced over to make sure Ramirez was writing in his notepad. "Strange how, Mr. Stuart?"

"Well, there was two things," George said. "The water pushes up sticks and driftwood from the river onto the bank, and when there's been a storm, the waves crash higher and bring the driftwood further up on the land. That's where most of the wood was last night, but there's been no storms recently."

"It's been a long time since you've been there. Maybe that wood was deposited a while ago," Dodd said.

George said, "Yeah, thought crossed my mind too, but for some reason it didn't feel that way. Maybe you'll see why if you go out there."

"We will definitely keep that in mind. What was the other thing you wanted to tell us?" Dodd asked.

"Oh, right." George furrowed his brow at this and took a long pull from his coffee. "We got these welds in railroading called thermites.

They're for when there's a section that needs to be replaced from cracks and whatnot. These thermite welds are hot. Real hot. Over two-thousand degrees Fahrenheit. They will burn your eyebrows off if you just get caught thinking about them too long. There's times where the vegetation starts growing up through the ballast rocks near the tracks, ya know. We are supposed to keep it down, but things grow up all the time, an' no roadmaster has all the hands he needs to keep up the rails, let alone push down vegetation. We did more than a few welds with that greenery under toe. When you have a thermite weld going on nearby, you can see how it scorches them plants and grasses. It's not so much a burn as it is a melting. That's what's out there near where Bella and me found that boy. The moss nearby looks like there was a huge thermite weld done there. Can't explain that."

Dodd took this in for a few seconds. "You've got more engineering experience than me or my partner here, Mr. Stuart. Do you think that could have been done by a drone or a helicopter of some sort?"

"Ain't no drone that could heat up like that and not melt, that's for sure, and a helo only swirls the grasses and mosses. It doesn't heat 'em. You'll see what I mean," said George. "Something out there got hotter'n hell."

Ω

Asmodeus found his way back through the hardwoods and lush undergrowth where he and his mother had been concealing themselves in the forest. Serenity held court until he descended into the ravine. The flora and fauna of the Catskills region didn't impress him. He was well traveled and timeless in mankind's perceptions, after all, but he *did* enjoy some of the same activities the humans he despised might undertake if they were inclined to listen to the darker voices in their minds. Catching and torturing the deer and small mammals in the area, for example, was not so unlike a child pulling the legs off an unfortunate insect. It was a bore, but it brought about a small degree of pleasure compared to the alternative of sitting destitute.

He was looking forward to hunting season, when more men would ignore the warnings of their ancestors and venture into the woods alone. Their squeals all the more satisfying to Asmodeus—a diminuendo compared to the rising torrents of crescendo heard when a being of such consciousness is extinguished.

"In dark woods, the right road lost. To tell about these woods— so tangled and rough and savage that thinking of it now, I feel the old fear stirring; death is hardly more bitter," Dante wrote in the first canto of the *Divine Comedy*. Many feel it's a statement relating to the fear of marching towards the twilight of one's life after middle age. A lamentation. But a being like Asmodeus would find its meaning to be taken quite literally, if such a being had the inclination to read such works.

The woods, the mountains, the sea, and the desert were where he and his thrived. These places were, after all, where the veil becomes thinnest, and the sprites poked through into circles of death's head mushrooms to invite people to dance astray until they couldn't find their way back. Where the leaves stirred for reasons unknown and all living things held their breath, listening. Where gateways to paths long forgotten barely hide themselves, awaiting those unencumbered by the distractions of modern life to chance upon them.

Through the ravine and into a small clearing traced Asmodeus, making not a sound as he progressed. Trees cleared and way was made for sunlight to caress the earthen floor ahead. Lilith awaited him atop a large boulder of granite deposited hundreds of years ago in a colder time of suffering.

She kept her face arched toward the light and asked, "Do you find your way here with good tidings? I've heard nothing from Nirah the messenger."

Asmodeus approached slowly and knelt before her. There was a time he would have laid himself prostrate before bearing news he knew would anger her, but his stature had been secured since those times, and he was less fearful of her wrath. He too was powerful.

"I did as we planned and put the boy into the water to drown. All was well until I felt a strong heat approaching and was forced to flee. I fear Nirah was consumed by their fire." Asmodeus raised his chin to show that he was not ashamed. "How one such as that knew where we were or what we were doing, I do not know, but it changes everything."

Lilith snapped herself from her leisurely pose in the sunlight. "The boy isn't dead?" she asked.

"He may be. He was all but consumed by the cold water before—"

She stomped on the embers of his logic. "No. If one capable of driving you off interfered, then the boy is alive. The nonpareils do not move without cause, Asmodeus, and cause isn't given without consideration. Eons have passed while they have debated on a course of action that would be pleasing to the creator. If one is watching the boy, then we have to revise our plans. And there's the loss of little Nirah, my sweet child... You are right, everything has changed."

He considered his next words carefully before speaking. "We are not in peril. Much has changed since we scattered before their upraised swords. We've become stronger. *I've* become stronger than all my siblings. I do not fear them."

"You have become strong from your work, and it is true that you may be able to stand before them, but that is not our goal. We must remove the boy before Azazel takes him," she said, staring into Asmodeus's black eyes. "It is not time for us to test our mettle against that of our rivals, my son, but that time draws close." She gazed through the rays of light flooding her body. Her milky skin drank none. "No. We will take a lesson from the humans and employ a tactic I've been contemplating for some time."

Asmodeus ground his nails into the palms of his hands. "What will we do?" he asked.

Lilith gently picked herself up from the rock and stood in the light. Her form was that of terrible beauty. No man, nor woman, had ever laid eyes on her and staved off the rising tide of lust she sent flowing through their hearts. Adam's first wife, the protosuccubus and mother of a vast host of demonic denizens who have ravaged the world since its transformation from molten amorphē.

She glided as a soft breeze and wrapped herself around Asmodeus as he sat transfixed. "We will release our own host from their partisan duties and allow them to walk in the light. They will disrupt this world in ways our enemies could never have predicted. We will use this to our advantage and spear opportunity when it comes up for breath." The words were a whisper in his ear.

"They will think we are at war, then?" Asmodeus asked.

"Yes, and they will be blinded to our movements as they choose their course," said Lilith, before placing her lips on his, pulling his thoughts from anything but her embrace.

They united in the grove, bathed in light from above, their union grinding dissonance within the forest.

Ω

Dodd felt the mossy ground gently reach above the wood soles of his brown leather shoes. He'd be giving a shiner some business if he didn't step carefully on this side of the tracks. Ramirez cursed and slid slowly down the granite rock ballast of the train tracks behind him. He looked out over a water-sodden expanse of green that he guessed disappeared in the wetter months of the year and revealed itself through the dryer summer weather patterns. The way it soaked in the river's moisture made him feel that the curtain was closing on its time above the surface, and it was not long to be swallowed by the Hudson once again.

"Doesn't seem very special. I wonder why the old man likes it so much," said Ramirez as he followed Dodd's progress across the soft ground, stepping clear of the craters the larger man left behind.

"No place really is when you pick apart the pieces, Saul," Dodd said. His eyes disrobed the ground before him.

Ramirez scoffed, "Ah, that cynical side of yours cropping up?"

"It isn't cynical, not really," Dodd said. "Everything boils down to the same building blocks. Our Legos and this moss's are all the same when the magnifying glass gets big enough. That's the nature of things."

"Really? You think that? I mean, I get the science behind what you're saying, but there's other factors at play. How about intent?" Ramirez shot back.

"Intent? What's that got to do with anything?" Dodd asked.

"Well," Ramirez said, "the moss is innocuous, like the Switzerland of fungus. It ain't here to hurt nobody, and it's fine with that, but those mushrooms over there see things a bit different. Their flag reads *Don't tread on me, motherfuckers*, and they don't leave scores unsettled."

"Ah, I see what you're saying. Eye for a fungi," Dodd said.

"Bet you're proud of that one, you corny old fart," Ramirez said.

"You bet," Dodd replied.

The men found their way past the driftwood that had been pushed up inland and walked to the water's edge, quickly identifying the spot George Stuart had spoken of. Dodd knelt and placed his hand on the obsidian black moss, half expecting to feel heat still trapped within. "This is not normal," he said.

Ramirez appraised the situation as professionally as he could by uttering, "What the fuck is that?"

The moss did look as though it had been melted, as George had surmised. Lush green color had defected to a thieving blackness.

"There was intense heat here," Dodd said. "Hot enough to melt this and turn the ground underneath into clay. Look." He rapped his knuckles against where the anomalous ground was, and then, pushed his fingers into the sodden soil a few feet away, releasing water two knuckles deep.

"Maybe there were explosives used here," Ramirez said. "We should get a forensics team to check and see if anything was detonated. Check for residue." He pulled his phone out and began scrolling through contacts.

"Get a rocket expert to come, if you can," Dodd said. "One of the retired demo guys, and somebody with experience using SAMs or RPGs. For the affected area to be this perfectly symmetrical, something shot heat down directly where the kid was laying. Look at his imprint there."

"Okay, I'll ask," Ramirez answered.

Dodd felt the water soaking his socks between the shoe leather and his flesh. Something had fired heat directly down into the ground here, and it had been hot enough to turn the area into a temporary kiln. The boy had been found unscathed.

The logic was becoming less and less firm and Dodd didn't like it.

Ω

Two sentinels set in repose atop dilapidated thrones heard the sound simultaneously as it thrust through the lobby.

To the larger of the two, with lupine features and clad in leather, the sound resonated deeply and rang harmoniously. His ears perked, and he cocked his head with unrestrained and outward pleasure. The slighter custodian closed his book, not bothering to mark his place with the black feather, which now slowly drifted to the floor. The sound reached his ears to quite a different result than his counterpart. It pealed through him as birdsong rang cacophony for Beethoven and to similar effect. He was filled with transient unease at the sound and its implications.

The man with lupine features stood and strode toward the inner hospital where the elevator banks were hidden away. The slighter sentinel stood and filled the vacuum of space in his path: glasses cast aside to reveal a conflagration behind his eyes, now seemingly twice the size of the visage who sat poring over a story.

His counterpart stepped a foot closer, near enough to smell the embers. Heat alone may not have made him break away from his course, for he was invigorated as he had only been on such occasions when he pursued prey under the light of the full moon. Even on those occasions, when his true predatory self was left untamed, he felt only a fraction of this fervor. But when the temporary custodian of Jericho Hospital uttered a word unintelligible to all but the most ancient of entities and a handful of scholars, the leather clad sentinel broke from his desired path and made for the exit.

The slighter man had said, "परीकृष्," which, if heard by someone who was of Indo-Iranian descent in the year 600 BC, would have sounded like, "Test me." The emissary of predation wisely chose not to but was emboldened to run through the day and the night alike and to act unencumbered by pacts and treaties long standing and long despised. The slighter sentinel knew this. However, his charge was to protect Jericho and the precious soul temporarily ensconced within it. Still seemingly larger than he'd appeared just moments before, he collected his belongings and made his way out of the lobby exit shortly after his counterpart. Nobody would take notice of him walking down the sidewalk and the next instant becoming a memory. No cab hailed, nor car entered.

Nobody save the vigilant woman at the front desk who'd helped Chelsea and Rose find their way to David. The whole occurrence was outwardly bizarre from her perspective but shouldn't have been frightening. Yet, for reasons she couldn't understand, she was covered in a cold sweat. Her breath keeping just out of grasp, she hoped to never see those men again for as long as she lived, but hope holds little sway when weighed against the hands of fate.

CHAPTER FIVE
JACOB

David and River traveled in silence for a short time. The placid nature of the water added to the unnatural miasma surrounding the boat. The feeling was reminiscent of The Old Mill ride at Playland in Rye, New York, as though they were being pulled by an unseen mechanism below the water's surface and floating on and on. The two seemed content with the company of silence until River broke the spell.

"Water's like me. Does things the easy way."

"Can you read my thoughts?" David asked.

"Not in the way you're thinking," he said, "but I can see through the murk as well as the keenest eye ever molded. It adds a touch of precognition, if you understand."

"I understand better than I would have over an hour ago, that's for sure," said David, remembering his visions through the living darkness. He moved closer to the front of the boat. "It's clearing up there."

Darkness had become so familiar to David while they were crossing the water that he hadn't imagined an end to it. Layers of opaque lifted one at a time, giving the sensation of forward movement he had not felt since they lost sight of the far dock. With it came a sudden shift in perception and a bout of vertigo that made David take a seat in the boat to let it pass.

"See how it fades right into nothing? That's just what you're looking for," River said.

David shook his head. "That's the problem. I've never seen darkness fade without light before."

"It is to be expected, David," River said. "You may have a foot in this world now, but you're not of it. An orchid raised on the sill of a window won't find feeling the desert air as easy a sufferance as its brothers and sisters who dwell within it."

"I did alright in figurative language when I was in school, Riv. You speak in a lot of metaphors, and I'm starting to think you're telling me I'm more than David Dolan of New York."

River began, "Anytime you learn, you—"

"Gain," David finished. "I heard that once on TV, when I pretended to be sick to stay home from school. I think it was channel thirteen. I've heard a few of the things you have said to me down here on that TV show with that painter guy, Bob Ross." Realization hit David's features. "You look exactly like him too. Are you Bob fucking Ross?"

River smiled so broadly it threatened to crack his face. "No, I'm not. I'm River the ferryman, taking you across the way." David gave him a look of distrust. "I take many across the way and many who come to the bell are tired and scared. A life's toils compound, and most don't enjoy their last memory of leaving because what they don't tell you is that dying is hard. And for most, dying is pain. A long time ago, I took to changing my form to match what is comforting in the traveler's mind. I can see it—"

"—through the murk," David finished.

"Yes. Through the murk," River added.

"Why didn't you take the shape of Gandhi, or Mother Theresa, or my girlfriend? Hell, you could have been Elmo if you wanted to make me feel comfortable. I barely remember Bob Ross. I mean, he was amazing on that show, but still." David sighed. "Sorry, it feels like I'm speaking about you in the third person even though I know you're not Bob Ross." David paused. "This just doesn't make sense to me."

"Much won't for some time yet," River said. "My ways are included, given that you aren't likely to be seeing me again. And if you *do* perchance come my way in the future, it means no good came to you in recent circumstance. This one parcel of confusion I can shed light on for you, though. I couldn't see far into your mind's eye. It's closed off to me in ways it never is for ordinary folk. A shutter in your mind blocked most all, but I snatched a tiny ray of light I saw coming through it." He smiled as he mimicked brush strokes in the air with his right hand. His left held an invisible paint pallet. "Happy trees, David. Happy. Little. Trees."

The outline of a shore became visible to David as he looked away from the ridiculous ferryman and past the bow of the tiny vessel. The utter similarity between this landscape and the side he'd left behind caused momentary panic until the absence of a bell atop the slowly emerging dock showed a variation. David thought he saw a figure standing off to the right. His vision was keen, but the murk had a way of making the available light waver.

Squinting, he could make out that the man was taller than average and wearing clothes that would be out of place in New York but were somehow fitting here. They were baggy, like what you might see extras wearing as they filmed a movie scene at a bazaar. The most striking feature the man held was a thick cloth covering over his eyes. He was blindfolded.

"There's he who paid your toll fee. It's not an easy fix, sending the ferry to the other side to courier the living, but he over there..." River lifted his arm and pointed across the water at the figure standing near the far dock. "He can move mountains if the ends justify the means."

"Wait, I'm supposed to be dead?" David said. "Why am I supposed to be dead?"

River sighed. "You aren't supposed to be dead, David. That's the point. I just told you—life courses through those veins, but you are where the dead pass, mistake that not." River gave David a serious look. "That man there is going to take you when we reach the dock, and you'd be wise to listen to him. I like you; you've light, and I don't see much light down here. I don't want to see you run off into the darkness and find your doom."

David tried to keep his eyes on the man he was being ushered to meet, but something about the glinting of the shores pulled his gaze away. The sparkling stopped well before the waterline over here. A survey of the dock showed the glow from the wood was also dimmer partway up the columns holding it aloft. "Why is the rock there not speckled with light?" he asked.

"The water eats the light it touches. S'why I cautioned you not to venture into it or let it splash you," River said.

"But there's no water touching those areas," David said.

"True," River said. "No water is there now, but there was a time when it kissed those peaks, though briefly. The river swells high when many souls come through at once. What you are seeing is from the river rise due to a great war in your world, probably before you were alive. Raised the water higher than it's ever been."

"The world wars," David said. "I think those are what you're talking about."

The boy sat for a few seconds to ponder this, then he turned to River and considered his next words. "I want to see the real you. Can you take off the Halloween costume?" he asked.

"Youths all wish to cast themselves from ignorance, but none ever know the burden knowledge brings," River said. "There are stories of once-untouchable titans perpetually rent and torn over this burden. Humanity is said to have been turned away from an eternity in the light over this burden, and a small child is being yoked with this burden at a funeral because she's just realized her own mortality for the very first time. You will never be able to look back. This is the nature of truth, David. Are you sure you want to see the truth?"

David nodded, never taking his eyes off River's.

"So be it," River said.

The murky cloud cloaking the boat descended upon them, but David wasn't touched as he expected. In a few moments, he relived the ethereal geometric shapes and colors he'd washed from his memory when he awoke on the shore. Windows formed in the shapes and through each he could see rivers flowing through different landscapes. There were thousands. So many that he shouldn't have been able to process the sheer amount, but he could, and he understood them as well.

He saw a river of deep sadness flowing in a space that looked similar to where he began this journey, juxtaposed next to a river flowing in Vietnam where a family was laughing and splashing. He saw a river of flames and chains flowing into the bowels of the earth, and also a river of pure forgetfulness. There was a river head of memory, and one of oblivion, a deep void of nothingness into which everything went and out of which nothing came. In this moment of pure understanding, David became disillusioned to many of the things he had once considered to be absolute.

As the windows flexed, reformed, and flew away, David's focus came back to his river and guide. He looked upon the boat, which he now knew to be propelled by lamentation, and saw the hue of light was gone. The ferryman continued to look at him, but now River wore a much deeper beard. Tendrils gnarled his face like the roots of an ancient oak, bearing age as iron wears rust, and out protruded a crooked nose akin to the likeness of a child masquerading as a witch in October. His eyes, sunken as they were, seemed like wells of wisdom colored in gray.

"A mask might have been your preference, then?" asked River, as he continued to appraise David.

"No, I prefer you like this. As you are," David said. "I've never liked being coddled."

River nodded. "Seems not, seems not. You know the Romans drew me more of a monster than a man, and Christians liken me more to death than the son of Night, but I guess the sight of me is easier to digest when things are in focus. And focused you are, David. Those young eyes have seen glimpses of where you are now. Not Kansas, nor

New York, nor any place you'd ever thought existed. But here you are. Tell me—do you now believe yourself in a dream?"

"No," David said. "For some reason, I know this is real. I can feel it is real in a way I can't explain. The longer we've been on this boat, the firmer the motion feels. It's odd, but I can also feel my mother and Rose. They are close to me somehow. I can't explain how I know. I just know it feels comforting."

"It's good you've no wool over those eyes, lad. You're not the first person ushered to me by that fellow there," said River, pointing again to the man they drew closer to on the shore, "and not the first who still draws breath. But you are the first in a long while. Even by my standards."

David straightened as they came to within fifty feet of the dock. "I know who you are now, but I don't know who he is. I still don't know why I'm here, either, but I do feel better than before. Thank you for that, Kharon."

Kharon the ferryman smiled broadly at David. "You've seen the rivers, seen through the murk, and from it you've gleaned my true name. We are well met, David, and we can part in good faith. In that spirit, I'll tell you one last thing. Those coins you have will weigh you down." Kharon reached out and patted David's pockets where the coins were nestled. "You should endeavor to lose them by any means you can. If I'm right about what I see in you, you are good, but time will tell as it always does."

David hadn't thought of the coins since he decided to walk off in the direction that took him to the dock. "I'll try," he said.

The boat smoothed to a stop as the wood from the dock kissed the bow. A moment of trepidation stayed David before he stepped off and looked back at Kharon, who had reverted again to his Bob Ross visage.

"Just let go and fall like a little waterfall," he said.

David rewarded him with one last smile and stepped off the dock, into the shadow of the man who waited for him.

Ω

Rose sat reading *The Penelopiad* at David's bedside. Days had passed since she'd first entered the hospital to meet Chelsea. Now, the petite auburn-haired girl had become a fixture in this room. The staff often doted on Rose, and it was a shift nurse who had handed her the novella. She found a reprieve from her thoughts as her eyes traced the pages, but the recurring idea of David being somehow entangled within his own odyssey would cause her to close the cover and place the story aside.

David hadn't yet shown any signs of coming out of his condition, yet the doctors showed little worry. Rose noted that there was an increased presence in the room, though the doctors' intentions felt more akin to those of Dr. Moreau than medical professionals who endeavor under the Hippocratic Oath.

The increased interest stemmed from when hospital employees began to take notice of subtle oddities in David's physique that didn't jive with the listed expectations in whatever book they took down and passed around. The support staff performed the tasks they would on any patient who was sedentary for long periods of time in order to stave off atrophy and bedsores, thus making Rose feel some comfort in David's body receiving care, but they too would comment on how David's condition was irregular.

Early flags included how David seemed heavier as they moved his limbs, and one CNA swore he had become more muscular since he'd been admitted. This was the opposite of what should have been happening, and they convinced one of the resident PAs to take BMI measurements. Sure enough, David's numbers were changing in the same way one's might if they were training for a triathlon. His body fat had plummeted. Again—not altogether abnormal as some patients may come in with a large amount, but his muscle structure was also taking on a form that became increasingly noticeable. She could have sworn stares began to linger as David's body became more akin to that of an Olympic athlete than an everyman. Rose made sure the nurses who bathed him took note of her being in the room. Vegetable or not, she had staked a claim on that body. She studied David's broader chest and shoulders with the thought of how they'd feel pressed up against her in their next embrace.

After some time caressing his hand, she stood, gently kissed David on his lips, and gathered her belongings to leave. Chelsea would be here soon to sit by David's bedside, and Rose needed to go to work.

She walked briskly past the nurse's station and heard a cheerful "see you later" from the staff. Rose thought they may have felt like the two young lovers were in some sort of Nicholas Sparks novel, their pain and lamentation being intertwined with romance in a way that had become insidious. Happily ever after didn't have to be punctuated by pain, at least Rose didn't think so. She and David were going to stay together forever; she had no more a doubt of that than she did of the sun rising in the East in the morning. If there was a price to be paid for that joy, she'd gladly wring the neck of the unfortunate soul who came to collect.

Leaving through the lobby, Rose's attention was pulled to a televised national news broadcast, a constant spew of information to stiff arm good tidings before they could break through. The story ticker read: MISSING PERSONS REPORTS SKYROCKET AS WARM WEATHER BRINGS MORE INTO WILDERNESS. The reporter, a mousy blonde backdropped by a trailhead, was speaking into a microphone and gesturing behind her as a sidebar of pictures showed three young men in mountaineering garb and flashing snow-white smiles.

Rose walked out of the lobby, hitched her duffel up on her shoulder, and trekked toward the restaurant as the rays of the sun softened and night began its gentle conquest over the sky. Twilight air held a hint of the crisp bite of winter chill to come, but the smell of fall in the evening had also roosted and it revitalized her. Winter in New York could be a tough lesson even for lifelong residents. It stretched on longer than one might ever remember, and its hold was firm. Rose took note of the absence of people who might be out walking their dogs or choosing to ride their bikes rather than drive their cars. Those were sparse, too, for the time of day when rush hour would just begin to ebb.

The solitude made her feel exposed, looking up at the swift moving clouds of an October sky as All Hallows drew closer on the calendar. She walked on, her thoughts occupied by David's situation. The detectives hadn't returned while she was in the hospital, but she knew that Detective Dodd had called on Chelsea a few times since they'd first met. The tone of the conversations, at least on Chelsea's end, seemed quite cooperative. The detective himself appeared a decent enough man from what Rose had been told by the doctor on call—and Chelsea, as well. There was an air of him chewing over a chunk of fat he couldn't quite swallow though, and Chelsea may have felt this way too, since she very easily divulged information to a man who, when you cut right to the bone, could be building a case that David was a terrorist. Rose was somewhat ambivalent toward the idea of the investigation. She wanted to know why that bridge collapsed in the first place. Forty-two was the number of souls lost to the Hudson's frigid waters that night, the story dominating the news for far too short a period of time in this age of scandal.

Rose arrived at The Bone Yard and entered the backroom to change into her outfit, thankful that the air inside was warmer than usual. She saw Victoria coming off her shift.

"Deep pockets tonight, Vic?" asked Rose as she shimmied her shorts on.

"Not a bad night," Victoria said. "There's a guy who has been here for a while, though, table started as mine, but you have to finish him off. He's devouring plates of food and probably had seven beers. Boss made me cut off the booze, but the guy switched to soda and seems even happier with that. He's a bottomless pit."

"Sounds like the kind of guy we like to see when bills need to be paid," Rose said.

"We'll split the tip, but even with that it might be the biggest of the night for both of us. I think his tab was over three hundred last I checked, and that was at least a half hour ago. He's ordered more since. The ticket'll be up soon." Victoria pulled her coat on over her uniform and lifted a battle-weary purse.

"Should be interesting. Seemed empty, so I won't complain. Is he a full boother?" Rose asked.

Vitoria shook her head. "He's not fat at all. Kinda skinny, actually. Has a face like Steve Buscemi."

Rose laughed.

"How's David?" Victoria asked, angling toward the door out of the closet they called a changing room.

"He's still out, but he's not getting worse," Rose said. "Makes me feel better to sit with him. I can't really describe it, but I think he knows I'm there for some reason. I need for him to know I'm there. I can't bear the idea that he's lost somewhere in the dark."

Victoria doubled back and wrapped her long arms around Rose. "He'll wake up, girl, and when he does, your face is going to be the first one he sees." She kissed Rose's cheek and walked toward the door. Vic always left in a rush because the daycare charged her a penalty if she was a minute late to pick up her kids. "He'll give that cute booty a grab, too," she said as she blew a kiss.

Rose laughed, waved her final goodbye, and finished dressing, checking herself in the full-length mirror. She spent a little extra time looking at her rear than she might have if Victoria hadn't said anything and walked out to the kitchen counter to sign into her shift. *ROSE: 6-CLOSE.* The dinner shift was the money-making shift, but the rush of customers seemed a little behind today. She hoped it would pick up soon. Working as a server might be one of the best ways to pass time at work, but when things were slow, the pendulum swung mercilessly in the other direction and time dragged for eons.

"Plates for table thirteen, Rose," Armand said from across the aluminum barrier. "Guy's trying to put Vic's kids through college. Easily had over fifty wings, ribs, and a good-sized T-bone steak. Keeps ordering. Don't stop him—I want to see if he explodes before he leaves." The cook winked at her before slapping the edge of his spatula against the table twice to punctuate the joke.

"Who's busing tonight? I doubt they will be eager to clean human remains off a booth," she said.

"Kid didn't show," Armand said. "Didn't answer his phone yesterday or today either. Looks like we lost him. Same thing with Perry." Meat hit the pool of hot grease and hissed.

Perry had worked at The Bone Yard for a long time. It was completely out of character for a guy who was probably next in line to be manager to pull a "no call, no show".

Rose wrinkled her nose. "Hope he's okay," she said absently as she turned and walked her zone.

There was a father with his teenage son sitting at a four top on one end and a vast wasteland of tables between him and the sole booth with an occupant. The red glow of the exit sign glinted off the green lamp shades that had replaced the jukeboxes from when this place was a diner many years ago.

Rose checked on the father-son team, being sure to give enough attention to the son to satisfy his father's need to see him make a lady smile. She could imagine the clap on the back and the "that's my boy" as they entered the parking lot after dinner.

She walked over to the booth with her hand on her hip, but the perky greeting she'd prepared caught in her throat. Armand had said over fifty wings, but he should have probably said over two hundred. There were half as many ribs stripped down to their osseous matter too, and the bone from the T-bone had been cracked, showing that the dark marrow had been stripped clean from within.

The man looked up at her through thick glasses. His face was odd, as though the skin linked to his facial structure was barely able to cling there, and his veins showed through his forearms devoid of body fat. The guy could have played Slender Man in a theatrical release movie version of the online game.

"Hi, I'm Rose. I'll be taking care of you from now on since Vic's shift ended. Can I get you a refill on your pitcher?" Rose asked, more flatly than she would have hoped.

"Yes," he said. "More. A different kind. I'd like more bread. Do you have different kinds? Bring them all. I want more of these fried onions. More fried potatoes." He shifted his eyes, unusually magnified by thick glasses, back to the last of his glass of soda and the small amount of shepherd's pie he had left. His progress as he consumed the food wasn't fast, but it was deliberate.

Rose's eyes followed a couple of flies hopping across the bones on some of the plates. She reached in to stack some. "I'm sorry about the mess, our bus boy couldn't make it ton—"

He grabbed her wrist. "Leave them," he said through a mouthful of food, releasing her arm as she pulled it back.

Rose managed to choke back a cry of surprise. "Um, sure," she said and quickly turned to walk away. The father and son duo had seen the exchange while appraising her from behind, and they'd taken note of her wrist being grabbed. The two stared daggers at the man in the booth, but he didn't seem to notice.

Rose placed the order ticket for table thirteen and Armand laughed as he mimicked a belly exploding from behind the counter, falling silent when he saw Rose's expression.

"What's wrong? Is everything okay at the hospital?" Armand asked.

"It's not that," Rose said. "That guy in thirteen. He's off, but I can't really explain it. He grabbed my arm when I tried to clear his plates."

Armand bristled. "He touches you again, you tell me. I'll roll him right out of here and double charge his card."

"Will do," Rose said and occupied herself with sorting the clean silverware before checking on her patrons again a few minutes later.

The father and son called for their check, and Rose walked to the back to the computer for the tally. She heard the buzzing of flies from the booth to her left but resisted the urge to glance over.

"Here's the check. Thanks so much for coming in," she said to the son before winking and turning heel to see to table thirteen.

The buzzing had grown to match the number of flies. They all but covered the spent remains, but none adorned the last remnants of the plate the man was working on. He was almost out of food.

"Where's the rest?" he asked through clenched teeth that dripped marinara.

"It'll be right out," she replied, not daring to ask about the flies or the plates.

"It needs to be now. I want more now. NOW!" The outburst

startled Rose enough to drive her back a few steps. Chairs scraped as the men from her other table stood.

"Hey. Take it easy, man. She's the messenger, not the cook," said the father.

The son followed up with less restraint. "You'll get your food, fat ass."

The man in booth thirteen took his bespectacled eyes from Rose and focused them on the two advancing toward him. "More," was all he said, but he muttered it in a bedraggled mania that Rose found more alarming than a shout.

"You're a little off, man," the father said. "How about calling it a night and heading home?"

Silverware clinked as the patron stood. His posture was crooked at the top of his back, and his arms were odd, like those of a praying mantis. His eyes devoured the father.

"More," table thirteen said.

Flies lifted from plates and swarmed the father en masse. The sight was stomach curdling as he desperately smacked at his face. The son, sensing the flies were somehow connected to the patron, rushed the man as Rose shouted for Armand's help.

Clicking sounds followed as two swift blows from the kid connected before he was seized by the shoulders and shaken to a quick and violent cessation.

"Stop." His speech turned to shrieks. "Let go of me!"

Rose looked on as thin fingers dug into the boy's shoulders. Blood cascaded, drawn down by the whiles of gravity.

"Stop! Stop!" Rose cried, hoping it would turn the man's attention back to his table. "Your food is coming out!"

He ignored her and studied the boy for a moment before he opened his mouth. His jaw falling impossibly low, the size of his maw swelled as teeth shifted out and around to accommodate the larger circumference. Two mandibles reached forward, out of his cheeks.

Rose watched in horror, continuing her protests. The father was too busy scraping his eyes and mouth to rid himself of the flies to yet notice. Armand had finally rounded the corner, brandishing his large flat spatula as though it were a battle axe.

The man from table thirteen's mandibled mouth descended upon the boy's head, and the sickening sounds of his skull snapping open drowned out the screams. Wet consumption followed.

The father fell, slowing his resistance to the flies, which had once again doubled in number and were clogging his airways. Rose backed away, and Armand placed himself between the young woman and the creature.

"Go to the kitchen and call the police," he said, tapping the spatula against his fist twice. "Go now."

Rose rushed through the swinging double doors and made her way to the phone. The 911 operator had just answered when she heard Armand scream, "Damn you!" The sound of furniture being overturned in the dining area followed, and she could hear the monster saying something to Armand. Rose only made out the word "Ekron."

"911, what's your emergency?"

"People are being attacked at the restaurant where I work. We need help!"

"Where are you, miss?"

"The Bone Yard on South Street. He's killing people!. We need help *now*."

"I'm dispatching the police. Does the man know where you are? Is he armed?"

"I don't know. Our cook is trying to subdue him right now, but the man is dangerous. Oh my god. He's eating people!"

"Eating people? Ma'am, you're not joking with me, are you?"

"No, he ate a teenager's head and..."

Rose sobbed. hearing the sound of the double doors swinging inward, she turned and dropped the phone.

Table thirteen was standing in the kitchen, looking at her. A deep mahogany had invaded his plaid shirt, and gore caked over his pants.

"More," he said.

Rose screamed. *This isn't real. How can this be real? A* final thought passed through her mind. *I don't want to die.*

"Miss, the police are on their way. Try to remain calm. Miss, are you there? Can you hear me?" The voice of the operator tried to assure her from miles away.

Rose backed away until spitting grease from the fryer bit through her shirt at the lower back. She hissed and sidestepped, but there wasn't an exit this way. Just the food prep window to her left.

The creature advanced toward her. His mouth had become smaller again, but mandibles still protruded from his cheeks, pushing out from beneath his fleshy disguise. Still chewing, his saucer eyes ravaged her from behind his glasses.

He rushed, looking to capture her with his long arms in the same way he'd grabbed the teenage boy.

She reacted by grabbing the first thing she could reach. The basket in the fryer lifted out and arched a spray of scalding liquid directly at the creature. He stopped to watch it soar through the air but didn't register it as a threat, and the main body of the grease landed on his face and chest.

Rose watched the appalling sight of flesh melting away, and boiling as the grease leached its way through its pores. Human skin parted, and scraps fell away, revealing horrors concealed beneath. His jaw was a nightmare of teeth, and his tongue, long and tubular, flicked like a snake. Black patches of coarse hair burst through particularly well-burned areas of skin, and his left eye melted away to reveal something bearing more resemblance to a window screen.

He spewed a green liquid at her from his tongue, but she was already rolling to her left. The cool metal from the counter kissed her skin as she rushed back into the dining room. She landed facing the kitchen. Her burning shoulder nagged at her, but she was too focused on her pursuer to give in to the temptation of checking it.

The man had reached into the grease fryer and was greedily consuming chicken wings. He had lost interest in Rose.

She seized the opportunity to rush back to Armand and the father and son who had tried to help her. The boy's body was absent to his chest. The remaining parts of his shoulder blades showed clean white, seemingly at odds with the bottom of his ventricles, which were exposed. The father, completely enveloped in insects, appeared withered under the bulbous flies. Armand was dead. His arms had been removed at the sockets and there was a large portion of his abdomen melted away. His eyes stared sightlessly at the ceiling.

Rose grabbed Armand's spatula less as protection and more to anchor her to reality, and ran through the front entrance into the night, holding it to her chest. The concept of time became foreign while she waited for the police to arrive, her focus slipping as she tried to catch her breath.

Responding officers exchanged glances as she quickly told them what had transpired, and she waited with one while two others investigated the scene inside. Red and blue lights danced on the brick siding of The Bone Yard. The third officer snapped the guard off his holster as gunshots rang out into the night.

Ω

David walked from the ragged dock to the man awaiting him. "You're likely already aware, but my name is David. David Dolan." David cocked his hand back with pointed a thumb at Kharon, who was making brush strokes in the air at them. "The ferryman said you paid for my crossing. Thank you for that." David paused and considered his passage over the river, then said, "I think."

The man lowered his face, giving the bizarre appearance of scanning David though his cloth blindfold. "I know you, David. You may call me Jacob. Now we are known to one another."

David ran his hand through his thick hair to slick it back from his forehead and relaxed his shoulders. A sigh blew the tension of his ordeal out through his well-aligned teeth.

Jacob turned his body and gestured for David to walk with him away from the river. "As I said, I know you. You are the only son of Chelsea Dolan, you graduated from high school as salutatorian, you studied well in college, but you lost the spark of inquisitiveness many boys do as they become men. You have been kind to strangers since you were a child, you are idealistic to a fault—stomping on pragmatism as soon as it rises to challenge you. I know you well. The time has come for you to begin to know yourself."

The words seeped into David as water silently invades a sponge, the porous mouths drinking steadily and slowly. He wasn't expecting this man to be quite so loquacious just after making his acquaintance, and David certainly wasn't expecting to get a positive Yelp review.

"You been stalking me?" he said.

"You are important," said Jacob, missing the subtle sarcasm.

"I'm getting that," David retorted. "I don't agree with it, but I see you have your mind pretty well made up." He scratched his cheek and sighed. "I just met a man I first read about in Edith Hamilton's *Mythology* when I was in seventh grade. If I use that logic as a guide, then maybe you're Sampson, or I guess you could be Hercules. Might be nice to be stalked by Hercules, though I'd run the risk of getting smashed should he take too much of a shine to me. Ever read *Of Mice and Men*, Jacob? If I ask you to look at the alfalfa, you'd better start running as fast as you can, buddy."

Jacob smiled at this. His weather-worn facial features gave him a distinguished look when they lifted. "Despite knowing you, I do enjoy how your wit keeps me guessing what you might say," said Jacob, indicating he understood the references. "I'm not Hercules, and though Sampson is closer to the mark, I am not him either." Jacob paused to consider his next words. "Do you understand celestial bodies, David?"

"Not strictly speaking," David said. "That is, I guess I haven't studied heavenly bodies further than, say, Scarlet Johansson or Bella Hadid."

Jacob spoke swiftly and struck the point like the tip of a sword. "I am of fires churning with such heat that they forge the elements of all existence in your world. I have been conscious since just after light first invaded chaos, and I hope to continue to usher that light for many eons more. My brethren and I are innumerable, though we shine with varying degrees of intensity. The further humanity peers into the unknown, the more of us they will find."

David didn't know how to respond to this. He knew he wasn't in a dream because dreams weren't this detailed, and he'd never had one even close to half as long as this experience. "Tell you what, Jacob, who describes himself in the form of a riddle… Let's say that's all true, and I am walking next to a raging furnace. What would a colossally powerful thing like you want with a person like me?"

"I've been communing with humans since they were able to feel my presence. Being allowed to feel the grace of your world is a gift that not all receive," Jacob said. "Some shine brightly, wielding power and responsibility. Some smolder and are meek. Yet, we all push back against the darkness."

"So, you're special?" David asked.

"That's a subjective question that would be narcissistic to confirm and unbelievable to deny," replied Jacob, as he turned his long stride slightly left and up an incline along the path. "You are the one who decides the answer."

The landscape around David had changed. The small comfort of the glow all but departed behind them, and the terrain took on a more open-air quality. The sky above was not yet discernible, but David could sense the lack of cover. It was dark, but it felt like a cloud-filled night more than an entombment underground. The edges of his vision picked up the shapes of what could be small plant life. It reminded him of camping at the Grand Canyon as a boy, so different than his jaunts up the Hudson River with the Boy Scouts, but lacking the vibrancy. Reality seen through a gritty window.

"I'll do that," David said. "Make up my mind, that is."

"Good lad." Jacob patted David's shoulder with hands that may have once molded stone into sculpture. "Soon we will come to a place of choosing. You will do the choosing, naturally. Until then, we may palaver if you wish."

David decided to walk in silence for a time. He thought of the truths within the murk that Kharon had helped him lift. He thought about his mother and Rose, and what they might be thinking right now.

Not wanting to sample much more than the fruit most accessible on the lowest branches of life had become David's calling card. No backpacking trip through Europe was worthwhile, unless Rose took an interest. Or a surfing trip in Vietnam, nor island hopping through

Greece. These took a backseat to slathering paint on the white picket fence that would wrap around their future home, sealing the happiness within and fending off the frivolity which may try to invade. This was the life he'd been vectoring toward, and frankly, it was the one he'd earned. Not making waves was looked down upon far too often, but waves break and ripple. Their lives were to be the lake's crystalline surface at sunrise.

"I don't think I'm capable of doing what you may ask me," David said. "I'm not the kind of guy who walks amongst the stars."

"No, you aren't," said Jacob, giving David nothing else to chew on as they walked.

Time passed as they continued, and David realized he had no idea how long they'd been walking.

"Why aren't I getting tired?" David asked.

"You're clever to notice something like that so quickly," said Jacob, grinning wide. "What if I told you you'd never want in the way of hunger or thirst ever again? How would you take that?"

"I'd say I was dead," David fired back.

"I'd say you were just beginning to live," replied Jacob, just as quickly. "Being a man means being compelled. Forced to act by outer forces and inner urges. I believe Abraham derived something to that effect. He wasn't wrong."

"Abraham from the Bible?" David asked.

Jacob shook his head. "Abraham Maslow. He found that a man in starvation will do things considered unspeakable to a man with bursting cabinets." Jacob did not give David time to respond to this, which David may have done because he knew of Maslow's work. "So, what would a man do or be like if he did not have to act in accordance with his environment or biology?" Jacob asked.

"I don't know. Maybe he would act with more kindness. He'd be more insightful. I guess he'd act more like an angel than a man."

"Right on half the point," Jacob said. "An angel is as different from being a man as a man is different from being a honeybee. There are similarities—free will for example—but the differences are far more numerous. At least until you get to the quantum level. Mankind finds it hard to differentiate themselves from angels because they put themselves into everything they see, and they only see the parts of angels that angels want to show them. Humans are shown what they may comprehend." The words flowed out of Jacob like a deep mountain spring. "The part about insight is closer to the point. *In sight*. Seems fitting, no?"

"I guess it does," David said. "Maybe that's why Native American's starve themselves when they go on vision quests."

"And why monks fast for months trying to separate themselves from their biological desires to connect their spirits to what's out there," Jacob said, waving his hand making the sky burst into the most beautiful display of the cosmos that David had ever witnessed. Above was now alive, as though the still picture you might spy on a rocky mountain top at night was sped up hundreds of thousands of times. Stars were born in nurseries of gas clouds, and they formed together by the billions into beautiful arms around an abyssal center that itself danced among many more like it throughout the darkness. Every moment brought winks as celestial bodies quietly died, and vast explosions as others cried out their demise, only to be brought back together into another cloud of calm where more were to be born.

David stared, stunned, unaware this was the first time he'd stopped walking since he and Jacob had set out together.

"Drink it in for as long as you like," Jacob said to David as the boy's wide eyes scanned the scene. "I thought you'd be less impressed with this now that there's such accurate models available for you to see whenever you wish."

"This isn't the same as seeing The Universe on the History Channel," David whispered, "and you're not Michio Kaku, Jacob. This is on another level entirely. I feel like I can jump straight up and become a part of it."

Jacob smiled as David's eyes drank in the universe.

Ω

Rose was taken to the police station by the same officer who had stood vigil over her. He was a younger man than the ones who had entered the restaurant and was keen on comforting her, though he lost interest in her statement quickly after the gunfire broke out.

Apparently the two officers who confronted the man from table thirteen had loosed their entire service issue magazines when they saw the bespectacled horror devouring raw meat from the refrigerator. Mr. Table Thirteen had chosen flight instead of standing against two officers much better equipped to deal with him than a fry cook and some civilians.

He had fled through the exit by his table and the pursuing cops couldn't make out where he'd gone afterward. The flies were absent by the time they'd investigated the scene, making Rose's account of events seem thin. Armand was found, and so were his missing arms. The two meaty appendages had been stripped down to the bones, as though they'd been painstakingly bleached by a taxidermist rather than expertly handling cooking utensils minutes before. The cops also found the remains of the father. Whispers of him sounded grim, but she was spared the more descriptive details. Rose was questioned a few times as more and more supervisors were brought in, until Chelsea arrived to pick her up because her own parents were unreachable.

"Thank goodness you're alright. You aren't hurt, are you?" Chelsea mothered.

"I've got a bad burn on my shoulder that the cops think was caused by the fry grease, but otherwise I'm okay," Rose said. "I'll probably get it looked at the next time I'm at the hospital with David."

"That's a good idea, love," Chelsea said and planted a kiss on Rose's temple while scooping her hand.

Dodd's large frame appeared and dominated the space within the station. Both Rose and Chelsea's attention was drawn to it.

"Ms. Dolan, I'm surprised to see you here. Parking tickets?" Dodd asked.

Chelsea had had a few telephone conversations with Dodd since meeting him in person almost a week ago. He had a disarming quality that was one-part charm and one-part character. She found that she looked forward to their conversations.

"Rose was attacked at the restaurant where she works downtown," Chelsea said.

"The Bone Yard was robbed? I wish I still used a scanner—" he said, his gaze cutting to offices on the left. "Give me a second."

Dodd stalked off purposefully toward a door that read, "Lieutenant Murphy". The doors to the left and right were assigned to a Sargent McNamara and a Captain Wallace. *Are all cops Irish besides Ramirez?* Chelsea thought.

She noted Dodd had dug deep enough into their lives to know where David's girlfriend worked.

Her hazel eyes left the wake of the giant and wandered back to Rose. "You sure you're okay? I know seeing that must have been awful."

Rose looked up at her with eyes that had once been young and doe-ish. The sea-green ovals David had fallen hopelessly for had a hard edge to them now.

"There's something going on," Rose said. "Can't you feel how weird it is out there? We were attacked by a monster tonight, Ms. Dolan. He devoured those men so fast, and he just kept coming for more and more. There was no stopping him."

Chelsea had noticed a charge in the atmosphere as of late, sure, particularly at night while the breeze brought in cool air to her basement workshop from the cracked windows on the floor above. It kept her sharp while she worked. Fewer people were out, too. Almost like they sensed something was wrong and instincts kept them indoors where the chance of meeting something averse to their wellbeing was slightly lessened. Chelsea could only nod and stroke Rose's long hair.

"You're a strong girl, Rose, but working in a place like that is beneath you," Chelsea said. "You're laying out the welcome mat and expecting men not to be angry when they find the door in is locked."

"It's not that. I mean, you're right, and I will be moving on from waiting tables in a volleyball player's uniform soon, but that's not what this was. Whatever killed Armand and the other two was not human. He was like a huge bug."

Dodd came back, seemingly unnerved. "Rose, that was one hell of an ordeal. You need a counselor to speak with?" he asked.

Chelsea shook her head. "She needs to be released so she can come home with me and get a meal and some rest. When can we get out of here?"

Dodd said, "She can go right now. She's given her statement enough times, that's for sure. I'll take any heat that comes, but I've known the captain for going on twenty-five years. The release order probably just got buried."

"That's encouraging. Are all cops so reliable, Dodd?" Chelsea quipped.

"I'm a special specimen, Ms. Dolan, he said. "You should have figured that out by now that you can't hold everyone else to the same standard."

"I told you two phone calls ago to call me Chelsea. I remember because you said to keep calling you Dodd." Chelsea gently picked Rose up and hovered over her.

"Why don't I tail you home? I wanted to ask you about something we found by the river anyway," he said.

"You sure you're not just trying to score a free meal from two damsels in distress?" Chelsea asked.

Dodd smiled. "I don't suppose it will help my cause to say that I won't turn down a hot meal or the company of you two fine ladies, but I promise my intentions are far from nefarious."

"Beware the charms of a man like that, Rose." Chelsea pointed directly at Dodd. "They'll talk their way right to what they all want."

"And what might that be?" Rose asked, returning a mischievous grin.

"Biscuits and gravy," Dodd said.

Ω

David and Jacob moved on for what could have been hours or weeks. Time had become fluid, and the two palavered, as Jacob had

83

said they could. Philosophy was discussed, as was cooking, hiking, wrestling, Genghis Khan, politics, Alexander the Great, Israel, sand, the number of stars in the universe, more politics, happiness, and finally, the idea of being a falconer. The bar didn't seem to have a limit for low or high on the topics they'd vectored to and from. David found himself enamored with his companion. He sensed a bottomless vat of wisdom harnessed in Jacob, and he enjoyed tapping into it, albeit for mostly cryptic responses.

"Why do you bother with humankind?" David asked. "I know you said you're one of the few who are allowed to interact with us, but why bother? Don't we seem kind of hopeless?"

"Mankind has been in the wilderness from the very beginning with a compass but no map. They wander lost and stumbling, picking their way through existence by striving for some semblance of certainty in it all. They have been dealt a tough hand, David. I can't imagine being able to perceive so very little while also being tasked to find so much. Being given the opportunity to receive a helping hand is supposed to even the odds for mankind, but I can't be sure. We don't know the grand plan in its entirety either. Ours is more a set of rigid guidelines to which we must adhere."

David had been fondling the coins in his pocket absentmindedly, and when he clinked them together, Jacob's attention drifted from the path ahead to the boy beside him. "I meant to ask you about God," David said. "What's He like?"

Jacob walked on for seconds that felt heavy in their emptiness before he answered. "The creator, as you understand it, is an incomplete picture. Many beliefs have some parts of the picture in the right places, but most have turned the table over and walked away. Given what mankind can sense and imagine, they've done well in trying to understand, but in this issue, the odds are against them. Many forces actively work to sway their perceptions to the wrong outcomes, and humanity simply doesn't know which is worthy of trust beyond a small nagging feeling they hold inside their moral compass. It's often easy to discount this feeling based on lack of information, David. The results are damning, however, and you will learn that a helping hand is absent for those who choose to do so. Righteous intervention is as fickle as fate or circumstance. You'll do well to remember that."

David nodded. "It's much easier to rationalize all of this when we get the inside scoop. Why haven't your kind just told us what we need to know so we can act appropriately? It seems *fickle* to leave us floundering with it all."

"The journey is the answer, not the means to it," Jacob said.

"I can't begin to understand that. It seems like the same bullshit answer a priest would tell a woman who lost her husband in a car accident. The same *he works in mysterious ways* response someone who doesn't know what they're talking about gives before handing over the collection plate."

Jacob took note of David's bluntness. "Don't mistake this reality for what some versions of religion say. You're wise to be skeptical of many institutions preaching 'the word' for how they've acted in the past and at present. You may wonder how people can pack into arenas lined with neon and feel they are being filled with light? They've no map, that's how. Don't be concerned about retribution, David, and there will be retribution. Snake oil salesmen burn brightly enough in the pits of Tartarus to warm the fields of Elysium."

"That's another thing! David said. "Which of these stories are true? I have met a Christian angel and a Greco-Roman ferryman on this trip, or whatever this is, and I don't know if I should be expecting to see Osiris or Buddha next."

Jacob chewed this over. He hadn't been certain the boy had made the necessary connections to understand he was in the presence of an angel. David's utterance of this knowledge came as a small surprise. Jacob said, "Imagine your favorite novel—"

"*Blood Meridian*," David said without hesitation.

"Yes, imagine *Blood Meridian* was written by Faulkner instead of McCarthy," Jacob said. "Would the story carry the same tone or theme, do you think?"

"Well, I guess the scenes and characters might change some given how different those two writers are," David replied. "Doubt Faulkner would have left so much unsaid. Can't imagine the story without the final moments with the Judge and the Kid. It wouldn't make sense."

"Precisely," Jacob said, "The avenues to enlightenment can be many, and this holds true for religion, folklore, and storytelling. Many of the names change, but the characters are facsimiled often. Jesus and Buddha have much in common, no? What of Gilgamesh? How about the titans and the watchers or demigods and the Nephilim? Do you see the vein here?"

"Can't answer that yet. What are the watchers?" David asked.

Jacob smiled and the beauty of it was more impressive than the previous times he'd shown his enjoyment of their discussions, almost as though David could feel his joy derived in the well-honed process of delivering information to be processed through the eager mind into knowledge. "The watchers were angels assigned to keep an eye on mankind. It's written of in the Old Testament and gnostic texts, too. They became enamored with humanity and began to interact with them without permission. The results weren't always beneficial to the journey of man. The Nephilim were the children born when a union was had between the two types of beings. They were often giants or possessed abilities not found in mortals. The outcomes surprised even us. You see, we didn't believe man, as a vessel, could contain celestial energy."

"Aren't they why Noah built the ark?" David asked.

"You are quite knowledgeable on these subjects, David," said Jacob, as though he hadn't known David would be.

"My mother's work brought a lot of these topics up," David said.

Jacob continued, "The flood was needed to purge these half-breed children from the gene pool, not for spite, but for safety. Otherwise, we might have lost all hope of mankind achieving... an ultimate understanding."

"Now we're mixing in Hinduism?" David asked. "This is becoming pretty hard to put together."

"The journey, David. It's not going to come to you until you're done with your journey."

"Well how do I know when my journey is over?"

"All humans feel anxiety about that subject, at least on some level. And no, your journey doesn't necessarily end at your death. Because your death isn't the end humanity fears it is or may be, but that's another topic entirely. Your journey's end will be so known to you that this subject needs not be fleshed out further. I hope that brings you some peace."

"Mysterious ways, Jacob," David said. "Mysterious ways."

"Yes, it's often frustrating. Perhaps knowing my kind undergoes similar frustrations will ease your mind?" Jacob offered.

David said, "Commiseration doesn't solve the problem, but it does lighten the load."

"Fair enough."

"Fair enough."

Jacob slowed his pace as the path wound its way up to a plateau ahead, and he reached his hand out to stop David.

"We've come to where your road branches," said Jacob, sitting on a rock and reaching to produce a small book. "Now comes the time for you to choose the path you'd like to tread upon as we continue our journey."

"Why do I have to choose?" David asked.

Jacob shrugged and remained silent as he opened the leatherbound reader. He concerned himself with only the inner contents and waved David off toward the area ahead.

David pondered for a tick and decided against questioning Jacob further. He had developed a trust in his guide he'd not thought possible when he first observed the blindfolded man standing on shore waiting for him.

He walked ahead a few paces and studied the surroundings. The sky was open, as it had been since leaving the cavern, and appeared quite familiar to him, but he'd noted this earlier. What was different were the three pathways forward. All of them seemed innocuous enough, and none offered much by the way of differentiating which would be the best choice. *Great.*

Pushing a tepid foot forward in the dust to take a look down the path on the left triggered the unmistakable low growl of a large cat. David swung his head toward the sound and spied glowing green embers rising from the brush at the path's edge. A leopard revealed itself and stalked onto the plateau.

"Oh shit," David said, stepping back toward the pathway in the middle.

The sound of claws clicking on the stone gave the boy pause. A timber wolf half the size of his car, which, as coincidence would have it, was now being tugged out from beneath the waves of the Hudson, swiftly walked up the middle path and pressed the boy further right. David was happy to find that the wolf did not growl, but he kept backpedaling, careful to keep both animals in view. He chanced a glance toward Jacob who hadn't concerned himself with this new development in the slightest.

"Jacob!" David whispered urgently. "A little guidance might be prudent here!"

The landscape shook under the pressure of a roar, and he was forced to forgo awaiting an answer to his hushed request for aid. So startled by it that he turned his back on the other two predators, he came eye to eye with a lion sitting no more than three feet from where his feet had planted him. The lion's gaze ravaged him.

Pivoting so his back was pointed to open space and not the leopard, wolf, or lion, David slowly retreated. The lion's tail swept back and forth, forming dust clouds as it walked him down in lockstep with the others. David kept his hands up and palms facing outward, trying to appear nonthreatening to the trio.

"You can't go back that way, David," Jacob said.

"What the hell am I supposed to do?" David said. Whispering seemed to be fool's errand at this point.

"A boy shouldn't say the name of the house of Satan so close to his door knocker," said Jacob, keeping his attention on the book in his hands. "You might call out worse than those kits and pup."

"What. Should. I. Do." David hissed.

Silence.

David realized he would have to make a move. He had brought the animals off to the right side of the plateau near the farthest path already. All he had to do was sidestep a couple of times and make a break for the left path. Maybe he'd get lucky and they'd shift their focus to Jacob, sitting there like a weather-worn plum.

One small step, then another, and David broke into a run. He'd always been fast, quite fast really by human standards anyway, but he knew he wasn't on par with the apex predators of three separate continents.

Still, he flew. They followed. It didn't take long for the hot breath of one to envelope him.

A yip issued from his right as the wolf nipped at his legs and David kicked them out ahead of him as he ran. Daring to snatch a look back, he saw the leopard and wolf were only a foot behind. *Are they messing with me?*

This thought seemed to hold water until the teamwork between the animals revealed itself. David caught sight of the lion just before it became airborne, long claws fully exposed and mouth agape. If it didn't spell the horrific end of his life, David might have found the sight to be one of the most beautiful things he'd ever witnessed. Front paws spread wide to wrap the morsel of a boy in the last hug he'd ever experience, the beast rode gravity downward.

David dropped his right knee and rolled three times, while hearing the lion land on the space he himself had occupied a split second prior. He made it. This time at least.

Something snapped in David, a feeling invading the vacuum of his mind and causing him to stand tall. He had never taken kindly to being bullied and the coordinated effort by these three animals felt very much like being harassed by a gang of marauding teens. If David had chanced a glance to his left, he would have seen Jacob studying him intently, fingers of his left hand pinching a page paused in the act of turning a leaf.

David bared his teeth and stepped forward toward the predators. They didn't shy away from the advance, not exactly, but their demeanor changed from pursuit to standing their own ground, the tenor the moment taking on the tone of a battle rather than a massacre. David hadn't been thinking, and he still wasn't, but he felt pleasure in facing down his pursuers. He felt as though he could tear them apart with his bare hands and relish in their demise by consuming them rather than being consumed.

The embers of this feeling began to rise within him and spread heat through his veins. The leopard and lion turned their heads toward Jacob, who had produced a small music box, but the wolf stepped toward David, not yet ready to allow its attention to be diverted. The look in its eyes matched David's lust for carnage with a mirrored perfection.

Jacob rotated the lever on the box, and what flowed was a cacophonous symphony of notes the likes of which David had never before heard. It chimed percussive beauty as pure as anything ever to have graced his perceptions. The tension in the air dissipated far more quickly than it took to build, and the two cats rolled onto their sides in a lazy display. The wolf followed soon after, now examining Jacob much in the same way a puppy might.

David no longer felt the murderous rush that had taken hold of him. A hushed memory remained, and he'd explore that later, but for now calm suffused him.

"Was this your plan the whole time?" David asked as he walked around to the front of the docile creatures.

"No, there wasn't a plan, Jacob said. "If there had been, your actions would have changed it. Not many make the choice to fight here." What he *should* have said was that none had ever chosen to stand and fight here. "Do you remember the coins, David?"

David had forgotten them but felt their weight when he placed a hand in his pocket. "I have them," he said, producing all three.

David walked up to the lion first, his initial fear having fled the scene. The lion took notice of David and the coins with keen interest, none of the prior malice remaining in its eyes.

"You're beautiful," said David, as he reached his hand out to run his fingers through the huge cat's mane.

The silky hair offered no resistance, and his fingers glided through and raked down the skin in a cordial scratch that any cat would welcome. It was the moment of contacting the lion's flesh when David was accosted by visions like those through the murk, when he was with River. He saw a great kingdom with a ziggurat at the center fall to ruin around a Fisher King whose smile faded with his empire. He saw a slight man with a silly mustache drawing battle lines on the western front as he organized the invasion of far eastern Asia. He saw a light brighter than all around it being cast into the deepest darkness.

Patting the wolf brought images of death and suffering around tables full of bounty but tantalizingly out of reach of those who were wanting, and the leopard revealed images of men and women who were robbed of the things they truly desired for the opulence of milky flesh they thought they needed. Countless images and scenarios raced through his mind before the experience lifted, and he had a similar feeling of having been connected to a vast database through time.

David surveyed the three coins: the black in his left, the silver and gold in his right. They no longer carried the images of the animals who sat docile in front of him.

The animals themselves had changed too. They had been reduced to comically small sizes and began to play with one another in a fanciful display of absurd camaraderie. David now knew, though he couldn't explain *why* he knew, that if the coins were used, he may follow any path before him and experience the thematic consequences of each respectively. The animals had been trying to stop him from that fate.

He stacked the coins together and watched as they melded into one another. As they did so, the animals also melded. A chimera the size of a spaniel remained, both adorable in its youthful look and haunting in the idea of what it might grow into one day. The paths converged into a wider roadway ahead.

"It appears you've chosen quite the difficult path, David. It also appears that you do so knowingly. Are you sure? Recklessness often masquerades as bravery."

David nodded. "I appreciate your concern, but I feel something. I feel this is right, and this is how I want us to move forward."

Jacob said, "Fair enough, David. Let us begin down your path."

Ω

Chelsea didn't have anything so Southern as biscuits and gravy, but she did lay out baked ham, sweet potatoes, corn, and a bean salad. Dodd did not complain one bit, and Rose found herself ravenous as she smelled the food on the dining table.

"How does David stay so skinny with food like this around, Ms. Dolan?" Rose asked.

"This isn't the usual fare served around here. I've got some leftovers from the Autumn festival the student outreach organization throws for downtown. Most of the low-income housing turns out, and the college donates a little money for us to cook up a small feast for everyone. This year we were able to send people home with leftovers, too. Big hit." Chelsea set the kettle to boil for the calming tea she was going to drink with Rose.

"How noble of you, Chelsea. That's great," Dodd said as he filled his plate. He wasn't kidding about not turning down food. Judging by the three servings of sweet potatoes he started with, he wasn't bashful either.

"Speaking of David being skinny, I noticed something odd," Chelsea said.

"The fact that he's starting to look like an Olympic swimmer?" Rose finished.

"Yes... that. The doctors have been chirping about it, but they're being cagey regarding the details," Chelsea said. "It isn't hard to see that most of them are excited. I get the feeling they don't care much about whether or not it's a good sign for David as much as it will be a great footnote for some research project they're cooking up."

Dodd perked up at this. "Mind filling me in?"

Before Chelsea could begin, Rose unloaded everything she'd heard at the hospital about David's bodily condition. She even added that she though he might have grown taller, but she wasn't sure.

Dodd made a mental note to speak to doctor what's her name. He'd taken her card.

"Rose, can we debrief a bit about what happened in the restaurant?" Dodd asked.

She nodded but kept her voice her own. After changing out of her work uniform into a pair of Chelsea's fleece pajamas, she had taken on the aura of a little girl, and Dodd couldn't help but wish to coddle her.

"Does anyone have any reason to target you or David, Rose?" Dodd asked. "The sheer amount of violence that occurred in there screams of a professional being involved. I don't mean to press the idea that David was involved in something nefarious, but this is not ordinary."

Rose took in a deep breath, "Dodd, you seem like a man of conviction."

He straightened at her pointed statement. "I'd like to think so, sure."

"Pursuing that idea is a waste of your time. David is a simple guy. He doesn't have a radical bone in his body, and frankly, he doesn't change his focus very often. That focus is on moving the two of us into a place of our own as soon as possible. Not much else."

Dodd said, "My intuition tells me the same thing. Still, weird shit keeps popping up around where he was or the people he knows. It's been keeping my focus on him." Chelsea shot him a sharp look, and Dodd added, "'Scuse the language."

"The guy in The Bone Yard wasn't a 'pro' hitter or something like that," Rose said.

"I just mean he caused a lot of bodily harm in a really short period of time, Rose," Dodd said.

"He wasn't human. He had a cloud of flies working for him, he had eaten enough food to feed Ms. Dolan's entire festival and more, and he devoured those people who stood for me. He didn't use any weapons, Dodd. He *ate* them." Rose leveled her red-rimmed eyes directly on the large detective, making him feel half her size.

Dodd had known every kind of liar the world could produce. One thing he knew beyond his intuition was that Rose was telling the truth—as she saw it. He let her tell the story completely, and he even checked out her shoulder after clearing it with Chelsea, who also took a look. The wound worried more than intrigued her.

They had finished their portions, and Dodd had finished two more, before they spoke about some odd areas of the case. Dodd felt comfortable enough to loop them in on the riverbank, the burn marks, and an odd footprint the investigative team found that had been in the hardened mud just beneath the waterline.

They told him about David, sharing stories about his childhood, embarrassing moments like when he first tried wooing Rose as a young kid and replicated the scene from *Say Anything* all the way down to John Cusack's wardrobe, or when he tried out for the wrestling team but dropped off after accidentally dislocating his first opponent's arm. Too squeamish for contact sports, it seemed.

Eventually, Rose retired to sleep in David's bedroom, which apparently happened from time to time while the boy was away at school. Dodd took note of this more from a paternal standpoint than that of a detective, as the girl's parents appeared to be out of the picture. After she retired, Dodd stood and went straight to the sink to start the dishes. Chelsea protested, but he claimed to be duty bound by the edicts of his now passed grandmother, and she'd curse him for not working off the food he'd been given. Chelsea settled for drying plates as he handed them to her.

"What do you think about Rose's story?" Dodd asked her.

"I think that kid is the farthest thing from a liar that someone can be, so I think she believes that man was a monster masquerading in human flesh. *I know* that burn on her shoulder may have been caused by grease from the fryer, but it also looks a lot like the burns some of my colleagues have gotten using acid to restore certain fabrics and artifacts for display. Nasty how it eats down farther than the surface. You can tell by the pitting."

"*Subdermal* is what that pitting is called," he said, thinking of the few millimeters of flesh that had been missing. "She also said he shot that at her from his mouth. Jesus."

"It's hard to figure out what's going on," Chelsea said. "I haven't worked much in the last week for obvious reasons, so I guess more news than usual has been creeping in. It seems so dismal lately. First the bridge, then people going missing on hikes, and now this horrible attack. It feels like things are spinning out of control."

Dodd turned to her, handing off the last plate. "I've been out there lately, and I can tell you something definitely feels off. Not just this case. The air feels weird, almost like there's a current running through it. Maybe a circuit's been flipped somewhere. I don't like the way it smells."

Chelsea dried the plate and grabbed him a mug of coffee. She took her tea, and they both sat on the couch. Usually, the love seat comfortably accommodated her and another, but with Dodd she was very close. She thought of the nomenclature of the furniture and flushed a little.

"Will we see you again soon?" she asked.

"If you keep a baked ham by the window, I'm sure to keep on checking in," he said, patting her knee. "I really just wanted to make sure Rose felt safe, and that you were alright. This is a lot to sift through for a couple of weeks' time."

"It is, but David's condition isn't getting worse, and the doctors keep telling me he can pop up any minute," Chelsea said. "Still, they did just get my clearance for a full body MRI, which is bizarre since he doesn't have any real trauma. I signed off to keep them happy in their little science project. They think David's physical condition is something to remark upon, but a boy taking his meals through the veins is bound to get a little leaner."

"That's true, and it definitely does happen," Dodd said. "After I touch base with Ramirez—he's working with the team out by the Hudson—I'll swing by the hospital and see if I can't get them to drop some answers. I don't think they know we've become chummy yet. They might slip me something juicy." He winked at her and showed that smile of his that belonged on a man wearing a bomber jacket in the 1950s. "At any rate, I'd better take off. Let you get your rest."

Chelsea walked him to the back door and switched on the light to force the shadows back across the yard. "You're a sweet man, Dodd. We appreciate you," she said. She stood on her tip toes, kissed his cheek by the corner of his mouth, and said goodnight.

Dodd stepped outside, where the cool breeze ran through his hair and the ghost of a smile lingered on his face.

Ω

Ramirez sat under one of the large, diesel-powered lamps illuminating the area under investigation. So far, they'd found no residue from a fuel source to explain the heat marks where they'd recovered David Dolan, no mechanical parts remaining from military equipment, and squat diddly fuck all else to explain anything around the rocket theory.

This checked out with what he and Dodd had assumed a few days ago, that there was no rocket and probably no terrorism involved, but the higher ups had hard-ons for rationalizing their tax burden on society. The pieces of the bridge they'd dredged up also corroborated his findings to that end. *They'll love that.*

The only good lead they'd come upon was when one of their contracted divers spotted the shoe imprint in the mud that had been kiln-forged into semi-permanence by heat. They'd carefully removed it, and it sat in the station awaiting a forensics team to check the tread design to match the style of shoe that left it, but Ramirez thought the impression was plain.

Slapping away the mosquitoes feasting on him, Ramirez surveyed the men who were wrapping up their search of the immediate area. The ground had become a grid of roped off sections with holes dug in some squares and evidence tags strewn throughout those and others. Much ado about nothing.

He fished his phone out and texted Dodd information that would put this line of inquiry to rest, or so he hoped. He hated it out here in the evening. His suits were probably fifty percent cotton and fifty percent DEET at this point, and he hadn't eaten anything worthwhile for about eight hours, so he was beginning to get cranky. The proof of this was in how wide a circumference the other men kept around him.

His phone screen lit up and he saw the response from Dodd: WRAP IT UP AND ILL SEE YOU AT THE MOTEL.

Good.

"Looks like we are calling it, fellas," Ramirez shouted. "Let's pack it up."

The men quickly transitioned to picking up the site. They weren't huge fans of being out here either based on how quickly they dropped their tasks and began throwing crap into bags and bins.

Ramirez walked to the water's edge and took a look at the reflection of the moon up in the sky.

"Super Worm Moon," said the diver who had found the shoe print a few days ago. He rolled his wet suit top down to the waist, a decision he might regret once the flying parasites took notice.

"Oh yeah? It's big," Ramirez said absently.

"Weird down there today and tonight," the diver said. "Like zero fish."

"You're normally a welder, right? Brought in to help with this part?" Ramirez asked as he turned and monitored the men packing items to be trudged up and over the tracks and placed into SUVs.

"Yeah, subcontracted for this. Wouldn't touch the bridge search. Too grim. Not cut out for it."

Ramirez imagined searching for bodies at the bottom of the cold, dark Hudson. "Don't blame ya. 'Least we're clearing out at a reasonable time."

Ramirez walked back to the little command center he'd made and packed up a laptop, some notes, and his cell into a briefcase then made his way toward the tracks. He had a date with Dodd at the motel, and he planned to get that location changed to a steakhouse real fast. Losing gallons of blood to flying vampires made a man hungry.

He was just about to begin his scramble up the granite ballast when he heard some commotion down by the water. "Fucking hell," he said and placed the case down to go see what was up.

There was a small crowd forming around where he'd spoken to the diver, and Ramirez saw he was pulling his wet suit back on. "Nothing but groaning and bitching while workin', but now that you get the all-clear, it's time to start looking for something?" Ramirez growled.

"Crowley saw something in the water that looked like a woman's torso," a beat cop named Steve Prince said. "Stauri is gonna go in with the lamp and see if he spots anything."

"Current doesn't push this way. The river flows south," Ramirez said.

"That kid ended up here," Prince replied, his palms flipped up.

"Hey Stauri, be careful," Ramirez said. "And if you do see a cadaver in there, pull her out with you. Might be grim, but the situation's changed somewhat."

Mike Stauri finished putting on his suit and waded into the water without his oxygen tanks or flippers. He had the grim resolve some people show when the spotlight is on them, but Ramirez saw he was scared shitless. Crowley must have spotted the body near shore. Ramirez thought it odd that the body wasn't there right now since there weren't waves pushing up on the shoreline or pulling back. *How did it sink and then float back out?*

Stauri took in a deep breath and turned on his lamp. The underwater light's green iridescence revealed the secrets of the shallows to the men on shore. As the lamp swept from left to right, they saw surprisingly little seaweed and no fish.

A few men peeled off to finish clearing the search area, but most stayed and watched the water. Ramirez was transfixed as well. There was something about seeing into an alien space that enticed the imagination. They were tracking Stauri's progress through the shallows, their attention spans being close to the breaking point, when they saw her.

"Back there on the south part of his light." Crowley shouted. "She's right there."

They all saw her—a woman at the bottom, facing upward with wide eyes and arms fully extended. Her hair was flowing in such a way that it covered the bottom of her face, but her breasts were fully exposed. Ramirez was getting ready to shut down any comments the boys might chime in with regarding those, but none came.

Stauri spotted her and came up for a breath. "Gonna grab her and bring her over," he said before taking a few deep breaths.

He dove. They watched.

Even without flippers, the man was quick underwater. He made his way to her in under ten seconds and reached out at tepid speed to grasp an arm.

Stauri wrapped her wrist in one hand and positioned his body to begin swimming back to shore, but she didn't budge. He dropped the light in the soft mud and used his feet to try and gain some traction, but she was anchored firmly. Her eyes, listless and vacant moments before, locked on him. Ramirez wasn't sure he was seeing correctly. Just as he asked, "Is she alive?" the woman wrapped her arms around Stauri's mid-section and pulled him off his feet.

The scene beneath the surface became a havoc of shadows and stirred silt from the upheaval of the river bottom. Ramirez kicked off one shoe, cursing.

"Human chain! Let's go!" he said. A few men also thought to preserve their footwear before heading in, but most began linking arms immediately. Had they gotten a better view of what was causing them to link arms, they may have been less inclined to wade into the river.

Ramirez took three steps into the water and wrapped his hand around the wrist of the closest man just how they were trained for fast moving water rescues. Arm locks were tight when tested and stressed, so he wasn't very worried. The woman was probably in a panic, like most drowning people. They pulled lifeguards under with them all the time.

About seven officers linked the chain, and the water had reached Ramirez's chest when he arrived at the spot where she and Stauri should be. He didn't usually wish he had Dodd's height—he was no shrimp himself at six-foot-one—but this situation would have been made easier by another six inches to see down into the water more clearly. He sucked in a breath and dropped in to look for them both. There was nothing but a cloud of silt dancing into his eyes. He popped up to the surface.

"Shit. I can't see anything. You guys," he called to the shore, "can you see anything from that light down there?"

"No, it keeps moving around. I think he's stuck with her somehow," Crowley called. He apparently felt most comfortable being in the group of men who'd remain dry while heaving them back in.

"Alright, I'm not gonna let go, but let's add another guy. I'll go in further and feel around with my legs," Ramirez said. He hadn't turned back around yet, so when some of the men's eyes looked down into the water and their expressions changed to shocked horror, Ramirez knew he was missing something.

"There's something pulling at my pants!" someone cried, and the whole crew began to pull back toward shore, Ramirez being dragged along for the ride.

"What the hell are you doing? A man's drowning down there!" Ramirez yelled, but the men paid him little mind. Their faces were locked in shocked unison, and nothing was going to tear their attention from the happening that had seized it. Ramirez followed their gaze to the woman who was now at the surface. Exposed from the waist up, she was alive, she was nude, and she was smiling at them.

Some of these men were war veterans, and some had been on the force for years, seeing terrible things day in and day out, but every man's veins cascaded with ice when they saw her smile. Her teeth were a riot of needlepoints, and her bright, moonlight-filled eyes belied the malice they'd hidden before.

Before Ramirez could ask another man to go get her, he realized the water where she was located was the same depth as where he stood. *How is her body so high out of the water?* The situation had finally overcome his protective instincts as a law enforcement officer, and a voice deep inside him rose to the surface.

RUN.

"Out of the water now, now, now!" he said, wishing he sounded more authoritative, but before they could all leave the water and fully turn to make their way across the thirty yards between them and the train tracks, the sunken woman began to rise further and further still.

As the water fell away from her, it appeared she was mounted atop an overturned boat, but Ramirez's sharp eyes noted the lack of legs on her—and that this boat had fur. Her top half was fused to the body of a colossal animal, bigger than anything he had ever seen this close.

Water had begun to rise on the shoreline.

Most of the men were scrambling to safety. Ramirez stopped, remembering his sidearm in its shoulder harness. The Glock 21 would probably be ruined after firing it wet, but he didn't give a shit. Government issued.

He pulled the weapon from under his wet jacket and immediately unloaded bullets into the sunken wench's torso at center mass. Whatever she was rose another two feet in response to being pegged over a dozen times by slugs. A gaping mouth that belonged in a Maurice Sendak book was revealed in the center of its chest below where the woman was perched.

The Glock barked three more rounds into the new mouth, and Ramirez felt a twinge of glee at seeing two teeth disintegrate before he dropped the empty gun and beat feet out of there. That thing had just taken fifteen rounds, and with those, all the bravery Ramirez had mustered. He was leaving.

Running at a full clip meant he should have reached the ballast line in about eight seconds, but his heavy frame and the mud pulling at his feet slowed him. Still, he was only behind the pack of men by about fifteen yards. Things took another turn, though. The water had caught up with him. It rose from his toes to his ankles and then his knees in the amount of time it took his brain to register it was there at all. Some of the men had fallen and some were pulling at comrades. None had reached the succor of higher ground as of yet.

Ramirez looked ahead and saw his briefcase begin to float as the water surrounded its base. He wished he'd never returned to see what was happening. He'd be halfway back to the motel by now.

"Up and out. Now!" Ramirez tried to spur the men into motion despite the lack of purchase the mossy mud afforded them.

He turned to see that the beast, now a full-fledged nightmare, had made it up onto land. Its legs were like tree trunks holding up an impossibly rotund belly that would have been at home on an elephant. Its mouth gnashed its teeth as it disgorged torrents of water at them. *That solves the mystery of the water level rising.* The woman who they'd tried to save remained perched atop and smiled.

Standing in the full light of the moon, Ramirez could see she was fused to the beast just below her navel. Her long black hair, used to temporarily conceal her features, was now swept back over her shoulders.

Even with the rising water, the beast hadn't stepped further toward them. They could make it to the tracks and dry land even if they had to swim the last ten yards.

The sound of spilling water ceased as the generator lights gave out, leaving them with only the full Worm Moon to illuminate their surroundings. Luckily it performed well in delivering yellowed light to the area, but they didn't necessarily want to see everything it revealed.

Ramirez glanced backward to see what the thing was doing now that it had finished spitting water. It was still pretty fat, but he noted the water it expelled had pulled in its ridiculous proportions some. The maw had been lowered down so that it was kissing the water with pursed lips. He found that to be a more welcome sight than seeing hooked teeth chomping in their direction. The sunken lady was pitched forward and running her hands across the surface like a cherub babe at the harp. She appeared to be at perfect ease despite brackish blood spilling from her wounds blotting the water. Ramirez began to register a reverse vertigo sensation. She was getting closer.

Men began to scream as they noticed the water flowing backward in contradiction to the previous current. Ramirez planted his feet and let the mud work in his favor. He craned his neck back again to see the cause to be the mouth sucking water up and inside the belly of the beast. The sunken lady lifted her face and smiled at him as if she knew the moment he'd realized they were going to die here.

"Bitch," Ramirez said, and then turned to order the men, "Push your feet into the mud. Hold on for as long as you can!"

If the thing was able to pull in water and expand, that meant it had a limit. They had a chance if they could stand firm and weather the draw. A scant few men picked up on his warning in time, but others had been swimming against the draw and were now slipping back. Those with the least luck had been upended and were rolling backward after being caught off balance by the unexpected change in flow.

Ramirez reached out to grab at men who slipped by. The closest were just out of reach, and if he lifted his feet, he'd just be riding back with them. Screams pierced the night as they flowed down and into the mouth. The woman gently pushed the heads of men down under the water as they reached her, silencing final protests. She took the time to pull Crowley in for a kiss, then tore off his ear with rows of needle-sharp teeth before sending him to his death.

The men being pulled into the monstrous mouth slowed the inflow of water, Ramirez saw, because the current had lessened substantially. He intended to make use of their sacrifice to save who remained.

"Move now!" he shouted.

The men took his order without hesitation and again began to make their way toward the tracks, redoubling over land they'd already cleared minutes before. It was maddening.

"Get to the tracks and we are out!" Ramirez said, his voice becoming less powerful as his words became punctuated by deep raspy breaths.

Hope took hold as they made steady progress toward their goal, but was tempered by a low bellow from the water. Ramirez almost resisted turning back—every time he did it was more bad news, after all—but eventually his curiosity tipped the scales. The river held nothing for them but death and hopelessness. It defied the human imagination to grasp how the veil over reality could lift and reveal the nightmare standing astride normalcy. In the end, it was the same instincts that made him a good cop which allowed him to bear witness to the harbingers of their demise.

After turning his head to see what the ominous sound signaled for his fate, he saw a half dozen more of the creatures pulling themselves up onto the moss-covered haven where George Stuart played with his dog Bella, back when the world still made sense.

Ramirez let himself sink to his hands and knees. It took seeing Mike Stauri perched atop one of the behemoths to break the last of Saul Ramirez's resolve. Mike's open eyes stared listlessly; the creature he had become one with opened its mouth and expelled the Hudson River at Ramirez and those who remained.

PART TWO
LEAVING MIDGAR

CHAPTER SIX
THE RIGHT PATH

Chelsea woke to the sound of soft rapping at the back door. She looked at the digital time display on her cable box. 1:47 a.m.

"This can't be good," she mused as she pulled herself into a sitting position on the couch. Falling asleep after finishing her tea would have been unusual if she hadn't spiked it. The sour taste of brandy stuck to the back of her throat, and she cleared the pipes with a rinse of warm tap water from the glass next to her mug.

Rap-ap. Rap-ap-ap-ap.

A snub nosed .38 sat in the hutch in the dining room, and she swung by to grab it before heading into the kitchen. The neighborhood where they lived wasn't considered bad by any means, but Chelsea grew up in a less secure city. Though not without its own charms, the ratty subdivision her family had resided in called for looking over one's shoulder. She employed the same strategy her father had used to "scare away the critters" by turning on the outdoor light and sneaking up to the window off to the left of the door. She could see out, but they couldn't see in. That was the idea, anyhow.

After pressing her ear to the wall, she peeked from behind the blinds and saw a hulking figure tall enough to obscure the porch light. She made sure to look for others hiding by the sides of the door and then walked over to it.

"Who is it?" Chelsea asked.

"Dodd, Chelsea. I'm sorry about the hour, but I need your help," came Dodd's voice.

Chelsea moved the blinds to make sure, then she slipped the lock and opened the door.

"We're out of ham," she said.

Dodd smiled, but the expression left his face in a hurry. "Something's happened to Ramirez."

"What?" Chelsea said as he walked into the kitchen. She noted his lingering glance at the bottle of brandy still on the counter and then the side arm in her hand.

"He got the all-clear to finish up down by where they found David," Dodd said. "There'd been a footprint found, but nothing else to fuel the rocket theory the higher ups are hoping to rubber stamp this thing with. I was waiting for him at the motel, but he never showed. Took a little while of him not answering his phone before I went down there to see what was up. Their cars are all there by the end of the road, but the whole investigation scene on the riverside of the tracks is completely washed out like there was a flood. There's gear still scattered around, but everyone and everything else is gone."

"Why are you coming to me with this?" Chelsea asked. "Shouldn't you be down at the station rallying the boys in blue?"

Dodd took a seat at the table. "I called it in. Normally heading to the station is exactly what I'd be doing, but this isn't normal. I found this when I was looking for Ramirez." Dodd held out his hand, and a three-inch-long section of tooth lay in his palm.

"This was out there?" Chelsea asked as she leaned in closer to examine it. "This is fresh, not from some necklace a hunter might wear."

"How can you tell that?" Dodd asked.

"For one thing, there's still soft pulpy tissue inside." She turned the tooth's base end to show him. "For another, there's flesh lodged inside of these cracks."

Dodd nodded. "There's something happening out there. It's hard to explain, but you can feel it, like we were talking about. People have started filing missing person's reports in larger numbers. Your girl who doesn't lie is upstairs sleeping after fighting off what sounds like the Brundlefly, and now shit like this"—he said and shook the tooth in his palm—"is on the banks of the Hudson. I just can't figure out what the connecting thread is."

"She really doesn't lie," Chelsea said.

"I know. I believe her," Dodd said and sighed heavily. "That up for grabs?" He pointed to the bottle of Cîroc on the counter. "I need something to take the edge off."

"If we are going that route, we might as well do it right," Chelsea said and left the room. Dodd heard her in the dining room, rustling around in the server. She came back with two crystal glasses and a bottle of Laphroaig 15. "Big guy like you doesn't shy away from the peaty stuff, right?" she asked.

"No, ma'am, a big guy like me does not."

Chelsea poured two fingers of Scotch whiskey into each glass and took the seat astride him. Dodd thought he might be falling in love.

"I'm not a biologist, so I can't tell you much more about this tooth than what I've learned pulling things out of the dirt, but it also looks like it comes from something like a sperm whale," she said. "The size of it is uncanny for even a grizzly, which we don't have in New York, and *that's* not even the whole tooth. Thing could have been two inches longer to the base."

Dodd nodded to the gun. "That thing loaded?"

"You're not about to give me a lesson on gun safety after showing me evidence that T-Rex is out there, are you?" she said.

"Wouldn't dream of it," he said. "I have a field trip in mind, and I don't have a spare for you."

Chelsea raised her eyebrows. "Little late for a moonlit stroll, Detective."

Dodd flushed from the whiskey and the implied undertones of Chelsea's statement. "You may not be so chipper when you find out what I have in mind. But first, what do you know about ancient gods?"

Chelsea contemplated this as she poured more whiskey. "You're thinking about what happened to Rose?"

"Yup," Dodd replied and took a deep sip from his glass. "I was doing some internet sleuthing, because the description reminded me of a guy we learned about in high school. The book had nothing to do with him, it was about a bunch of boys on an island killing each other or something, but there was a fallout 'cause somebody's mother sued the school for exposing us wee sprouts to pagan witchcraft. Golding wrote the book. *Lord of the Flies,* it was called."

Chelsea said, "The title is a pseudonym for Beelzebub. People think the name is for the devil, but it was Beelzebub's first. And, just so you know, the book has everything to do with the guy."

Dodd flushed a little at this. "Literary interpretation was never my thing. I had more interest in studying the teacher and student's behavior than grinding out metaphors. Paid off in the end, kinda. Guess it's a good thing I'm so dumb, Professor, else I wouldn't need you."

"There's that charm my grandmother warned me about," Chelsea said. "Rose mentioned that the guy seemed like a bug—"

"And controlled them," Dodd put in.

"—and controlled them. Then you immediately assume a philistine god is dining at The Bone Yard? Seems thin, Columbo," Chelsea said.

"That's where I started too, thinking this was a dumb idea, but I kept circling back to a kid who doesn't lie and isn't into drugs fully believing the statement she gave. There's also the part in her statement where she said she heard him mention the followers at Ekron. I don't know what that means, but the police put down Ekron as a possible place of dwelling or an accomplice."

"She didn't mention that to me. Ekron is the city-state where Beelzebub was first worshiped as a deity. It's thought that he was adopted by other philistines, mostly the Canaanites, and then his image was perverted through the texts to a demon afterward."

"The plot thickens," Dodd said as he got up and filled his empty whiskey glass with water from the tap. He took down three glasses before realigning himself in the kitchen chair. "Might explain how he got away so clean. Demons fly, right?"

"Sure, some might—if they existed. Beelzebub definitely would because one of the iterations of his name means *The One Who Flies*, but I think we are getting ahead of ourselves," Chelsea said.

"The kid doesn't lie," Dodd repeated. "How's she doing, anyway?"

"She's doing fine," Rose said, walking into the kitchen. "Fine enough to sneak up on you two in a house with creaky stairs."

Dodd smiled at her. He was only a few inches lower than her when sitting down, but she loomed over him in a mocked attempt to be threatening.

"How much did you hear?" Dodd asked.

"Enough to appreciate you two for not thinking I'm crazy," Rose said.

Chelsea said, "I'm not one hundred percent in that club yet. Stressful situations have a tendency to affect people in weird ways, Rose. I don't think you're lying, but what you think happened may not be exactly what *did* happen."

"Detective Dodd, did they ever find those missing pieces of the people who were alive and well twenty minutes before the police showed up?" Rose asked.

"Nope," Dodd said.

"Did they figure out how the father of that teenager got stripped of his skin so fast?" Rose asked.

"Not just his skin, pretty much everything but the internal organs, Dodd said. "Those were also nibbled away a bit. And nope."

"You already covered the part where he flew away, so we don't need to go there," Rose said. She snatched up Dodd's empty glass, poured a healthy amount of whiskey, and drank it before either of them could protest. Her eyes welled up with tears, but she managed to keep her glossy peepers on them. Dodd liked this kid.

"You've got my attention, Rose," Chelsea sighed.

"Good. Where we going?" Rose asked.

Dodd held his palms up. "I guess we've added a party member."

"First, I'm going to get something, and before I do, I'm taking this with me," Chelsea said and stole the whiskey bottle out of the room, placing it into the server before heading for the basement door.

"It was a good run while it lasted," Chelsea heard Dodd say, but she missed Rose's reply while heading down the stairs. Must have been a good quip because Dodd was laughing. His bellowing guffaws were so powerful that the walls around Chelsea felt as if they were flexing. She enjoyed how much she liked him. There didn't seem to be many people who put themselves out there as completely as Dodd did. It was like he was wearing a sign that said, "Here it is. Like it or hate it, this is what you get."

Chelsea rummaged around her photo books until she found the one that referenced her last trip to the Middle East. They'd been extracting artifacts in what was once known as Levant, located today in southern Syria. She was working with an amalgam group composed of representatives from many different countries. It was also the trip where she'd conceived David, a gift she'd not dreamed she wanted until it arrived.

She struggled to pull her mind from memories of that trip and focus on the task at hand. Rummaging through old boxes and tubs, she gently put aside idols and statues which were wrapped for protection save a few she had on the table. Iblis, Asmodeus, and various forms of the shaitans and jinns of the desert were all in attendance.

Chelsea's hands felt for sight within a tub until she found what she'd been seeking. Book in hand, she walked back upstairs to see that Dodd and Rose were still having a good time despite how screwed up everything was.

"This may be of interest to you, Detective," Chelsea said, sliding the open book of photographs across the table toward him.

Dodd studied an image of what looked to be a large pot from some ancient period with the image of a horrible beast etched into the side. The image had faded over time, but he could make out that it was dyed red and black. The depiction was of a four-armed demon with hooks for hands. The head, equipped with a spear-toothed mouth and exaggerated insectoid eyes, was shaded by wings splayed above it in a leathery canopy. Beneath were letters in a language that appeared to predate any alphabet he was familiar with, which was more than a few. He turned the book with some flare and slid it to Rose.

"That look familiar to you?" he asked.

She studied it quietly for some moments before she said, "The mouth is the same. You can even see the tongue he used to shoot the acid onto my shoulder."

"What's the back story on this?" Dodd asked Chelsea.

"It's from a dig we did in Syria back in the nineties. The image is of Beelzebub, Lord of the Flies," she said.

"That all it says on it?" he said.

"No, Beelzebub literally translates to Lord of the Flies, there are other theories on the translation, but the undisputed part is where it says *the gluttonous*. Rose, if this is who you ran into in The Bone Yard, then a three-thousand-year-old god from Ekron is here in the Hudson Valley with us, and I'd imagine it means we have plenty to worry about."

"Think he's the one who did in Ramirez and the team out by the river?" Dodd asked.

Rose raised her eyebrows at this. "The river? What happened?"

"We will fill you in," Chelsea said to Rose. "But no, based on the size of the tooth, I don't think he is the one from the river."

"So, we have multiple ancient deities roaming around?" Dodd asked. "This doesn't make any sense, Chelsea."

"I know, but you must have had this in your gut when you decided to come to see me," she said.

"Yeah, I guess I did. I knew I needed you, that's all I knew," Dodd said. "The question now is: Why is this happening?"

Rose spoke up. "It has something to do with the bridge and David, that much I know."

Chelsea put an arm around her. "Maybe, sweetie. If that's the case, we will make sure we keep him safe."

"That's just it," Rose said. "We can't. Maybe it's because you weren't there in the restaurant, but if you'd seen him, you'd know what I mean. I'm betting the police shot him and he was fine."

Dodd said, "They did *shoot* him, multiple times, and he still got away. That's another reason I'm here. Unless he was a man in a vest, you don't walk away from taking that much fire. Hell, even with a vest, you don't."

"We can't protect ourselves or David," Rose said.

Silence shrouded the round table.

"We will find a way to protect what we need to protect," Dodd said. "For one thing, Betelgeuse, or whoever it is, ran away instead of killing those cops. That denotes some kind of weakness. For another, this weird stuff is happening in the shadows, which means they need to hide. Another sign pointing to a weakness. We aren't dead in the water yet, but we need information."

Both Chelsea and Rose firmed up at this. "Where do we start?" Rose asked.

"We need to swing by The Bone Yard, and I need to go to the precinct and see what's being done about the missing men."

"Why do we need to take Rose back there?" Chelsea asked.

"I want to get a sample of the blood and the stuff he spit on Rose, Dodd said. "I know a guy in the lab who will run them for us. Maybe a chemical composition will give us something more to go on. The station stop will serve both purposes."

"I want to go to the hospital afterward and check on David, Rose said. "I don't like them poking and prodding at him when we aren't there to see what they're up to."

"Sounds like we know our route," Chelsea said.

"We can grab a little shut-eye when we get to the hospital," Dodd added.

"Things have gotten so unbelievably weird," Chelsea said. "It's hard to believe this is all happening. My mind keeps protesting against it." She sighed. "It's like it can't possibly accept this."

"I think it's always been unbelievably weird," Rose said. "Think about the upheavals and wars around the world. People hating others for no other reason than being in different clubs when they all serve a machine that's transparent enough to see and understand, yet impossible to escape. Having a face to place on the evil makes things easier. Now it's just believably weird."

Dodd and Chelsea glanced at each other, and Dodd smiled. He definitely liked the kid.

Ω

David and Jacob had set off down the new path immediately after his confrontation with the guardian creatures. Jacob had taken the time to briefly explain to David that the purpose the creatures served was to protect the realm from those who were not worthy of entering without a guide. When David brought up that he *did* have a guide, Jacob merely smiled. David felt there was more to things than what he was being told.

The small chimera trailed them as they walked and bounded round their legs in reverie. Jacob had taken to calling it Lycia, after the home of the famous chimera of Greek legend. David had let bygones be bygones and softened to Lycia's presence, but the wolf head still held an eerily sinister quality as he watched it chewing on the leg of Jacob's pants.

Their journey continued through the passing of days and nights, though the length of time never measured out to what might have been expected. Some nights passed in as short a span of time as a few hours, and others felt as though they dragged on for what could have been weeks in the living world. Time was an enigma, and he began to stop thinking of it as a construct and more like the ebbs and flows of a tide.

"Where are you taking me?" David asked.

"That is not the first time you've asked me this question," Jacob replied.

David looked at him. "And that's because you never give me a straight answer." He sighed audibly and reached back into his pocket to feel the coin. It was his only pastime as they walked for eternity, without needing to stop for food or rest.

Though, it wasn't all bad. David often felt incredible satisfaction from his conversations with Jacob. The man—the *angel*—held a wealth of knowledge like nobody he'd ever met, and he shared it freely, only punctuating some points with cryptic sayings or doublespeak.

"If I believed an answer would help you, then you should trust that I would deliver one," Jacob said.

"Okay, that's fine. Reasonable even, David said. "But tell me, what is the point of this? What is the point of everything? If everything is temporary, even the universe, then why bother with all of this toil and heartache?"

Jacob turned his face from the path ahead of them, something he rarely did in their travels. David felt as though eyes bore holes through him from behind the blindfold. "You are currently undertaking exactly that which you inquire toward," Jacob said. "You should also consider that while humanity's understanding of physics has come a long way in a short time, there is much left to be revealed. You can't be sure everything is temporary."

"Oh, man. *You* don't know either, do you?" David asked. "That's it. Your boss didn't offer up that information to us *or* to you guys. We're all in the dark here."

"That's a rash presumption to make, considering you have nothing further to prove it than your intuition, which is currently being fueled by agitation," Jacob said.

David hated when Jacob went Dr. Phil on him. "Alright, alright. How about this? You tell me why your eyes are covered by that cloth that looks like it was made when Hammurabi was making laws."

David immediately regretted the way he'd posed the question that had been on his mind since leaving the boat. Jacob was frustrating in the way untying a knotted line was, but conversing with him was often as satisfying as seeing the line straightened out at the end. He was kind down to his marrow; David knew that much. "Listen, I'm sorry. I shouldn't have said that," David said.

They walked on for a few more minutes before Jacob stopped. David stopped too, and the lack of inertia over-sensitized him. He looked to Jacob, waiting to be admonished. Jacob lifted his hands to his face, placing two fingers from each under the blindfold and slowly lifting it to his forehead.

There weren't two empty eye sockets, which was what David was expecting, considering the lead up. Instead, there was pure chaos. It appeared as the deepest abyss one could imagine, and David felt as though he was being pulled into the void by a force of gravity greater than the light-devouring darkness at the center of the galaxy.

He began to realize he wasn't just seeing this—he was feeling it, being it, and becoming lost within it. Just as his body began to stretch and be pulled away, a nagging bite on his leg anchored him.

Lycia's lion and leopard heads had each latched on and were pulling backward. He found he didn't need their help beyond being snapped out of his stupor; he was now doing fine, leaning his will backward against the draw of Jacob's true gaze. He became more comfortable with what he was experiencing, and the chaos transformed into a fiery chasm of light. As it did, Jacob brought the blindfold back down over his eyes.

David almost fell backward as the drawing sensation ceased. "Well, that's what I get for being rude," David said. He bent down to gently scratch at Lycia's heads and calm them. "What the heck was that about?"

The frown lines around Jacob's mouth and eyes filled in as his expression softened. "Would you accept that it is just too long a story for us to delve into at this time?" Jacob asked as he waved for David to walk on.

"You're the wise one, what do you think?" David said.

"I'll offer you this in lieu of your request. It will serve as something of an answer," Jacob said. Lycia rammed his shin and rebounded into David. "Do you know of the Norse god, Woden?"

"I know about Odin, David said. "The Zeus of Nordic mythology, big boss with an eye patch, lightning, and a bit of a temper."

"I'm not so sure about the temper, but that's right. He's also the namesake of Wednesday, the wielder of Gungnir, and the wisest of the Norse pantheon. Do you know how he became so wise?" Jacob asked.

"If I say book learning, will you hate me forever?" David said, smiling.

"No, but your clever witticisms aren't helping you find answers," Jacob said. "Woden craved wisdom in the stories so much so because he feared the destruction of the world. He sought out wisdom from the wisest people and gods he could find and sent his ravens to collect information, but it wasn't enough to satisfy him. You see, Woden was one who helped to craft the very creation he so wished to protect. To this end, he believed knowledge would be the best weapon."

David took this in as they walked and considered his own ambitions and how they fueled his need to know and understand everything. "He was the king of the gods, and he didn't know how to save the world? I guess that's a tough lesson for everyone to learn."

"It might be, if that was the end of the story, but Woden didn't stop," Jacob said. "He went to the tree of life they call Yggdrasil and attempted to drink from the well of knowledge, but, as in most stories, there was a cost. The payment for his prize was pain. He hung from the tree and endured the gravest suffering imaginable for nine days and nine nights."

"That sounds heavy. Why not seven days and nights, or fourteen, though? What makes nine special?" David asked.

Jacob paused and said, "The questions ceaselessly flick forth from your tongue."

"Sorry."

Jacob shook his head to show there was no need for an apology. Quite the opposite. "There are nine realms in Nordic lore. I assume that has something to do with the number of days and nights Woden hung from Yggdrasil. He didn't just endure this, though. He also impaled himself upon his spear and then ripped his eye from its socket as payment for the knowledge he sought."

"Are you serious?" David asked.

"This is the story, yes," Jacob said.

"Why did he have to keep finding ways to mutilate himself like that?" David asked, kicking a rock for Lycia to chase down.

"I'd imagine it was because the knowledge he was given didn't quite fill the void within him," Jacob said. "He had to continue to sacrifice in order to drink in more and more until he was satisfied he knew how to save the world."

David considered the deep chaotic nothingness he had just encountered within Jacob's eyes and became somber. "Your story helped me to understand a little," David said, letting Lycia pull at his pant leg while also jabbing needlepoint teeth into his shin. He thought of the suffering Jacob must have endured to gain his own wisdom. "Thank you."

"Let it never be stated that a good metaphor can't quiet the earnest needs of a youthful mind," Jacob said.

He kicked a rock into the air ahead of them. Lycia bounded past and leapt as the rock began to fall to the ground. The wolf caught it midair and promptly swallowed it.

Ω

The floorboards creaked under Marcus's bare feet as he rocked his four-month-old to sleep. Chester's small cherubic face, so pale that it seemed to glow in the darkness, peaked out of the ceremonially arranged clothes he wore before bed. The key to ushering him to his dreams was to watch his little eyes. The blinks measured at a slower and slower rate as the will to stay awake and watch shadows dance along the ceiling gave way to the siren's call of sleep. The timber groaned in rhythm with sways and steps at constant tempo despite the slowing of Chester's hands as they explored the stubbled terrain of his father's face. Daddy bops, a key tool in salvaging any adult time, meant Chester never stood a chance.

The infant's eyes lolled, and Marcus breathed in counts of one and two, three and four, five and six, until he reached a long sixty. Chester tended to pop up if he wasn't fully asleep when the motion ceased, and counting helped keep Marcus sane in the darkened nursery during the sleep ritual. Now, with his infant safely ensconced within the crib, the young father gingerly slinked from the room to help Janice complete their toddler's sleep routine: a far more in-depth

119

ordeal with multiple readings of *Are You My Mother, Goodnight Moon,* and *The Giving Tree.* The door creaked closed and carried with it the last sliver of light from the hallway.

Ambient home noises echoed to the nursery as the night wound down, but none would disturb the infant. Chester wouldn't hear Jimmy Fallon from the TV downstairs as Marcus and Janice enjoyed the scant wedge of waking solace afforded them. Not when the ritual was properly kept and an ounce of luck was on their side.

Against the tenants of rationality and fairness, when quiet filtered its way through the home and stillness reigned over night, Chester woke. If he could sit up, the boy would have seen a figure sitting in the rocking chair where his mother nursed him. Occupying the space now was not the adoring mother who looked down on him with love-glossed eyes, but a quiet antithesis of her. The woman in the chair was beautiful, an unarguable fact despite her aura of malice. She was as darkly beautiful as Helen of Troy had been a gift to men as a drop from the sun.

Lilith gently rocked the chair, and unease grew. Chester, a small creature, was completely dependent on his instincts for survival. Despite being known for their lack of any semblance of self-preservation, infants do have biological imperatives to help them to this end. Humankind managed to survive and flourish in the wild, after all. His brain, hard wired through years of gene memory, recognized danger was near, yet he could not muster the breath to cry out, his voice lost to him in the darkness. So, with eyes as wide and deeply blue as the pacific, he lay on his back.

Helpless.

Lilith rose from the chair and glided soundlessly over creaky floorboards to the edge of the crib. Chester regarded her face while kicking his legs and attempting to free his arms from the cruel embrace of the swaddle. Lilith smiled warmly at the boy while lowering her face to meet his, an act performed countless times in the past. Mere oxygen wasn't what she desired, but a tonic of his future, his potential, and all the love he would bring to the world. Lilith persisted this way, filling the vast void within her.

She was stopped just short of Chester's perfect lips. Much time had passed since she'd experienced anything that could give her pause. Anger swelled within her, and she pushed against the barrier just inches from the face of purity beneath her, her eyes aflame as a petulant child being warded off a coveted yet dangerous desire.

"Something amiss?" a voice queried from the far corner of the nursery.

"I should have known it was one of you. Their wards aren't nearly as powerful as this," Lilith waved her hand over the crib.

"Really? All I did was chant the Shema over the lad. If I recall correctly, the prayer is a product of the sons of Eve and Adam," the man said as he stepped forward from shadow. He placed a copy of *Love You Forever* on the little nightstand and pushed his glasses up from the tip of his nose.

"Samael, you're the last of the host I expected to meet during these times," Lilith said.

"I wonder why you might have assumed I would not arrive when you have sent so many souls to me in recent weeks. Did you think I'd lost all curiosity?" Samael said. "I've not changed much since we last embraced, Lilith."

"Yes, the ever curious and ever devoted Samael. Let me ask you, do you ever tire of their hatred of you?" Lilith motioned to the infant in the crib.

"Hatred? They don't hate me. They barely understand me. Fear. Fear is what they have for me, and can you blame them? They know next to nothing of the grand design within which they function." Samael began to make shadow puppets on the wall using the small glow from the night light. Chester's eyes followed the heads of dogs and the wings of birds as he lay silently in the crib. "They who have been tasked with enduring their existence all while thinking it to be finite. Some still believe in the continuation of their consciousness after death, but even those are holding on by their nails. Most are searching for meaning they can use to tie together their understanding of who they are and why they are here. You and yours are far more hated than I will ever be. Stop projecting."

"So you, the one who snatched the life of all the firstborns of Egypt as you were ordered, come here to judge me in my endeavors?" Lilith asked.

"I am here to preserve that which does not belong to either of us. That is all. This boy will live, and the reasoning of this decision is beyond both of us," Samael said.

"And if I was to call our son here to stand before you? Would you be so confident in your ability to stop us then?" Lilith asked in a softened tone. She began to move across the room toward Samael.

"Asmodeus?" Samael laughed. "He is your trump card?" Samael's lips parted in a toothy smile that gave Lilith pause. "Woman, what we had was not the product of your seductive wiles. I simply understood your anger after you were run out of the garden. You felt slighted and marginalized by your equal. Despite this truth, don't imagine you hold any power over me in this moment. I am beyond you."

Lilith bristled at the rejection. "You are a pawn and always have been. A delivery boy for souls torn from this world and a garbage man for your brethren. They laugh at you from on high as they slaughter my children."

Samael reached a hand out to cup Lilith's neck. "Garbage men have great benefits, whore of Eden," said Samael as he pulled Lilith within inches of his face. "We are both ancient and have traversed the void, but our similarities diverge well before this difference. I don't delight in pulling the life from those I deliver, as you do. Why won't you ever understand that it is a losing prospect? Everything has a purpose and a function. Your oily words don't change that no matter how you frame them. You wish more than anything to have death on your side because you are scared, and I'm wise enough to know it isn't me or mine whom you fear."

"I fear nothing. Not Raphael nor Gabriel—" she said.

"—nor Michael, nor Lucifer. Yes, I've heard the speech before," Samael said. "When you finally ceased speaking and were fully expecting your end, we united in our shared grief. You are afraid of something. I feel your fear and smell its perfume seeping from your pores. Why not tell me? We may be able to benefit one another."

"I'll never accept the aid of those who cast me into darkness," she whispered.

"You ran. There's a difference. Had you been ejected from paradise, your mortal body would have been consumed by flames and reduced to ash to nourish the soil. Everything has its purpose," he said, releasing her neck.

"Mocking me again? I am not one of them," she said.

"Close enough," he said.

"And where are your shackles, then?" Lilith asked. "Having coupled with a mortal woman gained many others of your ilk imprisonment here on earth."

"I'm sure you can understand the difference between me and the fallen watchers, Lilith. I memorized the rulebook first."

"Your arrogance reminds me of someone," Lilith said. "I wonder where it will take you someday."

"Be warned, mother of demons," Samael said, "arrogance or no, I'm still embraced by grace, and with it I burn so fiercely that nearly all in existence cower before my heat. Should the orders begin to come down again, as we think they will, you may find your neck under my sword."

"Your scythe, you mean? Would the Lightbringer cower, too?" she asked. Samael stiffened. "I guess that means the rumors are true. There's nobody at the helm anymore. He isn't pushing the buttons and moving the pieces on the board."

Samael regarded her, his smile faltering as he began to turn. "The one who destroyed Nirah was none other than Asmodeus," he said and disappeared through the open window, already a distant memory to the flowing curtains of the nursery.

Lilith regarded the child once more before making to follow Samael's lead, lashing at his face despite being repelled by the barrier. She shouldn't feel betrayed. The knowledge of Asmodeus's anger and unpredictability had led her to believe he had destroyed Nirah to a near certainty.

No longer willing to stay and drink in her own limitations, she turned her back on the crib and refocused her rage on those who had clipped her talons, the host who felt they were empowered simply due to being formed by the hands of the creator. Mankind who felt they were entitled to everything they could reach because they, too, were formed by those hands and fueled by life breathed into them directly from the source of all existence.

Breath she now must steal from innocents to continue her own life.

Was she not formed by those hands as well? She spat on the floor of the nursery, spittle glistening on the eye of the blue train engine smiling up at her in the moonlight as she left.

Chester inhaled deeply, and his eyes welled with tears. He began to cry a torrent of deep despair, filling the home with the sounds of his torment. Janice's sleeping dress swept the floor around her bare feet as she entered the room and pulled the budding life into her embrace. She sat in the chair and closed the window to bar the chill from the room. Gently, she rocked Chester and held him to her breast. Her warmth spread through him as he drank her in.

Ω

Dodd, Chelsea, and Rose arrived at The Bone Yard just after the sun crested the horizon. Driving in the dawning light of the budding day had kept them all in a state of unease. There was a weight to the darkness, so pervasive that the headlights in their car struggled to push it back.

Having arrived, Chelsea said, "Rose, you don't have to come in. I can stay with you while Dodd searches for what he needs."

"No, I'll be okay, Ms. Dolan," Rose said. "I can show him where everything happened."

"That'll make this faster, but are you sure?" Dodd asked.

"Everything will go faster when you two stop treating me like I'm about to break. I'm fine," Rose said.

"Well, I'm not your father, so I don't really have a dog in this fight," Dodd said.

Chelsea sighed heavily in the way that mothers tend to when

their attempts to shelter children are shrugged aside. "Guess we better get it over with."

Dodd entered the restaurant first, parting the yellow police tape for the women and then putting it back in place behind them. Rose said, "Over there is where the two guys were killed. Armand was killed right here." Rose pointed to the corner booth where chaotically arranged dark stains stood out on the floor. Chelsea had to tamp her imagination from running too far with just how the blood could end up arranged like that.

"There's nothing here for us from Beetlejuice," Dodd said.

"Beelzebub," Chelsea corrected.

"Yeah, him," Dodd said. "We need to find something that came from him."

Rose said, "That'll probably be in the kitchen. But the flies he had were all over there." Rose pointed to the ground carpeting where the men had been laying when she fled the scene.

"Alright, let's start here and then work into the kitchen. We don't need much, and we should probably get out of here fast. I don't want to answer any questions," Dodd said. They walked over to the area Rose had indicated, and Dodd knelt, taking a few small tools from his jacket pocket.

"Always carry a petri dish and forceps with you on your outings, Detective?" Chelsea asked.

Dodd didn't turn his head. "Only when it looks like it's going to be a fun night."

Rose remained silent while Dodd pulled fibers from the areas of discolored carpet. "Try to get the outside area where its darker. I think that's what the flies would have turned into. It's darker than the blood," Rose said as he seemed to be finishing.

Dodd pulled a second collection jar, did as she asked, and then stood. "Where to next, boss?"

Rose didn't bother pointing as she turned and walked to the kitchen. Chelsea and Dodd followed. When they arrived, they found things to be as Rose's story indicated, with small differences in the form of a phone broken on the floor, the fryer grease depleted and brackish, and spatters of black liquid on the walls from the bullets exiting the assailant's body.

"Jesus," Dodd said. "They really lit him up in here."

"It's scary. Like one of those crime dramas," Chelsea said, her arms crossed tightly over her chest and her posture stiff.

"He wanted to kill me in here," Rose said. "I think he settled for drinking the fry grease after I ran away."

"That can't be possible," Dodd said. "Those things are set to three hundred and fifty degrees, minimum."

Chelsea gave him a quizzical look.

"What? A guy can't have had a few odd jobs in his life?" Dodd said.

"Short order cook isn't that odd of a job," Rose said.

"Seems odd for you," Chelsea said with a smile.

Dodd set out collecting samples of what they surmised was Beelzebub's blood on the walls. Rose helped him by bringing over a bar stool so he could gather the samples higher on the wall, and Dodd laughed. "Not used to needing a booster. Thanks, kiddo."

He gathered some of the now-gelatinous grease from the fryer and what remained of the liquid that had burned Rose, which he found on the underside of the aluminum counter. Satisfied with their little CSI act, they hightailed it to the car and made for the police station. The ride was short, but in the time they were on the road, both Dodd and Chelsea noted the lighter traffic.

"Something is definitely off," Chelsea said. "There should be intersections backed up with cars at this hour."

Dodd grunted his agreement but made no attempt to further the conversation. He seemed deep in thought. Rose was in the back seat, and Chelsea could see her beatific features illuminated in the soft glow of the smart phone. "Anything in the news, Rose?"

"Yep," she replied. "Lots, actually. Here." Rose leaned forward to hand Chelsea the phone, which was already open to Reddit's news sub. Chelsea scrolled through a few stories and became more and more unsettled.

"There's nothing but stories of people seeing or being attacked by mysterious things," Chelsea said. "This one guy says he was camping and found a cast iron tea kettle on the trail he was on. He grabbed it, hiked some more, and finally settled in to make camp. When he came back, there was a man with skin like tree bark sitting where he'd left the kettle. Story says he sat up all night talking, and just before daybreak the tree bark guy just left. The hiker says he was talking about everything from mushrooms to spirits living in the woods. Says he was never threatened but felt like if he made the wrong move, he would be killed on the spot. Spooky stuff."

"That's not even close to as spooky as some of the other stories," Rose said. "And, didn't the hiker see the kettle again?"

"Yes," Chelsea replied, "it says he saw it when he was walking back out of the woods. He didn't dare touch it, though, and he ran the last few miles to his car."

Dodd said, "I'd have run too, and I don't run much. More of a stand and deliver type."

"Yeah, your track running days are probably behind you, Dodd," said Rose, leaning forward and patting his shoulder, "But we like having our very own giant to protect us."

Dodd smiled and said, "I live to serve, my dear."

When they arrived at the station, Dodd noted the absence of many of the police cars. It wasn't bizarre to see a few missing due to speed traps out in the early morning, although no cop will admit that they try to leave rush hour traffic alone as much as they can so that they don't slow down the commutes toward the city.

Today was sparse. Very sparse. Most of the unmarked cars were missing too. Dodd parked right in front of the entrance and threw himself out of the car. Rose thought the springs being released from their confinement might toss the left side of the car in the air and flip it with her still inside. *He truly is a behemoth.*

They walked in and briskly passed by the reception desk, where the attending officer nodded to Dodd as he stepped by. Rose hadn't been brought in through the front entrance when she came to the station just a few hours before, but she recognized the bullpen area when they reached it. She and Chelsea took seats while Dodd lumbered off down a dimly lit hallway.

"There's like no one here," Rose said.

"It might be normal for it to be like this in the morning. We're not in LA or Chicago," Chelsea said. They sat in comfortable silence for a while, listening to the tock-tock of a clock without ticks.

"I need some water. Want to come to the fountain with me?" Rose asked.

"Dodd will probably be a little longer. Sure, let's take a field trip," Chelsea said.

Rose bounced from her seat like only a twenty-two-year-old can on five hours of sleep. "I saw the officer bring it from this way when they gave me some last night."

Chelsea followed her in the direction Dodd had ventured, past the offices of the brass, and through a labyrinth of hallways. She couldn't imagine ever again working where sun never shined as she had at the museum, a world only visible through the artificial light of large fluorescent bulbs. Rose paused when they found themselves at a water cooler next to a set of stairs that led down. She drank greedily from a paper cone that looked like it belonged on a gnome's head.

"Do you hear that?" Chelsea asked.

Rose cocked her head to the side and listened. "Do you mean that sound like a music box?" Rose asked.

"Yes. that's exactly what it sounds like," Chelsea said. "My grandmother used to have one with a spinning ballerina on the top. It's not the same song, but it reminds me of hers."

Without warning, Chelsea made her way down the stairs. She leaned over the railing and looked down further before glancing back to Rose and shrugging. Rose tossed the paper cone into the trash and followed her. The stairs weren't long, and they soon found themselves at the entrance to the holding cells. The door was open and music leaked from within.

Rose looked at Chelsea and saw her jaw set with clenched teeth. Something was grating at her that Rose couldn't identify. Before she could raise a question, Chelsea entered the hallway, lined left and right with holding cells. It was a small space, housing four cells on either side, all seemingly empty except the one at the far end on the left. Chelsea walked on. Rose followed, being careful to glance around her as she did. Unease grew thick within her.

Chelsea reached the end and stopped to look into the cell. Three men slept inside. One clad in a tank top and underwear was on his side in a bunk with his back to them, two others were seated upright, propped up by where their heads met.

"This is weird, Ms. Dolan. Really weird," Rose said as she appraised the men leaning into one another. "We need to go."

The feeling of unease had transformed to full dread. The hair on the back of Rose's neck stood on end. She couldn't identify why, but her fight-or-flight response was screaming at her to run.

"Where is the music coming from?" Chelsea whispered. She leaned her face against the bars to the cell and studied the men inside. "It doesn't sound like it's coming from in there."

Rose wouldn't dare walk farther in, but she would never leave Chelsea behind either. "Look at the door," Rose said.

Chelsea looked and noticed the quarter inch gap where the door would normally be cinched closed to keep the men in the cell. Chelsea had moved a half step closer and reached for the door when Rose stopped her.

"The music sounds like it's right there," Rose said, pointing to the gray prison wall six feet farther, marking the end of the hallway.

Chelsea noted she was right and brought her hand away from the cell door. When she did, a squat figure revealed himself in the corner by the wall. He was not a man, but a male aura was felt by both women. His features were too compressed to be human, but despite this, he wore a wrinkled suit with the sleeves rolled up to reveal his wrists and hands. In his right was a small music box with a crank. He had been turning it to run the mechanism that played the song which had drawn them.

Releasing his lips from a pout into a smile revealed that his teeth were chaotic and angular. "Didn't go for the door? Why?" it asked.

Chelsea took a step back. Rose's arm caught her and guided her away from the cell bars, back and toward the door they'd used to get in.

"Leaving?" it asked.

The women were dumbfounded. Rose, having had some experience with the unexplainable as of late, felt the ground beneath her feet before Chelsea could.

"I don't know what it is," she said, "but I think if you opened the door, it would have killed you. It's wearing a cop's suit." Rose pointed to the barely clothed man lying on his side in the cell. "He was one of the guys who took my statement last night. I think his name was Tinderman."

The squatting creature narrowed his black eyes at Rose. "Hmm, do you think you can leave?" it asked.

Rose and Chelsea were backing away when the creature disappeared. The women instinctively crowded together when he vanished. Chelsea's yelping "ahh" echoed through the hallway when she heard the door behind them slam.

"Shit," Rose said.

Whatever it was had made it past them and closed the door to the cell area. The music began again, this time directly above them. Chelsea and Rose looked up to see the thing standing on the ceiling, still crouched, peering down at them from a few feet away. Its left hand spun the lever of the music box, its smile more insidious when it was inverted and dangling above.

Rose touched Chelsea's shoulders and spun her to the door. They both ran to it, Rose lifting the handle and pulling with all her might. Locked. The door was controlled by a keypad, and neither of them knew the code. Chelsea began mashing the code box, trying to get the door lock to disengage. The music tempo increased, and Rose turned to face where the creature had been.

Back on the floor, it asked, "Why are you leaving?" It took a step toward them and repeated, "Why are you leaving?"

The cell doors to their right and left disengaged with an audible click as metal slid against metal. One swung slightly on well-oiled hinges. "Why not stay?" it asked.

Chelsea gave up on the keypad and faced the thing with Rose.

"Don't touch the doors," Rose said. "I don't know what it's trying, but I know the doors are what the little geek wants us to mess with."

"Okay, but then where do we go?" Chelsea asked.

"I don't know," Rose said.

It shuffled toward them. The smiling face turned to a pouting frown with a few teeth still snaggled out of its lips. "Why not stay? Why not stay?" it mumbled as it ambled down the corridor, decreasing the space between them to no more than ten feet before stopping.

One of the leaning men let out an audible groan which caused their captor to turn its attention back toward the far cell. The man, not a cop based on his ripped jeans and half-tucked shirt, rose to his feet and stumbled a few steps forward. The other man who'd propped him up with his own body flopped to the bench like the foundation of a spoiled card castle.

The thing walked back, and stood a few feet from the cell door, and stared in, seemingly excited, before disappearing again. As the prisoner cleared his head, he noticed the door standing slightly ajar and made his way clumsily toward it. As he reached out his hand to push the coated iron bars outward, Rose shouted, "No! Don't touch it!"

But she was too late. The man swung the door and put one foot through the threshold before his shoulder and head were rocked backward, and he stumbled into the cell. The creature materialized, crouched atop the prisoner with its feet on his chest and its arms wrapped around his head. Its small size seemed not to matter given the element of surprise. The man hit his backside with an audible *humph* and threw his arm to push the creature off, but he was too late. It leaned in, its mouth open in a wide O shape in front of the prisoner's mouth.

"It's sucking his breath out," Chelsea said.

"I don't think that it's air he's sucking out," Rose said as Chelsea began to move toward them. Loud liquid sounds made clear Rose's meaning.

"We shouldn't try to help him, Ms. Dolan. I don't think we can," Rose said. "Think about the door. It didn't do anything until he touched the door."

The creature, seemingly too preoccupied with what it was doing to the poor man, didn't take notice of their conversation. "Should we lock ourselves in a cell?" Chelsea asked.

"I'm not sure it'll keep it out. He can turn invisible, but I don't know if he can come through doors," Rose said. "I do know that if we cross the threshold, it can get us. Maybe even if we just touch one of these doors."

"Why did it close us in then? Why not wait for us to run through the door we used to get in, or even just get us as we walked in?" Chelsea asked.

"I don't know, but that's a good point. It might just have dominion over the cell doors for some reason," Rose said. She looked and saw that all the cell doors were unlocked and slightly ajar. "It's eating something from inside him. What if it wants us to walk in to save us for when it gets hungry again?"

"And when we get too desperate, we come out and it is there to take us..." Chelsea said. The hinges of a cell door were betrayed by friction, bringing their attention back to the man on the floor. The creature was once again gone. Rose strode a few paces forward and stood in the middle of the hallway.

"We know how it works. You can't get us if we don't go in the doors," she said. Her defiant stance was immediately tested when the creature appeared behind her.

Whispering into her ear, it said, "Why do you think this will save you?"

Rose jumped and turned. The thing now stood between her and Chelsea. Not quite knowing what the next best move might be, she instinctively took a step back from the exit and closer to the men who'd been left on the floor in the cell.

Acting without deliberation, Chelsea planted her left leg and let fly a straight kick aimed right in between the thing's shoulder blades. If it was a normal height, it would have landed in the small of the thing's back, dealing more damage for sure, but Chelsea didn't care as long as she could land a blow. The kick hit nothing but air as the creature disappeared again. She could have sworn she felt some resistance though, as if she had maybe caught part of the suit fabric as the thing narrowly avoided her foot. Laughter rang from behind her now, and the music box began to sound again.

Rose quickly joined her side. "I want to keep it in front of us, if we can," she said.

It appeared, the trick losing its mysticism each time the women witnessed it, but still a sight which ground against their need to rationalize what was happening. It stood at full height now, the humor which had shown through in its obsidian eyes was gone. "Will you answer me? Would you believe I'd let you out if you do?" it asked.

Rose almost exclaimed the word "no" in a knee-jerk response before realizing what she'd been missing. "Don't answer his questions," she said.

The thing curled its lips back in a snarl. The hand working the lever on the music box stopped, standing rigid now. She'd struck a nerve. The squat creature began to advance on them, whatever agenda it had seemingly now lost. Its small footfalls echoing off the walls were interrupted by the sounds of the code being punched in from the other side of the door.

Dodd walked in with his head bowed to avoid hitting it on the jamb. The slow entrance gave the creature enough time to disappear again. "What in the hell are you doing in here?" he asked, more worried than angry.

"Be careful, there's something in here," Rose said.

"He went by on my side, Rose," Chelsea said. "He's behind us again. Dodd, don't touch the cell doors no matter what. Oh, and don't answer any questions, either."

Dodd blinked at them for a few seconds and said, "Alright, I think maybe we need to roll out some details, ladies. I'm not sure if you're aware of this, but you're not making a lot of sense." He let a grin grace his broad features while concealing the grip on his gun within his jacket.

Music began to play, and Dodd decided he would go ahead and pull out the sidearm. "Whatever you do, don't let him get too close to the door again," Chelsea said.

"Don't think those guys are going to be getting by anyone any time soon. Not sure why the cell door is open though—" Dodd said.

"Not them, they're probably dead. There's an invisible imp in here with a music box. That's what you hear. We know if you go through the threshold of one of the cells, it'll attack you. Might happen if you just touch the door, too. Not sure. Don't answer its questions, either," Rose reminded him in a single breath.

"Okay, no more whiskey for Rose. Chelsea, come on out of here. We have to talk about the—" Dodd cut off when he saw the snaggle-toothed imp sitting cross-legged in the hallway of cells five feet in front of the women. He didn't remember seeing anyone in front of them a second ago. Pointing his sidearm at it, he said, "Alright, why don't you two back out of here slowly. You down there. We are having a weird day, so I wouldn't suggest moving from where you are. I might just put a few rounds in you."

Chelsea and Rose took the opportunity to start backing away, but the creature did not feel inclined to listen to Dodd's directives. Dodd noticed the odd hair growth, stature, and how the movements of the thing were off. Still, he didn't fire. He never loosed the contents of his clip without being forced to, and as far as he could tell, the thing wasn't armed with anything but a music box.

"Stay put, bub," Dodd said.

"He's not going to. He's going to disappear again. Ms. Dolan, I have an idea," Rose said and leaned in to whisper something in Chelsea's ear.

Chelsea nodded as she considered Rose's counsel and said, "Okay, but I'll do it. Dodd, you'd better be good with that thing."

Rose looked like she didn't agree with the change of her plan, but she didn't argue. She stepped to the right a few paces, and Chelsea backed toward Dodd until she was next to the door of the last cell before the exit. The thing disappeared as Rose had predicted.

"What Criss Angel bullshit is this now?" Dodd said.

"Aim high, Detective," Chelsea said as she pulled the cell door open a few inches and quickly kicked her leg through the threshold, ducking her head and shoulders as best she could.

Dodd didn't know what the hell she was doing, but he saw—no, he felt—air flow the way it does when something is moving very quickly through it. He was happy he had spent some of his younger years boxing, because he didn't blink or flinch when he saw the squat creature beginning to materializing in midair, a mere foot from Chelsea's head. Its eyes were wide open, and its lips turned back in the snarl of an airborne lioness about to latch onto a wildebeest. Dodd fired.

The first three bullets took the creature in the chest and neck, but Dodd wasn't done. After releasing a half breath, he fired three more rounds, angling the weapon as far from Chelsea's hunched back and neck as he could. This made his second volley catch the creature in the collarbone, shoulder, and hand. The music box exploded as a bullet passed through it, before lodging in the concrete at the end of the room.

Before Dodd could yell for them to head out the door, Rose had swept across the hallway and grabbed Chelsea by the waist. Both ran hunched past Dodd and exited the room.

"Dodd!" Chelsea cried, and he woke from his daze. The thing wasn't visible anymore. He backed up a few steps and was clear of the door. Chelsea slammed it shut and said, "Is it locked?"

"Yeah, it locks every time it closes as part of the security protocol," he said. "What the hell was that?"

"Walk and talk," Chelsea said.

The two had relayed all they'd experienced and figured out by the time the trio had made it back to the bullpen.

"Not good," Dodd said. "Also, not good that the lab was empty. No way to test these samples we took."

"Do we even need to bother anymore?" Rose said. "That thing wasn't human, and I think I can speak for all of us when I say that some seriously fucked up shit is happening here."

Chelsea looked at her and then to Dodd. "Seriously. Fucked. Up. Shit. Detective."

Dodd said, "Let's go to the hospital. I raised a few patrols on the radio because this place is a ghost town, and it sounds like there's a lot of calls for weird crap and assailants from around the entire area."

Chelsea seemed to be turning over something in her head. "I

want to see my son, but I think we should make a stop somewhere first. I know a guy who specializes in weird crap, and he's not too far away. Works in an office nearby where mine is at the university. It's in the annex building, so we won't even have to go far into the campus to see him. I'll bet he can shed some light on this. Keep the samples handy, too. There might be a lab tech there as well."

They both looked to Rose, who swelled at their recognition. "Alright then, let's go to see the Monster Geek Squad."

Ω

Jacob, David, and little Lycia continued together until the sun was ablaze above. This didn't give any indication of whether or not it was actually midday, but it often signaled an upbeat vibe between the party members. Lycia chased and stomped their shadows as the absence of light mimed the movements of their bodies. The chimera's play drew Jacob's attention and made him smile. David, too, was happy to have her with them—A bright spot on a bleak landscape.

Walking in silence for some time led David to think of his mother and Rose. They were at the forefront of his mind during lulls in conversation, and he became depressed when he thought of the possibility of never seeing them again. The reality that he may, in fact, be dead was difficult to avoid considering. Maybe this was some kind of sick purgatory he'd been fated to endure, while the powers-that-be measured him against the gold standard of human behavior.

"Do you know what is happening to my family?" David asked Jacob.

"No, not specifically. But they are enduring your situation with strength and grace. This I know," Jacob said.

David said, "Is that a gut feeling kind of thing, or do you have a magic mirror in that pocket?"

"No mirror, and more than a gut feeling," Jacob said. "The world as you knew it is under siege by change. One so immense that it threatens the very perception of what reality truly is. Despite this, I

136

can tell you that your loved ones are in good hands as they traverse the new landscape. As are you."

"That's helpful, I guess," David said. "I don't know what I'd do if anything happened to them. I wasn't really concerned about their safety until you said that though. Are they in danger?"

"Yes," Jacob said flatly.

"And?" David asked loudly enough to distract Lycia from rolling in the dusty path ahead of them. "You're not getting off that easily. They are in danger... and?"

"Yes, they are in danger, and they are facing it with exceptional fortitude," Jacob replied. "I can't see more than that, David. I am sorry. I didn't mean to upset you."

"Will I be able to go back to protect them?" David asked.

Jacob shook his head. "This, too, remains to be seen."

David thought of how Rose's hair felt when he ran his fingers through it as she was falling asleep, how she made moments of languor vanish with her wit, the quirky sideways smile she reserved for when she was playfully antagonizing him. "Have you ever been in love with someone?" David asked.

"No, not with someone, Jacob said. "Love as you know it is not something I have ever experienced. Love, for me, is expressed more in a single moment than the collective breaths of every living human. Grass feels love for the sweet ichor of the morning dew, a child feels love for the moment its mother or father enters their room to rouse them for the beginning of the day, a pet feels love for the attention of its companion owner." Jacob reached down to pet Lycia's back. The little creature stretched up to meet his fingertips with earnest need. "Love is something I experience like this. I do not derive it from companionship as you do. That is how you were created, not me." He paused. "I feel love like the grass."

David absorbed this. "I see what you are saying. The best of people feel appreciation for the things you've described, but I doubt the word love can be attributed to that despite how often it is used that way. The only way I can describe how I feel about Rose is to say I am a part of her, or she is a part of me. Being without her feels like something was amputated. I'm incomplete. If she was to be hurt or gone, I'd never be able to become more than fractured."

"This sentiment is something I can understand as well. We are becoming better at these exchanges of understanding, are we not, David?" Jacob said.

"Yeah, we are moving past Abbot and Costello and reaching Oscar and Felix levels of communication," David said.

Jacob didn't get this reference, but he didn't press further to ask, which was rare.

"Got something else on your mind there, Jake?" David asked.

"We are drawing close to our destination," Jacob said. "I am somewhat saddened."

"Wait, really?" David exclaimed, "That's awesome! Why didn't you say anything before?" Lycia bounded around them with vigor at David's reaction.

"I've enjoyed my time with you," Jacob said. "We... I... don't often get to spend time with people, much less people like you. You're free of so many burdens, David. A young man full of inquisitiveness and hope. You share more similarities with Lycia than you do with much of your kin. This isn't to say humanity is lost, far from it, but I've watched them slip further from what they truly seek, and it pains me."

"I've never been anything special," David said. "I just wanted to spend time with the people I loved while I was still alive."

Jacob laughed. "You are not dead, boy, I've told you a thousand times."

"Thought I might catch you that time," David said smiling.

Jacob stopped on their path and gestured to his left to a side path that wound down through the shadowy crags and disappeared into a cavernous mouth. Lycia's hair stood on end as she faced the direction of the cave, and all three of her heads bared their fangs. David hadn't noticed just how beautifully all her pelts melded into one another until she showed her primal understanding of a dangerous foe.

"Where does that go?" David asked.

"Have you surmised yet that you are in the ether?" Jacob answered David's question with his own.

David sighed. "I've assumed I've been dead, and this is some kind of purgatory."

"You're wrong in that assumption. Though purgatory is as real a place as the one to which this other path leads. Do you see the inscription at the top of the entrance to the cavern?" Jacob asked.

David scrutinized the entrance and was able to discern writing. It read: Lasciate ogne speranza, voi ch'entrate.

"I know that from somewhere. I've read it," David said and shut his eyes, raking through his memories, but he was unable to place the quote. "I can't remember."

Jacob turned his face to the sun and began to speak.

> *"Through me you pass into the city of woe:*
> *Through me you pass into eternal pain:*
> *Through me among the people lost for aye.*
> *Justice the founder of my fabric mov'd:*
> *To rear me was the task of power divine,*
> *Supremest wisdom, and primeval love.*
> *Before me things create were none, save things*
> *Eternal, and eternal I endure.*
> *All hope abandon ye who enter here."*

David stared, entranced. "That's one of the most beautiful recitations I've ever heard. I knew you were, you know, amazing and supernatural and all that, but I didn't think I'd hear you go all Robert Frost on me."

"Alighieri, not Frost," Jacob said. "Although Frost spoke more of Hell than most people would care to realize."

David said, "I know it's Dante. Dope."

"Name calling at the gates of Hell is not wise, David," Jacob said, smiling.

David smirked. "I wasn't name calling. I mean it's *cool* as Hell."

"Hell is not all in one realm, and not all are hot, but cool would be an understatement for the latter. Or is this more slang you're using?" Jacob asked with interest.

David answered by broadening his smile.

"I'll learn your colloquialisms," Jacob said and wagged his finger.

"I know old man, I know." David clapped him on the back, "So Hell exists. That's crazy."

Jacob knelt to calm Lycia, who was beginning to froth at the wolf's mouth. "Most others would be immediately fearful for their souls, or at the prospect of eternal damnation. David says *dope*."

"Well, it kinda is. More metal than dope, actually. It's hard to explain," David said.

"Metal. I remember metal. It's definitely that," Jacob said. "Listen closely and you'll hear why Lycia is so anxious."

David stilled himself and tuned out the ambient noises around them. Jacob helped by stopping Lycia's growling which turned to whimpers and then quieted to calm.

David strained and could hear nothing from the entrance to Hell, but as he continued to breathe and quiet his mind, the wails began to come.

He heard them beginning with frail cries of anguish so pathetic that he thought he might begin to weep, but they were soon joined with more fervent sounds of torment, verging on animal rather than human. What David was too young to realize was anyone who has heard such pain rarely speaks of it, for to do so exposes the thimble of humanity.

"When I was a kid, a young kid, I would play in a plot of land near our house," David said. "It had woods. Not a deep forest or anything, but to a kid it might as well have been the Tongass National Forest. There were foxes in there, and I'd see them sometimes before they disappeared into the undergrowth in the way foxes do. One time, I saw a mother with her pups, or kits, or whatever... the babies. It was awe inspiring to see them dancing and playing in the twilight out there." David held Jacob's earnest attention as the angel looked up at him from Lycia's side. "One night not long afterward, I heard a pack of coyotes out in those woods whooping and screaming the way they do when they're onto something. They'd cornered small animals for the kill. It's a horrible sound to hear, especially when it's close, but I heard a sound that night far more guttural than the coyotes. After their chorus died down, a wailing noise I'll never forget for as long as I live rose from the woods. It was the mother mourning her babies. It was the sound of unbelievable sorrow. That's what it sounds like in there." David pointing to the entrance. "It sounds like a mother losing a child."

Jacob nodded. "A very accurate description, and a good argument for Hell not just being down there."

David mustered as much courage as he could and steeled himself for what he was sure was coming. "Well, if we have to go to Hell, to hell with it." He began walking on the path that led to what seemed to be much worse than oblivion.

Jacob reached out with fingers of iron and pulled David back. "We aren't going to Hell, you fool."

"Wait, what? Then why did you stop to show me?" David cried.

"I stopped because I thought it'd serve you well to know. We don't have any business down there, and, even if we did, you and I can't just walk in like tourists. There are rules," Jacob said. He surprised David by laughing.

"What's so funny?" David asked.

"You! You making ready to take on Hell with no purpose or reason." Jacob howled as he spoke, and Lycia pulled away fearing he was angry. "You said, *to hell with it*!"

Jacob repeating David's saying, which had felt so cool and perfect in the moment, was now beyond emasculating. He tried not to pout.

"Yuk it up, buddy, yuk it up. I never know what the hell you have in mind," David said defensively.

The unintended pun made Jacob laugh harder, and Lycia joined him with howls and yowls. Jacob took David by the shoulders and ushered him forward on the path they'd been on.

"Thank you," Jacob said. "I haven't laughed like that in such a long time."

"Glad I could be of use to you," David said. "Are we continuing on the never-ending pathway again? Great." David began to walk on his own, relieving Jacob of the need to push him. "Ever hear this one, Jake?" David began to sing the lyrics to the theme song of *The NeverEnding Story*, but he replaced the word *story* with *journey*.

"I'm familiar," Jacob said. "I told you that I am familiar with most all of humanities great works of art."

A bit tickled by the sentiment, David sang louder, "AND THERE UPON A RAINBOW IS THE ANSWER TO A NEVER-ENDING JOURNEY, AH, JOURNEY, AH..."

"You know, we are near the end of the path," Jacob said. "This is a crossroads, after all. That path leading to Hell being but one. There are more leading to other places."

"You better not be messing with me," David said. "I don't know if I can take much more walking. It feels as though we have been walking in place. Things change, night and day, the terrain, but I can't shake the feeling we are on a treadmill."

"You're closer to the mark with that feeling than you might think," Jacob said. "In order to come to this place, any entity must be guided or taken, lest they've been before. Think of it as a journey of the mind rather than physical distance."

"So, we haven't been traveling at all? I knew it!" David said.

"We have, but not outward. We've been traveling inward, David," Jacob said.

David stopped walking, taking a moment to think about this. He noticed they were on a smooth, rocky plateau overlooking endless wilderness—mountains that rivaled the Himalayas, large expanses of desert both sand and frost, forests of trees sized to dwarf the tallest redwoods in the world of the living. All climates and terrains were represented before him, but to a degree of perfection he'd never imagined.

"This may be the most beautiful thing anyone has ever seen," David whispered.

"Yes, it is quite breathtaking," Jacob said. "Much else is its match and more, but that depends on perspective. There are people who appreciate piles of paper as much, if not more, than that forest of magnificent trees."

"Where do we go now? This is the end of the path," David said.

Jacob strode to stand ahead of him and held up his hands. "Your path will end somewhere, David, but the end is not here."

As Jacob's hands stretched above him, he once again let his head fall back as though taking in the warmth of the sun. David watched, transfixed by the elaborate gesture from Jacob, who'd previously been so reserved. The fabric on the tunic at Jacob's back began to shift, and out emerged two wings of the deepest sapphire, their oily feathers catching and reflecting the rays of light from the sun in all directions. As they unfurled, the sheer enormity of their size baffled David. He'd never imagined what human-sized wings might look like up close.

"You really are an angel," David said.

Jacob turned, his wings folding over his back, creating arches above each shoulder, the feathers at the tips hovering inches above the ground. "You doubted this was true? Tsk, tsk," Jacob said. "I thought we'd forged a stronger bond than that."

"I didn't doubt it, but seeing is believing, I guess. Those are beautiful. Your true form, I mean. You're beautiful," David managed to say.

"Thank you," Jacob said. "You should know that this isn't my true form, though. Even I don't know what that will look like. I hope to experience the beauty you see now in what I find at the end of my path, where I will one day find myself complete."

"It is time for us to head to our destination. It is a place where only wings will take you." Jacob looked down past David's legs. "We had better say our farewells to Lycia."

"We can't take her?" David asked.

"No. She belongs back there to test anyone who might find themselves on this path," Jacob said. "You should feel honored that these three, Lycia, chose to be in your company for so long. Most often, they choose to push those who are finding their paths back and back and back again until they are deemed ready. It seems endless."

David knelt and laid his palms out in the gesture that told Lycia she'd be getting some good pets if she came close, and she darted from the periphery to meet David's hands and rejoiced as they danced around her.

"I don't know how long we've been together now, but I feel like we've become companions. I'm going to miss you," David said, wrapping Lycia in his arms to hug her, a gesture he'd never tried before due to her very primal nature. He was happy to feel no tension as she collapsed into him. The two cats licked and nibbled at his arms playfully. The wolf had its eyes cast down but turned its head to the side when David scratched behind its ears. *We're friends,* in canine speak.

"Don't eat anyone," David said and stood up to watch her. She looked to Jacob in what seemed to be a far too knowing way than such a tiny, cute creature should and turned to leave them. As she made it to where the path began to descend from the plateau, she split back into three separate creatures. The lion didn't look back but bounded off down the path ahead of it. The leopard walked sideways away from the wolf before slinking into the foliage, vanishing. The wolf held its place, glancing at both of the others as they went and then looked back to David with the same eyes he remembered from their first meeting. Now they seemed filled with a different emotion: melancholy.

The wolf raised its head and howled deeply into the sky. The sound reverberated off the rocky outcrops around them and danced into their ears from all sides. Then the wolf, too, was gone.

"Parting is such sweet sorrow," David said.

Jacob laughed.

"So how are we going to do this? Do I get wings now?" David asked.

Jacob somehow managed to switch from miraculous to incredulous in an instant. "No. No, you most certainly do not just get wings now," he said. "I will carry you over, as the souls of many others have been carried."

"Aw man, that's no fun," David said. "Can't you make an exception? I'm the guy who turned those zoo animals into a cute puppy-kitty thing. You can give me some wings for that, right?"

"Come here, David," Jacob said.

David sighed. "Alright." He walked to Jacob, and they made their way to the edge of the plateau together.

"Are you ready?" Jacob asked, looking directly at David.

"Yeah, I think I am," David said.

They rose into the air and flew.

Ω

The annex Chelsea led them to was not as sparsely populated as the police station had been, but there were very few students and faculty in attendance. Rose pointed out that it was around finals time, when most colleges were barren, so they made an attempt at denying the nervousness that fought to take residence at the forefront of their minds. The incident at the jail cells kept them peeking over their shoulders. Chelsea, in particular, had her stomach tied in knots from the guilt at being the one who'd led Rose down to the creature.

The trio made their way to the tan brick building, emboldened by a sign etched above the front door reading, "For those who believe, no explanation is necessary; for those who do not believe, no explanation will suffice." Chelsea guided them upon entering, and they found themselves at a large, mirrored elevator bank. The three stared at their reflections as the elevator descended.

"I hope we aren't going down again," Rose said. "I've had enough catacombs for one day."

"I'm sorry about that, Rose. You too, Dodd. I put both of you in danger." Chelsea looked down at her clasped hands. "It was the music that called me down. I had to know if it was my grandmother. I know it doesn't make sense. Hell, she's been dead since around the time David was born, but I couldn't help but see her in my mind, and I just knew the music was coming from her."

"Nothing makes sense right now, Chelsea," Dodd said. "It'd be odder if the reason you were drawn down there was, well, reasonable."

"Thank you. And thank you, Rose. You're why we made it out of there alive," Chelsea said, giving Rose a shoulder hug as they heard the egg timer *ding* of the elevator and the doors slid open. The three entered, and Rose was relieved to see Chelsea choose the seventh floor.

145

"It had a pattern. It was weird, like an evil leprechaun or something. He had to follow rules. Maybe that's how we get ahead of these things," Rose said. "We figure out their rules."

"Maybe," Dodd said.

Chelsea appraised him. He seemed drained. Losing contact with his partner and not getting sleep seemed to finally be taking its toll on the aging detective. "All I know is, I'm glad I'm not alone in this. I'm even more glad you two aren't alone, either. I hope we can stick together until we understand what is happening. Maybe Leonard will know something more than we do."

"What does he do?" Dodd asked.

"He studies ancient demons and folk creatures," Chelsea said.

"You know a demonologist?" Rose asked.

"Well, that's not really accurate. There's no formal title of demonologist. He's an anthropologist with a specialization in theology. Leonard's the guy who identifies the ancient deities and other creatures of yore we might find depicted on the artifacts we dig out on site. He's a little eccentric, but he should see us." Chelsea paused. "I think he likes me."

Dodd smiled. "Ah, the power of a woman."

Chelsea elbowed him in the ribs. It was all the more amusing to Rose because Chelsea had to angle her elbow up to a ridiculous angle to do it. A bell chimed, and the doors slid open, revealing cold tile and a lone potted fern. Rose exited first and waited for Chelsea to look around for a moment to get her bearings. "This way," she said.

They walked for a brief time before entering one of many doors, seemingly identical to one another—at least to Rose. The inside of the room was such a stark contrast to the atmosphere of the rest of the building that she took a second to make sure they hadn't just flipped realities.

The immediate area had two desks adorned with simple lamps and a television mounted to the wall streaming the news. It was muted, but Rose saw words furiously scrolling across the bottom as news pundits barked vitriol fed to them by teleprompters. Her attention was pulled to the area behind the desks, where long tables were filled with treasures alien and wonderful. Rose could hardly keep herself from running over to explore them. She saw idols and vases under lamplight, with brushes and stencils strewn about and around. Among the delightful oddities was a squat figurine with what could have been fangs and a long-forked tongue protruding from between them, a rock cracked open to reveal what looked like half of a female face and hair, and something she could swear was a tiara on a table toward the end. *I have to get in there.*

"Leonard?" Chelsea called.

"Hello, hello, hello! Who's there now?" came a voice from the back of the room.

"Leonard, it's Chelsea Dolan. I came with some friends, so don't be alarmed," Chelsea said, looking for where he had squirreled himself away.

"She's making sure he doesn't crap his pants when he sees you," Rose whispered to Dodd.

"You're not looking too great yerself, little sis. He might think you're the girl from *The Ring*," Dodd lofted back.

Rose smirked and wondered about how she must look a mess. She was sure she had bags under her eyes, and her hair was not tended to at all. She might stumble upon a hair tie and some makeup soon. If not, she could possibly spruce up at the hospital just in case David were to wake up while they were there.

"Chelsea!" Leonard called from back. "Good to hear your voice. Hold one moment, and I'll be right there."

They watched as a tiny man crawled from under one of the far tables. He was wearing a face shield and had lights on the rims of his glasses. It was so ridiculously geeky that Rose instantly found the man charming.

"What were you doing under there?" Rose asked with genuine intrigue, though deep down she knew the answer. He was hiding.

"Oh, I was looking for a thick bristled brush I dropped while working on the Gerasene idol there." Leonard motioned to a figurine of about eighteen inches that didn't appear to have been close enough to where he emerged to have been his focus. There weren't any tools nearby the artifact, either.

"Don't worry, we come in peace," Dodd said.

Chelsea spoke to side-step the awkwardness. "Uh, Leonard..." She cleared her throat. "We need a little help. Some things have happened, and we think you might be the only person who can help us understand what we are, uh, dealing with. Do you have time?"

"Of course! It's been a bit spooky here without anyone about today. The regular techs seem to be taking a day off. One or two here and there, but still," Leonard explained. "I don't mind the distraction. Plus..." he motioned to the work behind him. "These aren't going anywhere."

"Oh, good, thank you," Chelsea said.

Leonard pulled some chairs around so they could sit, and he pushed a leafy pile of papers back onto his desk before he took his own seat atop it. Dodd went first, explaining what he saw around town over the last forty-eight hours and detailing what he found when he went looking for Ramirez. He produced the tooth and handed it to Leonard, who examined it through his thick lenses. He paid special attention to the inside, as Chelsea had.

Next, Rose explained what had happened to her at work and spared no detail regarding the murders of her patrons and the short order cook.

Chelsea rounded out by going over the events at the police station, speaking with pride at the part where Rose's plan had paved the way for Dodd to drop the creature.

"So, do you have someone around here who can study these samples we have?" Dodd said.

"Don't need to," Leonard said.

"I know it's a big ask, but we really need to know what this stuff is to figure out what to do next," Dodd said.

"Oh, no, I don't mean that I can't help you," Leonard said. "I mean that I don't need those samples. From what you've told me, I think I know what's happening."

The three looked quizzically at one another.

"Here, this might help," Leonard said and produced a remote for the TV. He turned the mute off and rewound the DVR until they saw the Governor of New York speaking a formal address none of them had been aware of.

"Right about here," Leonard said and pressed play.

"—unprecedented events and disappearances. We can, at this time, rule out terrorism or formal interference from other countries. This includes attacks and sabotage. Let me be clear here. There is no insurgency occurring, despite what some have been led to believe from certain rumors circulating on social media. What I can say with absolute honesty is that we do not know exactly what is transpiring at this time. We have requested the national guard to come in to help with the roughly"—he looked down at the papers on the desk before him— "four hundred square mile radius that has been established, based on police reports of incidents. I am signing an executive order now to declare martial law and a shelter-in-place order for all non-essential workers and personnel. Unless you are working with the folks who are getting to the bottom of these... happenings, you should be staying home. We do not anticipate this to last for more than a few days, so please do not worry about long term supplies. However, you should take the time to make sure you have what you need by five o'clock tonight, as we will begin sheltering in place at this time, and all stores will be shuttered. I know you are scared and uncertain during this unprecedented time, but know that your elected officials and law enforcement are working diligently to keep you safe and return things to a state of normalcy—"

Leonard turned the TV to mute again.

"You guys are right on the money," Leonard said. "Weird things are happening, and you've been at ground zero from the beginning. It looks like incidents have been ramping up steadily as time goes by. The real danger seems to be after sundown, but some are occurring during daylight hours. Most are outdoors, but I think these things are getting bolder. There may be an uptick in home invasions."

"What are they?" Rose asked.

"Exactly what they seem to be. The creatures and demons

from your nightmares have been loosed on the world somehow," Leonard said.

Dodd cracked his knuckles. "Even with all we have seen, that's still a tough pill to swallow, Lenny. Why would these things just show up out of the blue?"

"I have some ideas about that. Unsubstantiated, of course," Leonard said. "What's more important is the information I have on what you've encountered so far."

"Was it Beelzebub who attacked Rose?" Chelsea asked.

Leonard clicked his tongue loudly. "I don't think so, at least, not quite. Beelzebub was not a low-level entity. What attacked Rose was likely something made in his likeness. An avatar of sorts. Many of the deities, demigods, um, demons... They have been known to do this in anecdotal tales passed down through the apocryphal texts and folklore. It seems to be a slight toward God for creating mankind in his image, at least from the readings I remember." Leonard nodded to Rose. "She threw burning oil on a Beelzebub copy. That's my assessment." He flexed his fingers and placed his hands on the edge of the desk as he leaned toward them, seemingly excited to speak about the subject. "The thing in the station sounds just like the ancient Babylonian demon called a rabisu. They, well the ones known as crouchers, they used to wait near doorway thresholds and pounce on the unsuspecting people who crossed over them. The music box part is odd to me, but there's a lot I don't know, too."

"And what got my partner?" Dodd asked. His downcast face hooded his eyes and threw shadow over his normally jovial features.

"That one isn't as tough, so I think I've got an idea," Leonard said. "It is much more commonly spoken of in the modern day. The Aboriginal people of Australia have folklore surrounding a monster or demon called the bunyip. Indigenous and agricultural peoples today use the story as a cautionary tale to keep children away from riverbanks, so they won't be taken by saltwater crocodiles, but there is a moral aspect to it too. If one is too greedy and takes too much from the river, the bunyip may appear and wreak havoc and floods on the village responsible. They've been described as water horses, or large-bodied beasts with great intelligence who can cause floods at will. Some even describe them with human features, like the mermaids of European lore or the sirens of Greece. There's a degree of cross-over in most myths because cultures blend together, but you get the idea."

"So, you think that a children's story is what killed almost fifteen men out on the Hudson last night?" Dodd asked.

"Well, the Hudson would be a good river for a bunyip to covet. It was heavily polluted for a century and continues to be a dumping ground for plenty of corporate trash. There are stories of bunyips destroying whole villages, and if those are true, fifteen men doesn't seem too outlandish. In any event, the logical conclusion isn't necessarily what you want to work with when you are dealing with things beyond current understanding. Keep your mind open to the illogical, and a path usually appears for you."

Chelsea reached over and took Dodd's hand. "If he is alive, you'll find him."

Rose looked to Leonard. "Can we kill them?"

He was taken aback by the question. "There are movies and comics that always have some mystical weapon a hero uses to vanquish demons and gods, but in what we've read from canon, there aren't any such items. What it does detail are limitations of the demons. Ways to outthink them or use their rules against them. That's how people have survived in the past, and it's what they tell in folk legends to inform their kin of how to deal with these things. I'm sorry to say, but I don't think waving a bible in their faces is going to do much. No spear of destiny, or magic rocks. Some old prayers and markings have been said to be useful in deterring them, but they are specific to cultures and in that way specific to those demons or creatures. You, for example, defeated the croucher by outsmarting it and making it reveal itself so that the detective here could harm it. Those are the types of things that we see in legends."

"That makes sense, now that you mention it," Chelsea said. "Even God didn't kill the fallen angels or demons in the scriptures. The punishment is just imprisoning them or casting them away until a time of judgment."

Leonard said, "That's in the Abrahamic religions, but yes, it is a common trope. I'd venture to guess that these things aren't meant to be killed in the same way angels aren't meant to be killed. Seems odd discussing it as a truth of the world of science rather than a religious teaching, but here we are."

"Speaking of science," Dodd said, "it might be that their biology is alien to us, too. Maybe they can be destroyed, but the weaknesses of creatures from the natural world doesn't really apply to 'em."

"Well if they are here now, then there was a time when things were keeping them away, or at least hidden. What changed?" Rose asked.

Dodd said, "I'm going to venture a guess and say that our learned friend here probably won't know that."

"Accurate," Leonard said as he rose from the desk, taking note of Chelsea's hand on Dodd's, "but in ancient Chinese traditions there exists the story of the Yin and the Yang."

"Don't the Taoists worship the Yin, and the Confucianists worship the Yang?" Chelsea asked.

"Close, but not quite accurate, Chelsea," Leonard said. "Both religions form philosophies pertaining to conflicting forces, but not necessarily the concept of good and evil. The Yin and the Yang were formed from the chaos and represent opposites. One, the Yin, is considered darker and involves reclusiveness. The other, the Yang, the light, is about engaging with life. These two major forces are kept in balance by many smaller outside forces, but the balance is a must. If we consider this, and apply it to a cosmic scale, then the Yang will have to come up to meet the surge of Yin. What has caused the imbalance in the first place, though, is impossible to tell based on what we now know."

Dodd said, "Nuts to what we don't know, but all things considered, this has actually been really enlightening. Thank you, Leonard."

"I don't often get to enlighten," Leonard said. "It's nice to be able to use my life's work to help, even in circumstances such as these. Is there anything else I can help you with?"

"You wouldn't happen to have a hair tie in here, would you?" Rose asked.

Chelsea laughed. "You look fine, Rose."

"Not according to Goliath over here," Rose said and inclined her head in Dodd's direction.

Leonard went to the adjacent desk and opened the drawer, producing three different colored hair ties. "I don't know how sanitary they are, but Molly, my associate, she tends to be hygienic. I doubt they are soiled." He handed them to Rose, who put two on her wrist and began to tie up her hair into a ponytail. "Wait here a second," Leonard said and walked into the back of the room to rustle around within the contents of cabinets and drawers.

Dodd observed Rose as she straightened her hair in the well-practiced way women make seem so effortless and fluid. She looked so little to him in that moment.

"How can we fight back against these things if we keep running into them?" Dodd asked.

"We have to outsmart them, like Leonard said," Rose chirped.

"Yeah, but we don't have his lifetime of studies to back us up," Dodd said.

"Rose managed fine without that," Chelsea chimed in. "I have faith in our quick thinking, and your muscle behind it."

"I'm going to assume that was meant to be a compliment to my physique and not a slight to my mental prowess," Dodd said.

Leonard returned to the front of the room with two items in his hands. "He's right. You may need more than quick thinking out there. The more you venture around, the more likely you are to meet something you won't understand. Here..." He handed Chelsea a book. "It's a field guide put together by a colleague for identifying entities. I think it was written in jest, but in this circumstance, we can consider it quite literally. There's also this..." He handed Rose a small necklace with a larger-than-normal, ornate charm on it. "That is an interesting find. It is an apotropaic ward against evil, but what makes it unique is its attributes from many traditions. The paper wrapped in the middle has the face of a sheela na gigs to ward off malevolence, but her mouth is open, revealing a Greek evil eye as well. There is rowan wood being used to encase the hemp paper with the image, which is also traditional in warding off black magic and spells. The necklace itself is modern silver, but the encasing of the charm is composed of pure silver, and if you came in here knowing anything about this subject matter, you'll know silver is often referenced as a ward against evil. Lastly, the cylindrical charm has shungite at the top and kunzite at the bottom. We assumed it was to create a polarity of sorts, to amplify the effects of the charm itself, although this theory *was* challenged by a research team in California. In any event, and regardless of the amplification theory, it would be the most powerful charm I have at my disposal. I want you to have it."

Rose studied the charm for a moment before slipping the chain around her neck. "I love it," she exclaimed and rushed to give Leonard a hug.

His eyes widened. "It's my pleasure," he said as she released him and looked back down at the charm, feeling its smoothness between her fingers, spying the coarse wood hidden deeper inside. Leonard took a half step back from Rose and scratched the back of his neck.

"Leonard, we can't thank you enough for the help, and for these." Chelsea held up the book and nodded her head toward Rose.

"Couldn't help but notice there's no huge sword or special bullets for me," Dodd said.

"No, there's not," Leonard said. "I told you before that you shouldn't focus on trying to kill these things or even harm them. The croucher you shot is likely doing just fine, waiting by the cells for someone else to come so it can feed off them like it did the three men left there. But there is something I think I should tell you. Rose called you Goliath before. Do you know much about the philistine warrior of the same name?"

"He was a big boy who got taken down by a kid with a slingshot. It's one of the reasons I never sleep on a little guy who wants a piece of me. He probably knows something I don't," Dodd said.

"Yes, David did vanquish him with a sling, so there is a killing in the story, however the Goliath of lore was only half human," Leonard said.

"You subscribe to the theory that Goliath was a Nephilim?" Chelsea asked.

"Nephi-what?" Dodd asked.

"The Nephilim were said to be the children of humans and angels, known as watchers," Leonard said. "Their presence was what was said to be the cause of the flood in the stories of Noah and Gilgamesh, and I don't mean respectively. Most who study them consider the floods in both tales to be one in the same. Yes, Chelsea, I do believe he and his brothers were Nephilim. I also have findings that show the Nephilim did not always share the same properties, gigantism for example, but instead had many forms and powers. They were powerful enough beings to validate the purge of most life on the planet, after all. When Rose brought up the name, it made me think. These are the things of folktales and legends; even Beelzebub wasn't considered a big deal until he was written into the pantheon of hell as a lieutenant to Lucifer. But, you guys, if you keep this up, you may run into something more powerful and far more evil. Something that has not come out in some time. It all depends on how long the Yang lets them run amok, but it is possible. I wouldn't cast doubt on any religion or story, if I was you. If you see something you recognize as a real threat, Chelsea, you run. There might be nothing you can do against it."

Dodd fiddled with the buttons on his cuffs while Chelsea pressed her pants with her palms.

"You should come with us," Rose said. "I know you don't feel safe here, or you wouldn't have been hiding under a table when we showed up."

Leonard blanched at this. "Was it really that transparent?" he asked.

"Fooled me," Dodd said, giving Chelsea a sideways glance.

"You are welcome to join us," Chelsea said.

"I appreciate the offer, but I think I'll stay in here. I'll be safe if I keep the demons I deal with bound within the research papers here in the annex," Leonard said. He stuffed his hands into his pockets. "I'll just be a liability out there, anyway. Yes, I do know them and know about them, but stories don't favor those who know about them. They favor those who are good and quick witted. All the same, call in to check on me. If I don't answer, maybe swing by?"

"Sure," Rose and Chelsea said in unison. All three took his cell number.

As they made to leave, Leonard placed his glasses inside of the face shield he had donned upon their arrival and headed back to his work. "Remember what I said. If you see something bigger, you get away."

"How will we know what the big baddies are compared to the others?" Dodd asked. "Rose's account had us thinking we were in with the big baddies already."

Leonard shook his head. "Trust me, Detective. You will know."

Ω

David expected to find himself in yet another awe-inspiring place after flying over a vast distance, faced with views so like the picture of perfection that they were impossible to differentiate from a master's camera roll. What he wasn't expecting was for Jacob to leave him there like he was being dropped off at a bus station with a dollar bill and a note pinned to his shirt.

"Wait, you're leaving?" David asked Jacob as he bounced around to ease the stiffness from being carried aloft for so long.

"Yes. It's important for you to experience this without me," Jacob said.

David reached into his pocket to feel the coin. "I know I'm going to sound like a baby, but I don't want you to, Jacob. I don't feel like I belong here."

"You don't," Jacob said as he stood in the same spot where he'd landed. "Neither of us do."

"See, so let's go together," David said. "You can fly, so you can take us pretty much anywhere, right? I'll take you to some great spots back on Earth. Ever been to Ben and Jerry's? Bet you haven't. It's amazing. Let's go to Ben and Jerry's, Jacob."

Jacob smiled. "I promise you we will meet again. One way or the other, our paths will merge."

"Gotta tell ya, you're not inspiring me here with your little speech. Sounding quite ominous there," David said. "Don't think I'm too interested in finding out what any of those merges look like."

"David, I've told you much without telling you anything at all," Jacob said. "You and you alone must find your truths, or, at the moment when they come within your grasp, they will ring hollow. Good luck, my friend."

Jacob took off with a leap into the air and a flourish of movement from his wings. The sheer speed at which he accelerated and moved was subtle and sublime.

David wanted to kick him. "Well, here I am," he said. "Wherever here is."

David turned and walked in the direction he was facing when Jacob had set him down. He thought he might have to keep walking, because the theme of this experience had been thus since he'd woken up and met River—or Kharon, or Bob Ross, take your pick.

However, he crested a small hill, and the sight of an enormous structure realigned his thinking. It was the largest and most extravagant wooden lodge he'd ever seen. A building— no, a *hall*— the size of ten stadiums all side by side. To say that the place was huge would be to say the ocean was big—not untrue, but lacking in scope for true understanding.

Felled trees, the huge redwoods he'd seen earlier, were stacked precisely to a height of what seemed like five-hundred feet, and the roof was shingled with what appeared to be spheres of pure gold. The light being reflected from it was a second sun. Adorning the building were massive, mounted heads of beasts far too large to be taken seriously, yet there they were: a wolf, a stag, a serpent, and what looked like a woolly rhino. And more, all portraying ferocity in their stasis.

"Okay," David said aloud. Speaking did have the effect of grounding him, and he began walking toward the building before he could think better of it. Swirling, large birds circled above the structure, and David hoped he wasn't going to seem like a lone bunny crossing the open field to the extravagant building.

Before he could learn if he'd become lunch for the birds —*eagles, gotta be eagles. It's always something with claws*—his ears were shattered by the bass hum of a horn he could see atop the hall. He fell to his knees and clapped his hands over his ears as the grass blew back around him.

Gritting his teeth, he managed to open his eyes and looked up to see the hall's doors being cast open at all sides. There was a litany of them, and from these portals, a volume of people poured. They raged forward across the field at nothing. David couldn't see an adversary until his eyes were drawn far to the left, and he spotted that there, along a ridge line serving to conceal their true numbers, another horde had been amassed. They too began to advance, but with much more precision and purpose than the group leaving the hall. For them, it seemed like a free-for-all. They raged across the field, swarming toward the lines of the well-disciplined force.

David had no intention of moving closer to the impending battle. He would stay here and see how things played out. At least, that's what he had planned before he felt the ground trembling beneath him. He noticed the cold, but the spectacle in front of him must have distracted from just *how* cold, or the fact that it was becoming more frigid still. Frost overtook the green grass and transformed it to a series of infinite glassed spears, imperfectly arranged. The ground began to feel slick and then brittle underfoot. He leapt from his knees and ran. Intuition for this sort of thing seemed to be growing within him. The ground groaned as though waking. Portions of it diverged, and large chasms opened around the fleeing boy.

Unable to outrun the cataclysm, he began to navigate the ground by tracing over the areas which remained wider and taking small leaps over rifts which hadn't become large as of yet. It was working.

"Don't look down, don't look down, don't look down," he recited as he ran.

He gained enough confidence to look upon the battle raging ahead of him. The field there was intact, and the two sides had met while he was worrying about falling.

He had become distracted, leading to carelessness in plotting his route. Looking ahead, he saw there was a tear in the ground far wider than he felt comfortable trying to leap—and it was becoming wider every second. His heels dug down to put on the brakes, but the slick grass had placed a doorstop on this intention. Unable to stop, David decided he had to try and propel himself forward as fast as he could.

Committed, he timed the final step perfectly and launched himself through the air farther than he had thought possible. Not a chance he could have done this before he had taken his journey with Jacob, he knew, but he also knew he was going to be coming up short. There was no comic moment of surprise on his face like in cartoons or movies, just the resigned sadness of the realization that he was going to hit a wall of frozen earth a foot below where his hands could have taken hold.

His body slammed into permafrost, and his will forced his fingers to ignore pain as they dug for purchase, but they weren't able to do more than slide uselessly down. David's despair was lifted when he felt his left foot connect with something firm, and he transferred his weight to that side while desperately sliding his palms on the cruel frozen earth. His neck bent to see the pale-gray head of a ghoulish creature that had been climbing. It seemed as surprised as David was at their chance meeting, and it wasn't alone. There were scores of them rising to the field.

"What is happening?" he shouted down at the creature with human eyes. It offered no explanation.

Shirking its head to the side to cast David off only served to make the boy's knee buckle, and he fell onto the thing's shoulders. Riding it like he was a kid at a carnival he said, "Woah, woah, okay, wait a sec, buddy. Just give me a minute." Instead of reaching up to dislodge him, the creature resumed its ascent.

David's eyes scanned for anything to grab, should the ghoul have second thoughts about its new cargo, and his eyes halted on a very close view of the long claws protruding from gnarled hands. Black talons tore into the frozen earth and emasculated his puny fingernails that had evolved into more of a fashion statement than anything of practical use here. The creature used his own quite practically and continued up the five or so feet to the surface.

By now, they had been overtaken by many others already at the surface and beyond. David assumed the creature would want vengeance for his unwarranted intrusion into its activities. As soon as he had breached the surface enough to pull himself up, he rolled away turning to face it. The creature regarded him for a moment, then turned its attention to the field and ran with its brethren toward the embattled warriors. The ghoulies were a third faction, it seemed.

Not interested in finding out if indifference would be the choice of all the creatures around him, David ran sidelong, dodging them and the holes until solid ground could be trusted. He sat with his legs splayed out in front and his hands propped up behind to gain his bearings.

It took him a moment to realize he wasn't gasping for air like his intuition told him he should be. He wasn't fatigued at all. There wasn't much time to ruminate on the odd development, though. The sound of a small bell loosened him from his thoughts. He rolled his head back to see behind and found a goat, a large goat, was slowly walking his way. It lazily chewed on the remnants of a leaf the size of a serving platter. A tarnished cowbell—*goatbell?*—hung from its neck.

The animal looked docile enough and had beautiful gold-rimmed eyes which were fixed on him despite the battle raging about a mile ahead of them. Movement in the periphery of his vision made him loll his head over to the other shoulder to see a woman had also walked up from behind. To his surprise, she simply settled herself on the ground adjacent to his plot in a similar position to his own.

"Hi," David said.

"Hello," she replied.

David tried not to stare as he observed her, enshrouded in robes of pure white. Her feet were bare, with only a small golden chain wrapping around her luminous skin from her ankle up her calf, where it disappeared beneath her clothes. Beatific links reappeared and wound around her opposite arm up to the wrist she was using to prop her head. So pure in its color was the chain that it nearly appeared to glow, yet the beauty was diminished in comparison to long, gilded locks of hair that flowed over her shoulders.

"Did you bet on a side to win?" David asked.

"No side ever wins," she said. "The battle will end in a stalemate, and each side will carry their fallen home where they will be made whole once more. Some will plan for the next battle, some will feast and drink to their valor on the field, while many others still will go back to an existence most ceaseless and bleak—only to be turned berserker once more by the call of the horn." She began to flex and squeeze her toes in the grass.

"That sounds interesting," he said. "My name is David. It's nice to meet you."

She turned her blue eyes onto him and asked, "Is that your only name?"

He swallowed and responded, "I don't like Dave, and my last name is Dolan. David Michael Dolan is the only name I think I've got."

"I've so many names. It would be nice to have just one, like you," she said. Her golden hair lifted as she turned her head to the men fighting before abruptly falling to the ground, stretching under the sun. "You may call me Mardoll, if you like. Unless you wish to give me another name, that is."

"Mardoll is fine," David said. "Well, you seem to know a lot more about this place than I do. Where are we?"

"You, a warrior, don't recognize the gates to the halls of Valhalla?" she asked. "That's not likely. Even if you were new, you would surely know by now." She turned on her side to face him, the golden chain chiming gently on her hand as it rested on her hip. "My-oh-me, it is a bit strange that you aren't taking part in the melee. You *aren't* a warrior, are you?"

"I don't believe I qualified for warrior when I took the careers survey in high school," David said. "I was brought here by a man.

Actually, he's an angel in the form of a man. His name is Jacob. He left me here and didn't bother to give me lunch money."

"Poor thing. You won't last long here if you aren't a warrior, I'm afraid. Pity. You seem so interesting. Full of light." She said and rolled to her stomach, pushing herself into an upward dog position, and then up and striding toward the goat. She pulled two cups from beneath her robes. "You must be sad, seeing as you will die soon. If you've hunger, I can't help, but I can offer you the most delicious mead you've ever tasted."

David didn't bother to tell her it would be the *only* mead he'd ever tasted. He watched her crouch down and begin to milk the goat into the two cups she'd placed on the ground underneath. Her precision was commendable; not a drop spilled to the grass below.

She returned to his side and handed him a cup. "Enjoy," she said and promptly set to the task of emptying her cup.

David was a little more tepid in his approach. He looked into the dark liquid. "It looks like apple cider," he said and took a small sip. The flavor was sweet, and his body filled with fragrance rather than his senses relaying taste. "This is remarkable."

"Thank you. I don't often partake in the gifts of Heidrun." She lifted her cup to the sun. "But when I get the chance, I steal a cup of divine mead. There's nothing to match it."

David tried to be reserved in his consumption, but the taste beckoned to his lips, and he could not refuse. Soon, his cup was empty as well. He felt his worries ease, and he welcomed the change. "Who is Heidrun?" David asked.

Mardoll slapped the goat on its flank and sent it galloping toward the expansive hall. "The goat is Heidrun," she said. "He belongs to another, and he doesn't often like to share. So, not-yet-a-warrior David, what do you surmise you should do next?" she asked.

"I don't find it too objectionable to stay here and watch the happenings with you. Maybe the boozy goat will come back, and we can have seconds." He grinned as he gestured to Mardoll with his empty cup.

She returned his smile and plucked the cup from his hand.

"One cup should suffice for some time. It isn't a natural mead, after all. You may notice your reservations have fled from you. This effect will not be as fleeting as the harmonious feeling you have in your belly right now."

"I guess I can take a walk to the hall there and see what's happening with whoever owns it," David said.

Mardoll let loose a guffaw of laughter out of sync with her angelic demeanor. "I'm not certain you'll be so well received by him, young one. Perhaps mingling with the warriors of Valhalla will suit you more. They tend to be welcoming."

David looked at the battlefield. It appeared the three sides had broken up for the day. The fighters who remained were mostly picking up after themselves. The odd creatures from the ground were beginning to crawl back toward the chasms and rifts from where they'd emerged, some with their own body parts in their mouths.

He scanned the field to observe what the warriors from the hall were doing and was not encouraged to see them sparring and fighting amongst themselves now that the others were leaving in the direction from which they'd come.

He turned to Mardoll. "You sure about them being welcoming? They seem a bit barbaric to me," he said.

"They're far more barbaric than my chosen warriors, this is true, but they maintain a sense of brotherhood and camaraderie you'll likely understand more than I," she said. "Don't fret. When the time comes, I will rejoin you for what I hope is another nice moment under the noonday sun, David. You have my word on that."

Mardoll stood without any further words and angled in the direction of the warriors from the ridge line. He noted the ghoulies gave her a wide berth. Resisting the temptation to stare after her, he stood.

"Guess I'd better go make some new friends," David said. He made his way toward the hall of Valhalla with the sun kissing the nape of his neck and the warm breeze dancing about his hair.

Ω

The trio arrived at the hospital at around eleven in the morning.

Dodd, despite the feast from the night before, had begun to get a little ogrish, as Ramirez would say. The classic signs of hunger were evident in the car: raving at other drivers, speeding, and being a little "snippy" with the guard manning the entrance gate to the hospital.

Chelsea suggested he pick up some breakfast sandwiches for everyone from the hospital café after Dodd told the guard he would sooner crap a gold nugget than pay fifty-four dollars for an overnight parking pass. The two ladies had gone upstairs to see David, and Dodd was to rendezvous with them when he was suitably fed. He didn't have an issue with the hospital food—in fact, he found it to be pretty damned good. The café was equipped with a deli short-order cook who had been slinging fresh home fries, bacon, eggs—the whole nine. Dodd made a platter of cold breakfast potpourri disappear and snagged five fresh bacon, egg, and cheese sandwiches to bring upstairs. Whatever the ladies didn't eat, he'd take care of.

Upon cresting the short stairwell that led into the lobby, something made Dodd pause before turning left toward the elevators. The little glasses-wearing twerp with the khaki jacket and book was still in the waiting room. Dodd may not have noticed the cover of his book was different had he not been keenly aware of such details as a detective of many years, but notice he did. *This guy's been here for a while. If he was waiting for a patient, wouldn't he be in the room during visiting hours?* Questions ran through Dodd's mind as he lumbered into the lobby. He took the seat next to the man.

"Whatcha reading there, friend?" Dodd asked. He had been striking up seemingly harmless conversations with persons of interest for so many years that it felt second nature now. Life must be hard for people with social anxieties. The lack of those birthed one of his most valuable attributes.

"It's a collection of works by John Milton," the man said. "Do you know of him?"

"Can't say I do. I'm more of a Grisham and Clancy guy. Maybe Crichton too, but the early stuff. I don't really do the classics. Looks like a big book," Dodd said, setting the grease-stained brown paper bag down on the tile floor.

"Yes, a lot in here. It takes the whole of eternity to read and understand, you might say," the man said.

"My name is Brendan," Dodd said, extending his left hand crosswise to shake.

"Sam," the man said and gripped Dodd's hand firmly.

"What brings you into the hospital, Sam?" Dodd asked. He stretched his legs out before him to make it look like he was settling in for a lengthy wait.

"Well, Brendan, it's serendipitous that you should ask," Sam said, "I do believe we are both here for the same reason. That being to check on a person who is of great interest to us." He continued to scan the words on the page in front of him, and Dodd's eyes danced across the title of the play he was reading. *Samson Agonistes.*

"Oh, you are?" Dodd asked. "I was just curious because I think I've seen you in here before. You stick out a bit."

"Do you know of fate, Brendan?" Sam asked.

"Sure. I see the hands of fate quite a bit in my line of work," Dodd said.

"Are you aware of the nomenclature assigned to the fates of Greek lore?" Sam asked.

"If you're going to keep talking like we're in a class at Harvard, I'm going to need to buy a dictionary from the gift shop to stay in this conversation," Dodd said.

"Forgive me, Detective. I assumed you would know," Sam said.

"Ah, and there it is," Dodd said. "You seem to know more about me than you should, Sam. I think our conversation should probably turn over to that. Let's start with how you know I'm a detective."

"Seems a prudent request. I know you're Detective Brendan Dodd, now retired—well, not entirely. You were born in Yonkers, New York at St. Joseph's Medical Center on a rainy Thursday night in 1965. I particularly enjoy that hospital for its namesake. So paternal, don't you think?"

Dodd kept Sam square in his focus now but said nothing, and

Sam went on, "Clotho spun your humble beginnings and cast you out onto a path that eventually lead you into the New Rochelle Police Department, where you climbed the ranks to lieutenant for exemplary service and honor to the badge. You had many victories and a few failures along that path, but your moral compass guided you well.

"The inner workings of that compass were set in place by your mother, a woman who never took for herself without thinking of others, and your father, a mason who believed a man should be able to stand steadily on any wall he built. There were other artisans who contributed to the man you would ultimately become, Brendan, and some were even nearly as instrumental to making you who you are as your parents were. They acted as base plate, scales, rulers, and orienting arrows within your compass which set you to true north. Your morals, newly laid and not yet set, one day served you to decide to call out a colleague who had used, shall we say, unnecessary force on a dark-skinned youth who was being questioned. I doubt it would have mattered to you at the time to have known the boy was quite unimpeachable. You would have spoken up doubtless of his guilt."

A warmth just shades away from hot coursed through the back of Dodd's neck and sweat prickled his brow.

"The last part was unnecessary prattle on my part," Sam said, "but I thought you might like to know of the boy being innocent of any wrongdoing. Yet, without prior knowledge, you stepped in to stop your colleague's actions just the same. This defining moment set in stone what those who built you had cobbled together with wet mortar just twenty-eight years earlier. Quite the pin in your lapel, deciding to be a man of principle. It was more important than being a *good old boy*, as they say. Yes, some called you names like snitch or canary, but you didn't waver in your conviction. Conviction, worn like a suit of armor, protected you from those who saw you in a less-than-flattering light, and they never received an opportunity to strike you down. That's the key to being a person of principles. If you pick and choose when to have them, then you cast aside the very thing that defends your spirit."

Dodd was becoming less comfortable with every detail this stranger divulged about his past. He opened his mouth to speak, but the words were slow to come, and Sam continued, "Many years later, you still don the same armor, and here you are to sniff out the root cause of the ugly mess you've stepped in. You have also found people. People for whom you care and people whom your convictions scream at you to protect. Yes, Brendan Dodd, I know you. I know every soul striding the earth at this moment, and all those who have left footprints in the sand before today."

When Sam stopped speaking, the softly singing songbirds of morning lifted Dodd from a dream. "A lot of things have happened in the past few days that stretch my ability to reason. This might be the most sobering one, though. Who the hell are you?" Dodd asked.

"I think you will learn this without my having to tell you. The divining hands of Lachesis tend to be predictable in that way, at least to me. What will probably surprise you is that if you had the slightest idea of who I am, you'd find you know quite a great deal about me. Until that time, to you, I am Sam," he said as he licked his finger and made ready to turn the page in his tome of epic poems, plays, and masques.

To Dodd's surprise, Sam extended his right hand to him. He looked at the open palm for a moment before he reached to grip it. "I expect that this won't be the last time I see you," Dodd said, picking up the bag and making ready to leave.

"I can say with certainty that we will meet at least one more time," Sam said and returned to his book.

Ω

Jacob's wings opened in a flourish as he landed near the top of a mountain overlooking the field of battle. Below, the warriors appeared like two football teams walking back to their locker rooms. Wings neatly folded behind, he scanned the ground for David to see what may have befallen the boy. He smiled at the sight of him drinking mead with who could only be Freja. She and her cats always enjoyed toying with mortals. Her open and coy posture comforted him. She'd taken a shine to the boy, which wasn't so hard to imagine. He did have charm. Brains, too. Mettle was what needed testing now.

"I thought you were trying to protect him, though now it seems you're endeavoring to get him killed," a deep voice issued from his back. Jacob didn't bother to turn. He knew this voice as well as his own.

Jacob said, "I wasn't hiding my actions from you or any of the others." He heard the sound of feet hitting the ground and stepping lightly through the dusty remains of sandstone and shale. A man with sun-kissed features didn't betray emotion as he stepped beside Jacob, but the air was heavy with his anger. "What business do you have with me, Michael?"

"Your brazen actions have been more insulting than if you'd skulked in the shadows," Michael replied, his tense jaw betraying a legendary temper as he followed Jacob's gaze to David and Freja. "You are the one wrought with hard-won wisdom, yet you still play this game with him? He is a danger to us all. You've no right—"

"He is a danger to not a gnat in the sky, and you know it," Jacob said. "We are not in the position to dole out judgment based purely on odds and predictions. I took him to guide a boy into the man we know he can become." His posture had become tense as well, but he and Michael both knew he'd never take up arms. His passion flowed from the tip of his tongue. "Why have we remained unmoving while the denizens run rampant on Earth, despite knowing we can wipe them away with the flash of just one of our swords?"

"We do not move without guidance," Michael said. None thirsted for battle more than he, and Jacob knew it.

"Not once have we acted upon such urges, and those who have were met with a grim fate," Jacob said. "Yet still you point your anger at that boy there. Sometimes you confound even me."

"Uriel," said Michael, although Jacob's true name being spoken did not disarm him, "I do not move without warrant. Once, long ago, a directive was handed down to purge Earth of all Nephilim. It was done despite the great sacrifice required to carry out such a task. We waited in silence for direction, because surely something must come, yet nothing. Not a word." Uriel let him finish. "This led us to discuss the matter at length, and we surmised the lack of an order was due to one having already been given. We must purge the Nephilim."

"Sounds as though you were skewed to one side when many viewpoints existed. Shall I guess... Raphael? Sounds of his brand practicality," Uriel said.

Michael balked, "Should you have been present, perhaps your insights would have changed the circumstance. We would have surely benefited from such wisdom. Instead you were taking the very threat we needed to address through benchmarks in the afterlife. You've no right to judge."

"None of us has the right to judge, that is my point," Uriel said. "I wish to put my opinion on record now. This boy is no threat and deserves no ill-treatment. If we are worried about his existence, we need only show him the light. He stretches toward it at every opportunity, Michael. He is as good as we. Maybe more so."

At this, Michael turned to face Uriel. "We've never once in our existence been deaf to the word, Uriel, yet you dare compare us to him? He who is not even old enough to have garnered the wisdom to know what lies beyond his fingertips? I won't suffer your righteous indignation, brother."

"Are we not deaf to the word now?" Uriel responded, without an ounce of mirth at his logical victory. "Perhaps this fact alone should give you pause." It was never a serious challenge to outwit Michael. This held especially true for Uriel who swam in the rivers of physics, literature, mathematics, cinema, and all forms of artistry as often as he was able, but none among the angels was more lethal than Michael. He was the incarnation of might for right, and he was not putting on airs about how he felt. If he saw the opportunity to, he would destroy David.

"Only a fool would ignore you when you've set your mind to something," Michael said. "Know that I still hold you in high regard despite your actions of late, but we cannot allow Azazel to break free from his prison. Should he manage to join with the boy, the Nephilim, Azazel will have a vessel strong enough to carry him forever. This certainty moves me and no one else."

Jacob's chin lowered as Michael's words rolled over him. Azazel, a watcher of great power, had been imprisoned along with the rest of those who acted to cajole humanity without warrant. It was often thought that this act was committed with just human women, but men fell victim to the celestials' wiles as well. They sired offspring who contained characteristics deemed improper for the balance established at the creation of humankind. For this, they fell, but not to the same dark depths as those who had the audacity to stand against their creator. Those who, when they landed, burst the underworld into a furnace of woe and pain known only to those who've been cast out of the light. The watchers were cast into the Earth, deep within the Earth, but no further. They were not beyond reach, and Michael's worries were not without warrant. Azazel would certainly free his brethren at the first chance, should he manage to escape, and this would cause a war with ramifications none could predict. Especially since they no longer heard the sweet seraph songs calling them to action.

"You have right to worry, Michael," Uriel said. "You, especially. Not tasked with guarding the gates of Eden, the trees of life or wisdom—no, not you. You, who were tasked with defending the very celestial halls crafted to hold us and the creator. I do not begrudge you your need to do what only you can do, but I implore you to consider that boy as our kin and not our killer. He has the same potential for benevolence as for harm. Mark my words. He will surprise you, should you give him the opportunity."

Uriel turned to face Michael. His posture, with wings in and palms out, contrasted Michael's with perfection designed for verse. "Humanity is in a fragile stage now. Anything may change their course on the intended path. We cannot allow for this variable to be us."

"And we should allow it to be him?" Michael asked.

"He is one of them, after all," Uriel said.

"He can be one of us or one of them, not both," Michael said. "That is the warrant handed down, resulting in the deluge that wiped the Nephilim away, and we've counseled and determined this warrant still stands. There's no other explanation for the silence, for the lack of direction. The only question remaining is whether or not you will try to stop us."

"The plan in place is not for us to determine or undermine," Uriel said. "I will not stand against you, nor Gabriel, Raphael, Selaphiel, Raguel, Jophiel, Barachiel, Jegudiel, or Ramiel. I don't believe I will have to, Michael. Destiny is at play. We are moving 'cross the board of our own whim, but to a greater plan, and perhaps for the first time without the hand to guide us. I believe we've been handed free will to see how we may measure against the din within ourselves in these times."

Michael relaxed, but his glare remained as threatening as his posture had been. Physically taller and more imposing than Uriel, his body the archetype for violence—though to merely worry about his body was a fallacy. Within Michael burned a sword with heat dwarfing those of all others, perhaps even the disgraced Lucifer. Should he choose to turn it on Uriel or David, there would be little to be done about it, though Uriel did have some measures at his disposal. He was not too idealistic to simply allow himself to be engulfed in a fire hotter and brighter than his own.

"I'm going to weigh your wisdom and take it back to the others," Michael said. "Not because I believe you, but because it is not my place to act alone as you have. Not with this concept on my mind for the first time. Understand, Uriel, should we return to take him, you will not be able to stop us. Not after we've taken your counsel into consideration."

"I am thankful for your decision," Uriel said.

"When you were forged, the creator should have only left half a tongue," Michael said. He didn't smile, but Uriel knew this was as close to an olive branch as he would get.

"Does the angel who loves battle above all else approve of the display before him?" Uriel asked, motioning away from David and to the field now soaked in blood.

Michael glanced over. "A pitiful effort by all sides, save one.

Freja's army emerges the clear victor despite being stopped before overrunning both hordes. I grew tired of watching long ago."

"I suppose Beethoven wouldn't find much joy in watching piano lessons either," Uriel said.

He turned to see David making his way to the halls of Valhalla and, Uriel hoped, what lay beyond those massive doors in the mountain behind it. He turned back when he heard the silt and soil churning in the wind.

Michael's wings, as crimson as arterial blood, were a marvel to all who beheld them, even Uriel himself—the angel who had been calling himself Jacob, who embraced the beauty in all things.

Ω

Chelsea and Rose were tending to David and the knick-knacks in his room when Dodd entered. Rose took notice of his beleaguered features. "Why the long face? Did they run out of Scooby Snacks at the cafe?" she asked.

Dodd shook the paper bag in her direction. "Nope, had plenty of grub that's fit for a cop. Not sure if you'll like it, though."

Rose stopped straightening flowers in a plain white vase and ventured over to peruse the contents of the bag. "No ketchup?" she said.

"Packets at the bottom. Not my first rodeo, rug rat," he said and took the seat by the window.

Chelsea had been holding David's hand and combing his hair while listening to their exchange. "I'll take one without," she said and came over to the small round table to sit with Rose. She studied Dodd. "You do look a bit burdened. Maybe you should get some rest."

"I do need some, but that's not it," Dodd said. "I met someone downstairs."

"Oh, will we be getting an invitation to the wedding?" Chelsea asked.

"Har har har. Not like that," Dodd said. "It's a guy in the lobby. Ramirez and I saw him the first time we were here."

Rose swallowed her mouthful. "The one in the khaki jacket?"

"Yeah, him," Dodd said, becoming less and less surprised with her observational skills. "He's been here for a while, sorta sticks out like a sore thumb, but I couldn't really pick out why. I decided to chat him up and see if I could rattle him. Thought maybe he was a part of"—He waved his hands around in the air—"everything. Turns out I was right."

Chelsea and Rose both looked at him. "Does he have anything to do with David?" Chelsea asked.

"I think he does. He knew everything about me, soup to nuts. It was uncanny. I think I fully understand what Leonard meant now about turning and running. The guy, calls himself Sam. He wasn't threatening at all, kinda the opposite. Thing is, I'm three times his size, and my intuition told me he could have snuffed me out in an instant without any effort at all. Things are getting real thin, ladies. Don't really know what to think about what to do next." Dodd sat with his shoulders hunched forward, hands on his cheeks.

Rose crumpled up her tin foil into a ball and popped it into the empty paper bag. "You don't have to. So far things have been rolling along without us doing much of anything. I think all you need to do is enjoy a break. That chair pulls out into a bed. Maybe take a nap and recharge."

"You could call it a bed. I call it the rack," Chelsea said. "Thing does unholy damage to your back."

Dodd laughed. "Yeah, I've slept on a few over the years, visiting injured guys in the hospital. They're brutal. I'll probably stretch out on the ground right here in a few."

"Before that, come here for a second. I want you to look at something," Chelsea said, returning to David's bedside. Rose came too. Chelsea rolled the blanket down David's body to his waist. "Look at him and tell me the first thing that comes to your mind."

Dodd did as she asked. The kid had an impressive physique. His shoulders and arms were muscular, sure, not odd for a boy his age, but the kid's midsection looked like he was an athlete at the top of his career. His abdominal muscles were tightly formed and protruding from his abdomen in the way they do in some athletes and movie stars.

"He looks like he just left the gym," Dodd said.

"Rose and I have both noticed he is putting on muscle instead of atrophying like he should be," Chelsea said.

"Not just the muscles, though," Dodd said. "There's a heat coming off him like he just finished a marathon. Look at his veins. They're full like he's just put down weights."

"Guys who work out call it a pump," Rose said.

"Yeah, like he's just finished pumping iron," Dodd said. "Not what you'd expect from a kid in a coma."

Chelsea pushed down on David's forearm, and it barely gave under her fingers. "This is what the doctors are all going crazy over, but I don't think they've noticed that on top of putting on ten pounds, he also looks like he's grown a little taller. Maybe even a couple of inches. I swear his feet didn't reach the end of the bed the last time we were here."

Rose reached out her hands and placed them on David's chest. Dodd thought he was going to see her begin to explore it with her hands—she was at that age after all—but both remained above his heart. "Wake up now, okay, David? It's time to wake up now. We need you. I need you."

Dodd saw the tears beginning to well up in her eyes and placed his large hand on Rose's shoulder. "He's gonna wake up, Rose. No man wouldn't find his way back, knowing a girl like you is here waiting for him."

To Dodd's surprise, she took her hands from David and turned into him, placing her hands over her face and burying herself in his stomach. He wrapped his arms around her and held her there while she softly wept. He and Chelsea exchanged a look of soft understanding, and he turned his face down to look at Rose.

Such a small thing, this girl, but she was so much stronger than most people he'd ever known, even those who had stood beside him in some hairy situations and held their water. The first moment of vulnerability she'd shown was brought on by her love for David.

Dodd thought it spoke volumes about who this kid was.

Chelsea studied the way Dodd cared for Rose as his white shirt dampened with her tears. She was finding herself drawn to him more and more during their time together. "Let's get some rest, guys," Chelsea said.

She closed the door to the room while Dodd led Rose to the makeshift bed because she sorely needed some sleep. When Rose didn't leave the protective cavern of his embrace, Chelsea layered a few blankets on the ground and motioned for Dodd to set Rose down in Chelsea's arms. He did and removed his jacket and tie before setting down on the blankets too. He stretched out on the floor, and after some time, felt warmth nestle into his right side. Rose had snuggled into him. Chelsea made to do the same on his other side. He offered her his arm to use as a pillow and she accepted it, placing hers over his chest. They huddled together like pups in a den, releasing tension in their collective comfort.

The three lay on the hospital room floor and were ushered off into a deep sleep soon after. David's sensors continued to deliver their readings to computer screens, and the boy who'd traveled leagues to find himself lay motionless in his white bed. The room temperature would rise by a half degree by the time the group awoke but none of them would make the connection to David as the glowing ember warming them.

CHAPTER SEVEN
A WARRIOR

Droves of people poured back inside the great hall as David approached. He became overwhelmed with the same eerie feeling he had experienced twelve years ago on his first day of middle school. Everyone appeared to be traveling in groups, their camaraderie evident with slaps on shoulders punctuated by howls of laughter. Nobody noticed David existed. This worked in his favor, to an extent. Being invisible made it easy for him to walk right up to the hall, but it also froze him out of the groups.

Through people-watching, David observed that some groups heading inside counted women amongst them, though far fewer were female than male, and they were all clad in clothes spanning multiple eras in history. One mongrel group ahead was made up of two squat men from the bronze age: a Persian, tall by comparison to his counterparts, and a woman adorned in warpaint and worn leathers who may have hailed from the tribes who birthed the Celts. A man in gray fatigues and a helmet seeming to indicate the era of

World War One walked by, and there were a handful of men clad in leather armor and animal furs, brandishing brutish-looking swords and axes close behind.

They fraternized with no communication issues, and David himself couldn't discern a difference in languages at all. Everyone seemed to be speaking the same tongue here, despite their clear cultural differences, and he also understood it. David began to wonder if the language was English at all when he was bumped from behind by a fast-moving man in khakis and a tan chambray shirt. He hustled past, not stopping to discuss the incident, which was a relief.

"Don't mind him, he always rushes inside. Not sure why, with there always being enough food and drink for everyone and all," a female soldier in digital desert fatigues said to David. "Are you new? I don't think I've seen you before."

"You could say that," David said.

"It's a little weird at first, but you'll get used to it. You might even learn to like it," she said. "I'm Mina Gallagher. Was a staff sergeant in Afghanistan. You American?" She removed her helmet to reveal black hair of modest length.

"Um, yeah, I am," he said. "David Dolan."

"Where did you punch your ticket to get here, kid?" she asked.

"It's an interesting story. Maybe I can explain better when we get inside," David responded. He still wasn't sure how any of them would handle learning he wasn't a warrior like they were.

"That's a good idea. You can sup with us." She gestured to two others who walked behind her, discussing the day's events. One wore a kimono with a katana affixed above a smaller sword at the waist, his white shirt so saturated in crimson gore that it was hard to believe he was behaving in a casual manner. The person he spoke with was a more modern soldier, maybe from the Korean War or World War Two, although it was tough for David to tell based on the scant black and white footage he'd seen growing up.

Mina led them inside where the people were dispersing across the hall to innumerable long tables before them. Each held vast assortments of food and carafes of drink, as David had been told.

Illumination floated down from hanging chandeliers and candelabras aplenty. Despite the expansiveness of the dining hall, the sheer number of people made David feel slight claustrophobia.

They walked down the aisleway, and David took the time to observe the scene. The bounty of food elevated the atmosphere from joy to mirth. People sang with arms round the shoulders of neighbors, and cares were left miles behind. Such unkempt celebration was a novelty to David, and he found himself being carried away with it. Perhaps it was Heidrun's mead, or maybe it was true that joy could permeate the mind from outside and spread within.

Mina motioned for him to sit at a table carbon copied from the same source as the others, and David set himself down in front of a large platter of bone-in steaks. The samurai patiently motioned for David to slide further on the bench, and he did so. *Don't want to piss him off.* Resettled, he stared forward at an enormous fish, its mouth stuffed to comical size with fragrant herbs, and still wearing its silver scales. One tea saucer eye bore a hole in David's forehead, and Mina had to jostle him away from staring back.

"Don't worry about the food. You'll find trying new things is the best pathway to making yourself happy," she said from across the table.

The semi-modern soldier sat next to her, and opposite the samurai to David's right. "Who's the new kid?" The soldier asked. Before anyone answered, he said, "Hey, new kid, I'm Boris."

David took his outstretched hand over the fish's tail and felt a bit sheepish about the formality in front of everyone around them. He still didn't want others to single him out if he could help it.

"My name's David Dolan," he said. "Good to meet you." Instinctively, David turned and offered his hand to the samurai and was surprised when the man stood and bowed. "I am Jubei Kibagami. We are well met."

"The honor is mine," David replied and offered his own bow, hoping it didn't seem too awkward compared to Jubei's well-practiced greeting. He returned to his seat after Jubei stood tall and smiled.

"Mina, are there many Americans here?" David asked.

"Sure, there's a few, but way fewer than some other cultures," she said. "We've been to war, but there's countries that have been fighting for centuries longer. There's just more dead soldiers from history than you can imagine, though not all come here."

This piqued his interest. "Where do they go?" he asked, hoping the answer wasn't someplace horrible.

"Helheim for some," Boris said. "The weaponless oplakivals who crowd the field after we meet the warriors from Folkvangr, they're from Helheim."

"Yeah, some end up there. We don't know exactly why, though. There are theories that it's punishment for shirking their duties during battle or running, and others think it's because they acted dishonorably. Jubei here is in the latter circle of thought." Mina pointed a fork toward Jubei, who didn't take the bait. "Regardless, they're probably not enjoying the feast we are right now, not based on the look in their eyes on the field. They seem so sad."

"Sad until they're within a hair's length of you. Then they show their true colors," Boris said.

David took a cue from Boris and filled his cup with water from a carafe next to the fish. Mina and Jubei seemed to be drinking other beverages. David couldn't figure out why or how, because all the containers looked the same to him. He was surprised to see the fish had turned into a honey spiral ham like the ones his mother made for special holidays, down to the way she'd pin the pineapple up the middle with toothpicks. He took a slice onto his plate and tried it. Heaven.

"They are wretched creatures," Jubei said.

"What about the Folkvangr?" David asked.

"Those are more like us, but they seem to have some kind of leadership," Mina said.

Boris looked at her. "We have leadership. What of Bulwyf?"

"He's like a boss," Mina said. "I mean clear leadership. I was a staff sergeant in the army. We had a pecking order from the top down, and that's how we operated. Kept things clean and smooth."

"Da Meam, we did too, though I never made it past Ryadovoy in the Soviet army," Boris said. "Bullet tore through my skull before it could swell with enough pride for that."

"That means Private, right?" David asked.

"Da." Boris nodded and drank from his cup, which he'd filled from the same source as David's, yet Boris's breath smelled far more medically sanitized after his drink. The Soviet soldier poured more clear liquid into his cup.

"What I don't understand is how I knew that when I don't know a word of Russian," David said.

Jubei turned to him. "For some reason, this place allows for us to know these things. I think it is for us to communicate more easily. I learned of what a mercenary was from a Hessian soldier who fought during America's Revolutionary War. We have a similar term in my culture for a samurai who did not hold allegiance to a lord or territory. These samurai are called ronin. When the Hessian told me his story of being conscripted to cross the sea to fight in a war that was not his own, the words mercenary and ronin became one in my mind."

"Interesting. I wonder if that has to do with why you are all here," David said.

"Why *we* are all here. You are here now, too" Boris said through a mouthful of food.

Mina appraised him for a moment and then turned her attention to David. "What brought you here, David?" she asked.

"I don't exactly have a story—" David said.

"Everyone has a story to share," Mina interrupted. "I lost my life clearing a building of friendlies. I can't be sure, but I think there must have been a Taliban soldier hiding inside. I was sweeping the room and moved to check my blind spot, and then nothing. Next thing I knew, I was standing outside, and Jubei and Boris offered me a seat at their table."

"I was shot by a Nazi sniper in Stalingrad," Boris said. "We were circling in on him, getting a read on his location, but he was good. He took two of my comrades before me. I think he had a line of sight from a window I wasn't paying attention to."

"I was cut down by three rival swordsmen," Jubei offered.

Mina said, "The messed-up part about his story is that Jubei struck a killing blow on one of the other guys before he was killed. The other guy is here, too."

"Sanada Masamune," Jubei said, looking diagonally across the dining hall to a few tables over. "He is there."

Sure enough, David spotted a Japanese man who looked older than Jubei and who was eating alone.

"He met me with honor," Jubei said. "My blade pierced his middle before others met me. They did not have honor." He looked to David. "Never release your guard."

David acknowledged this as he took note of Jubei's plate. It was sparsely populated by food. The majority of his sustenance was full, clean vegetables and fish. He found himself wanting to try an experiment and thought of the same type of cuisine. Sure enough, the platter before him had become filled with it.

"Do you all see the same food as I do?" David asked.

Mina laughed. "I asked the same thing my first time. We do, but only when it's on our own plate. Everything in the middle of the tables seems to be more... customized to us." Mina gave him a coy look. "Now it's your turn. How'd you punch your ticket, David? You're in plainclothes, so you weren't fighting with an organized group. Are you CIA? Seem too young for that, but I've been wrong before."

"Nope, not CIA." David laughed. "Wouldn't know how to even get into that racket."

"What's the CIA?" Boris asked.

"Like the NKGB, Boris, but American," Mina said. "He didn't live through the Cold War, so he doesn't know. He didn't know about the KGB either, until I told him. You'll find a lot of history lessons being slung around here."

"I see. It's a good place to learn about others," David said.

"Bingo," Mina said, her expectant eyes never left David as she waited for his story. When he still didn't offer one, she said, "Some people are here who died fighting off intruders or home invaders. Not many, but some. Is it something like that?"

David decided to come out with it. "No. The truth is I was brought here by a guy, an angel. He's kind of my friend now, I guess.

His name is Jacob. I didn't die. That's what Jacob and the river guy, Kharon, said. So, I didn't die fighting, and I really don't think I belong here."

"New one by me," Mina said.

"Same here," Boris said.

"Unprecedented in my time," Jubei rounded out.

David found himself telling his story from the beginning. He didn't know why, but after starting with the bridge collapse, hazy as his memory of it was, and then waking up in the underworld, the torrent of experiences opened. He shared everything. Boris seemed intrigued by the near pass by the gates of hell, Mina loved hearing about Lycia, and Jubei listened quietly until near the end. Only then did he ask about the collapse of the bridge.

"David, you should not fight at the horn if you don't think you've already died," Mina said. "I mean, if you didn't kind of wake up at the front door there,"— she pointed to the front of the hall—"then I don't know if you'll come back if you fight."

"What do you mean, come back?" David asked.

"When we battle on the field, we are reborn at the door if we are to die," Jubei said quietly. "It is unpleasant at first, but many fight with true abandon when they see death may no longer reach them. Reach them again, that is."

"It is as our Japanese comrade says," Boris added. "Same rules apply if we were to be killed inside." David raised an eyebrow at this. "Happens during disagreements or sparring. Jubei here has killed Masamune over there two more times since I've been here. He's really good with those things." Boris motioned to his swords. "He calls them his dashu."

"Daisho," Jubei said.

"I can never pronounce it right after a few drinks—" Boris said.

"So, never," Mina added.

"—but the image of them slicing through the air is clear as day in my mind." Boris motioned his cup to Jubei. "He's a real-life master. If I was half as good with my rifle as he is with those swords, I may have finished living my life an older man."

Mina said, "Boris did I ever tell you the one about selling Russian rifles?"

"I thought those were called katanas," David said before she could get the joke out.

Jubei pulled the hilts of his swords into view. "I have heard your word for my main tachi, it is the larger sword. I did not call it katana when I was alive. The smaller sword is the wakizashi. Together they are my daisho."

"They are magnificent," David said.

Jubei humbly responded, "Thank you."

"He gets to keep those on all the time," Mina said. "Looks badass, too. We don't get our weapons until we are about to fight. They just appear. I don't know why, but a very few people have them on them all the time. There are general weapons in the arena, though."

"That's interesting," David said. He wondered if Jubei's swordsmanship allowed for him to carry his swords at all times. Might be the case, given that Mina and Boris were not self-proclaiming their skills in marksmanship.

"Another who always has his weapons is Bulwyf," Boris said. "You should see him before the horn blows for the next battle."

David found himself very nervous at the prospect of leaving the table. "I'm not sure that's the best idea. Nobody else is standing yet."

"Most won't for a while, but they always do," Mina said. "There are other areas of the hall to enjoy. Bedding areas, brothels, practice arenas—anything you want, really. We have some time before the next battle, but the horn tends to surprise you. It's hard to understand time in here. The candles don't burn down. Bulwyf isn't scary, by the way. He may be intimidating at first, but you'll get over it fast. He's pretty wise."

David thought this over. "Okay, well, if I run the risk of being killed on the battlefield, can't I just stay here?"

"We don't know," Jubei said.

"Nobody has ever stayed behind," Boris said.

"When you hear the horn, it compels you to the field. You'll want to fight. Unless you're different in that way too," Mina said.

"I don't know why Jacob brought me here," David said to nobody in particular.

"My guess is to meet the great Soviet warrior, Boris Zhukov," Boris said and smiled broadly before taking in half of the liquid in his cup.

"Slayer of spirits and Stroganoff," said Mina, wrapping her arm around his shoulders.

Boris began to sing and slap his palm on the table to beat time. Mina joined him, and soon other tables were involved. Cups waved in the air to signal the absence of care.

"She is right," Jubei said. "You must seek Bulwyf's counsel."

"How will I find him?" David asked.

"I will take you now," Jubei said.

"Can we just leave without saying goodbye to them?" David asked.

Jubei looked so intensely at David that the boy thought he'd angered him. "I have been here for far longer than many you see around you. What you have told us is unprecedented in this place, even to me."

David said, "I'm just not sure it's the right time."

"I feel you are in grave danger, and I have learned to trust my unconscious feelings even if I do not understand them," Jubei said. "David, we should go now. They will be here supping at this table after the next battle, but my gut tells me if we do not do something, you will not. You may not be anywhere."

David nodded to Jubei. "Alright, let's go."

Ω

The attention David was worried about receiving when they stood to leave never manifested. Boris had seen to that, though whether it was by design or by chance, David did not know. He walked behind Jubei as the warrior weaved through the throngs of people ambling about the hall. The war song started by Boris leapt from person to person like wildfire through the hall, and many took it up and added their own cultural spins. It was a remarkable sight to behold. Thousands of the world's warriors all together in celebration of nothing other than being in Valhalla.

Jubei's presence carried with it an unspoken respect from most of the warriors. They split and created a path for the samurai as he speared through the crowd to the far end of the hall, where a myriad of doors awaited. Jubei rapped on one three times with the back of his upraised hand. The door opened, and he spoke with someone unseen.

"We have news that will be of great interest to him. Please hurry with our message," Jubei said, finishing his hushed conversation. The door closed on them, and Jubei turned to David. "We must wait."

"Okay," was all David could think to say. He leaned his back against the wall and crossed his arms, his eyes raking the scene before him.

"At the bridge, you remember nothing?" Jubei asked.

David said, "Not much. I remember hitting the cold water and bailing out of my car, but after that, things get hazy."

"There is more to your story," Jubei said. "Try to find it."

"What makes you so sure?" David asked, letting his arms fall to his sides.

Jubei responded swiftly but softly. "There is something I believe about this place. A requirement people must have to be here. It may be more important than dying in battle or conflict. I cannot yet see if you have fulfilled this hitsuyo joken. Keep thinking about your fall."

"What is the requirement you are thinking of?" David asked.

"I fear telling you will taint your memory. I must not do this," Jubei said.

David thought of the bridge, of the cold water invading the car as he regained his composure. He thought of the air filling his lungs and restoring life to his body as quickly as its absence robbed him of it. As the idea of inhaling air flitted through his mind, he realized there was something dancing at the edges of his memory, and he'd just brushed it with his fingertips.

Jubei was right. There was something more.

The door opened, and a young woman wearing a cassock and

cowl thrown back on her shoulders stepped out. "He will see the boy, but you will stay, Jubei," she said.

Reading the panic on David's face, Jubei said, "Do not worry, David. Bulwyf will look after you in my absence. Would he not, I would not leave you."

"I hope you're right about that, buddy," David said.

Jubei smiled for the second time since meeting David. "I am. I wish to hear your full story. I cannot do so if you are gone." With that, Jubei performed a deep bow for David, which he returned, and then one to the woman. She simply nodded. Then he was gone.

Turning to David, she said, "I am Sarena, Bulwyf's aide. Please follow me and do not wander. I will not come to find you if you become lost."

She turned and moved beyond the door. David followed. The door led to a hallway markedly different than the hall they'd left. Wood flooring had been exchanged for white marble. Statues of monsters and warriors lined the walls as they advanced. There were a myriad of creatures David could connect to certain myths, like a chimera much larger than Lycia had been. It wore a snake for a tail, wings, but it also had the lion's head. After it was a pathetic looking creature with a missing arm whose face was twisted in a pained upturned howl of rage.

David's attention was on Sarena's back and these statues, so he missed most of the human warriors on his left side, but one figure stood out. A gilded Achilles clad in ornate armor, wielding a spear as thick as his arm, the cruel, flat-leafed point aimed at the archway near the exit. Once through the hall, there were paths right and left and a circular stairwell comprised of stone. Sarena mounted and climbed them.

The monotony of the stairs allowed for David's thoughts to wander, and he found himself kicking at water within his mind. He was back at his car, watching it sink below him as he hovered freely in the water. A set of lights flickering to his right caught his attention. Feeling along it and finding ingress to free the cherubic child trapped within, images of Tim filled his memory.

Little Tim, whom he'd tried to save from the autumn-cold grip of the Hudson. A visage of their journey through the water and the stars twinkling down on them flashed. He could feel his strength leaving his body as it had when they began to sink. Anchored by the clothes ladened with water as it endeavored to consume them, they'd slipped under.

David took a knee and gasped as though he was drowning here on the stone steps of a stairwell in Valhalla. Sarena never looked back, rounded the stairs out of sight, but David heard her say, "I will not come back for you." He pushed himself to his feet and trudged onward, grief making the movement almost unbearable.

"Where did he go?" David mused aloud. "How was I brought to Kharon without him if we sank together?" The questions assaulted his spirit, as they often did when fate and righteousness met one another head on. The idea that Tim may be on his own path in this place was consoling him when David completed his ascent.

Despite her warnings, Sarena was watching for him as he crested the top. "Not out of breath after three hundred stairs? Interesting," she said. "Come, Bulwyf is just beyond this passage."

The two continued onward. She, standing upright with pride and strength. He, cowed by lamentation. His reservations slipped away, and he asked, "Sarena, how did you die?"

She stopped in the middle of the hall and turned to him. Eyes alight with anger, she said, "I fought under orders of the archangel Michael to restore the rightful heir of the throne of France. He had been speaking to me since I was a young girl as well as on the day I met the English in battle. He was with me for each skirmish thereafter. The divine was on our side. We slaughtered the interlopers and forged a path to realize Michael's wishes. Misfortune took hold when our own countrymen attacked us. I was captured and forgotten by the very man I'd helped restore as the king. They delivered me to the British, and *they* fed me to the fires. This is how I died."

David could only manage, "I'm so sorry."

"Do not pity me. Pity those who must burn for far longer than I for their choice of malice and avarice," she said. Sarena strode the remaining ten paces to a large double door with iron mullion. The door belonged to a different era than the ornate surroundings of the hallway. Sarena did not knock but placed both hands on the doors and cast them inward. David followed her inside.

The room was large but not lavish. Sconces lined the walls and cast dancing shadows on a large table holding pieces symbolizing armies and what was clearly the field outside of the hall. There were two other areas for battle on adjacent maps. The first looked to be a separate field backed by an ornate fortress, and the second looked like a subterranean cavern littered with obstacles. A group of men discussing the maps sat at the end of the table. They paid little attention to Sarena and David as the couple entered the chamber. Away from the table and maps, sitting in a chair appearing to be hand carved from a large tree trunk, sat an enormous man. He was dressed in battlefield attire, covering all save just below his knees. From there, the leather and metal gave way to his scarred flesh until it met his fur lined boots. Two battle axes, roughly David's height, leaned on each side of the chair.

The man stood and took up each in his gnarled hands. He stalked toward David and Sarena, the latter moving swiftly to the left and away from David, and raised the axes to waist height. Their cruel double faces pointed to the floor and ceiling; the spear tip at their tops pointing at the boy.

"Hey, now!" David said, raising his hands in defense and sliding his heels back. The men at the end of the table looked up as they took notice of what was happening. "Sarena, I don't think your friend knows that I have an invitation," David yelled and tried to move in her direction, only to have this path cut off by the sidestepping axe-wielder.

"He knows," Sarena said. "He is the one who invited you. David, meet Bulwyf."

David said, "This is the guy who's in charge?" David didn't wait for an answer because he didn't have time to. Bulwyf hadn't stopped closing the distance between them and, as he drew within ten feet of David, he crossed his arms in front of his chest with the axes, making to slash the boy in half.

David, stopping his leftward trajectory, feinted right to prompt Bulwyf to strike. Just as the huge warrior's muscles tensed in motion, David dropped to the ground. The boy wondered if he'd acted too early just before he felt the axes brush through the hair on the top of his head. *Impossibly fast*, David had time to think as he hit the floor and rolled back to the left until the wall stopped him. He stood and grabbed a torch from the wall, spun, and faced Bulwyf, who was spectating from the same spot where he'd tried to kill David.

Bulwyf placed one of the axes on his back and pulled the other close to his face. He grinned broadly at Sarena. "Not a warrior?"

"That is what Jubei explained," Sarena said.

Bulwyf pulled one of David's hairs from the face of his ax and said, "I believe our reliable friend Jubei may be mistaken in this instance." He held the hair out toward David. "What say you, boy? Could someone without a fighting spirit have dodged such an attack?"

"I didn't think, I just moved," David said. He didn't lower his haphazard weapon and stayed crouched in case Bulwyf revisited the idea of letting his torso take a vacation from his legs.

"Exactly," Bulwyf said.

Sarena walked calmly to David's side, gently lifting the torch from his hands and replacing it on the wall. "He won't harm you."

"I am not confident in your judgment at the moment, miss," David said.

Sarena smiled. "He was measuring you."

"He almost measured me into the grave," David said.

"Warriors do not find death here in the halls of Valhalla, son," Bulwyf said as he placed his second axe on his back. The men at the table had once again lost interest in them and were back to placing pieces on the board. Sarena had made her way to the chair at the back of the room and poured drinks into three cups. Bulwyf followed her, and David stood where he was, honing his new skill of not knowing what to do.

Bulwyf drank and thanked Sarena. She emptied her glass and placed it on the tray beside his chair, and Bulwyf reached for the carafe to fill her cup once more before handing it back to her.

"Drink and find ease," he said. She took the glass from him and looked to David.

Awkwardly, without much choice in the matter, David walked to them. Bulwyf handed him a tankard. "Mead, the drink of my countrymen. Sip and rest. We have much to discuss."

David took the large cup and drank. The mead was the same as he'd tasted from Heidrun when he was with Mardoll. The liquid coated his throat and stomach and eased his tensions. This time, he drank it more greedily. "Thank you," David said.

"Good. We've shared strong drink. Now we may share our stories," Bulwyf said.

David looked to Sarena who nodded to him. He detailed the events of his journey from the bridge, stopping when Bulwyf pressed him for further details. The chief seemed particularly interested in Jacob and Kharon.

"I've never met the ferryman of souls," he said. "We who come to the gates of Valhalla do not cross the rivers. Not by boat, anyway."

"How do you come here?" David said.

"We arrive at the doors of the hall much like waking from a dream," Bulwyf said. "Those who fight with Freja are carried by the valkyries to their hostess, and those who dwell in the ices of Helheim do not speak to us, so we do not know their tales."

"Helheim," David repeated. "I've heard that's where the monsters came from."

"Aye, they claw their way up from the pits of Helheim and meet us in battle or, at times, we take a path down to their realm," Bulwyf said. "It's a joyless place, Helheim, but many great battles have been fought there. The creatures seem easy prey at first, but a spark awakens in them when they are engaged that makes them worthy of standing before our warriors here and from Folkvangr alike."

"Why do those creatures go down to that place?" David asked.

"For the opposite reason warriors come here or go with Freja," Sarena said, but offered no more.

David mulled this over and thought better than to press further.

He needed to figure his situation out first. "Do you have any idea what I should do?"

"Aye," Bulwyf said. "Jubei is right. You may die if you are cut down in battle here. We can't be sure why your angel..." Bulwyf glanced to Sarena who met his gaze. "...took you here, but I have a few guesses."

"Well, your worst guess is probably better than my best," David said.

Sarena filled Bulwyf's glass again, and he thanked her. "Why would anyone drop you off at the doorstep of the greatest warriors ever to live?" she asked David.

"Other than to be brutally cut in half by a Viking warlord, you mean?" David asked. Bulwyf smiled broadly at him. The flames from the wall danced in his eyes before he closed them to empty his cup again.

"I honestly don't know," David said.

"To fight, boy," Bulwyf exclaimed as he slammed his cup on the tray table. "He brought you here to cut your teeth."

David shook his head. "Why wouldn't he just teach me to do that? And why would I need to learn to fight?"

"The angels are not all warriors," Bulwyf offered. "Your angel, very likely an archangel of the holy sephiroth, may not have felt he possessed the ability to teach you what we here can."

"Archangel? What is the sephiroth?" David asked.

"From time to time, we are visited by members of the host, and archangels have been among them," Sarena said. "They each have traits specific to their nature and exemplify them in how they carry out their orders from on high. The sephiroth is the trait the archangel was imbued with upon creation, but there's more to it than that."

"Christianity, mythology from around the world, monsters and demons—this doesn't make sense," David said, exasperated. "Why are all these things here? Why are we in a place that's in Nordic mythology?"

"Your questions are not unfounded," said Bulwyf, clapping David on the shoulder with his massive hand, and the boy was surprised that he didn't crumble under the weight of it. "Many traditions and stories told in the world are pieces of a larger whole. It's best if you consider that many are overlapping truths of the reality of the realm beneath the veil of the living world. This is the name we've come to call it, though we consider ourselves to be very much alive here in this place as well."

Sarena filled David's tankard even though he was not finished. "There is more to it, but what Bulwyf says is the foundation of the truth," she said.

David stared at the mead in his cup, the color of the vessel giving the liquid a dark hue. No waves touched the surface, serving to remind him of his steady hands. "Who is the archangel in charge of learning?" David asked.

Bulwyf said, "I know this angel to be Uriel."

Sarena said, "They take many names through different traditions, but Uriel or Ariel for knowledge, yes."

"Thank you," David said, keeping this name in his back pocket for later. "So, how will you two go about teaching me to be a warrior?"

"The best way I know," Bulwyf said. "By making you fight. Sarena will oversee you, so you won't likely be killed."

David sighed, "As much as I trust Joan of Arc to keep me safe, I'm not too sure I'll survive for an instant on the battlefield."

Sarena's shock was given away by her eyes flicking back to David.

"Don't be surprised. Be glad your name is still in the history books," Bulwyf said. Sarena was quiet as she contemplated this. "You would die in an instant within the mayhem of an open battlefield, this is true. You will cut your teeth in the arena housed within the walls of this hall, and your trainers will be among the greatest men and women to ever wield weapons, David."

David stood, wondering what the future held for him. Sarena looked in his eyes and said, "I'm reasonably certain you won't die."

Ω

David spent some time in the chambers of Bulwyf, discussing a myriad of characteristics of the afterlife, before being sent back down the staircase with Sarena. They didn't rejoin the members of the hall, instead entering another door on the fringes of where Jubei had taken him. David could see the crowd had become more boisterous. Men and women were entangled carnally on tabletops and in corners of the room and around them people sang, scuffled, and danced.

"Come," Sarena said, leading him through yet another door. The area beyond was not ornate, as had been the case for the hall leading to Bulwyf's staircase. It was a short walk before the ceiling fell away behind them, and they were standing in a massive indoor arena.

Men and women were spaced out around the area practicing with various weapons. Some sparred, but the contrast between how the horde engaged in combat at the horn and this disciplined exercise was evident at first glance. The fervor during their engagement on the battlefield having ebbed, there was control and concentration in their movements.

"They are careful not to kill one another or inflict severe wounds," Sarena said. "The risk of being injured before the next call of the horn is too severe a penalty for most here."

"Why do they care so much about a battle that is meaningless?" David asked.

"Consider how they died, David," Sarena said. "Imagine being locked in mortal combat with an adversary and finding yourself blinking from existence before your spirit is able to process your departure. Mightn't you find solace in the cycle then?"

David thought about this for a moment before the weight of whom he was speaking to fell upon him.

"I am sorry for what happened to you. You are an incredibly inspiring person," David said.

Sarena nodded. "Thank you."

"Why did you hide your true name from me?" David asked.

"There are many reasons a person will hide who they are or were," she said. "Those who choose to use a pseudonym do so because they don't wish for people to take their measure based on stories of the past. Some have known me in life, but they are a scant few. Many have merely seen my likeness in movies or read of my endeavors. That is not who I was, flattering as the depiction may sometimes be."

David smiled. "Milla Jovovich did a pretty bang-up job in her role as you."

Sarena said, "I heard it was a bit contrived."

David saw in her the warrior she had been. Perhaps not the most skilled warrior in France at the time, but certainly the one with the biggest balls. Now, he surmised, she had risen to be one of the deadliest in the hall. "I imagine it is odd to hear what someone who was born hundreds of years after your death thinks of you."

"It's unnatural, but so is much that transpires here," she said. Changing the direction of the conversation, she pointed to the arena. "Do you see that man there?"

David's eyes traced the vector of her finger and found a man who was carefully repeating his footfalls in the sand. He wasn't brandishing a flashy weapon, just a curved sword with a simple hilt, and he was in plain linen clothing.

"I think I do," David said. "The one dancing?"

"It is a type of dance, yes. His name is Mukhulai. He will be seeing to your development," Sarena said, turning to leave.

David had become accustomed to her brevity, but it was still unsettling. "Will I see you again soon?" he asked.

"They will not kill you, don't worry," was all she said in return before pulling up her cowl and striding out of the arena.

David stood for a few minutes before meeting yet another dead warrior. The people fighting may have been holding back, but it still didn't look as though they were too reliable at not drawing blood. Plenty had open wounds as they sparred. One man fought with his off hand while clutching two lost fingers in his other.

I am going to learn how and then I'm going to kick Jacob's ass for leaving me here, he thought, and made his way down to the sandy arena floor and toward Mukhulai. He was sure to keep to the perimeter as much as he could, but he was forced to wait for a few skirmishes to move on after they invaded his path.

Once he reached Mukhulai, David raised his voice in salutation, only to be stopped by an upraised finger. Mukhulai was looking down at his feet as he continued to trace his steps. After a time, he would raise his eyes and continue the steps while looking forward. A few minutes passed before he stopped.

"David?" he asked.

"That's me," David said. "You're Mukhulai? I guess they told you my deal, huh?"

Mukhulai said, "Nobody made a deal with me. I was just told to teach a boy with infirm legs to walk."

"Well, that's one way to put it," David said. "Were they clear on the part that if I die, I probably won't come back?"

"Yes, they did say you were strange," Mukhulai offered. "I'll be sure to not kill you or give you a lasting maiming."

David rubbed his hands together. "Sounds super reassuring. So, are you Chinese? There are so many warriors here from around the world, and everyone here has a story. What's yours?"

Mukhulai's features showed mayhem as his lips parted in a smile and his eyes barked fire. "I'm a Mongol, boy. A Kheshig. We were warriors so feared that the Khan himself dared not show disrespect," he said, slowly drawing his sword. "I would not speak of the Chinese again if I were interested in remaining whole. Now go to the rack and choose a weapon."

David was not excited that he'd pissed off the mad Mongol. As he made his way to the rack filled with swords, bows, and spears, he said, "I meant no disrespect."

Mukhulai waited. Focusing on the rack, David noticed there weren't any swords like Mukhulai's. He settled for a medium-sized, straight sword with a sturdy looking guard on its hilt. He returned, crouched, and stood ready.

Mukhulai laughed, "We will need to correct your balance, but first I get to have fun with you for assuming I am Chinese." He lunged at David, swinging his curved sword. David would later find out it was called a scimitar, a weapon which found popularity in Europe and the Middle East for how effective it was. He felt that effectiveness run through his bones as he blocked the attack and its follow-up, which hurled twice the force due to Mukhulai's expert spin.

"You do well to not wince or cow, but blocking is just seeing your death slowed down," Mukhulai said, ducking low to sweep David's legs. David hit the ground on the flat of his back and rolled to avoid any would-be attacks aimed at him while he was downed, but Mukhulai stood his ground and waited. "I am pleased to see that you show promise. You are afraid, but it does not hold dominion over you. This is good."

"Thanks. And thanks for not going easy on me," David said as he brushed dust and sand off his pants.

"Oh, I am, boy, but I won't for long," Mukhulai said as he advanced.

Both souls danced on a tightrope slung between life and death and lost themselves.

Ω

David and Mukhulai trained together tirelessly, except when Mukhulai heeded the call of the horn. The horn held no compulsion for David, a relief since Mina had worried it might, and he spent his solitude exploring the passages and halls of Valhalla. David studied ornate architecture and works of art that would have been priceless artifacts on display in museums back home. Here, they were left to the mercy of the elements.

Mukhulai would come to the arena at a trot when the warriors returned and avidly resume training. David noted he was slightly more dangerous after returning from the field, as though the blades affixed to his palms desired still more bloodletting.

Time drew on, and other fighters would come to offer their services, allowing for Mukhulai to coach them and David simultaneously. The Mongol was well respected amongst the warriors. A British longbowman told David tales of how Mukhulai had never fallen in battle on the field. Others said he had, but it was rare. Regardless, he was the spirit of combat personified. David could see how he breathed as he fought, how the air around him became an ally as his body moved through it.

It was rare for people to have missteps or lapses in fealty around him, but it did happen. In one instance, a training partner specializing in the pike had plunged his spear into David's shoulder. He cried out but managed to keep grasp on his sword. Mukhulai's expression did not change when he said, "Kill him, David."

Without thinking, David flipped his weapon to the other hand, stepped back from the snare of the spearhead, and ran down the length of its shaft. The pikeman's head rolled through the sand before David could take the measure of his own actions.

"How did it feel?" Mukhulai asked.

David responded by retching into the sand. The event shed light on one question, though, and it was not the one regarding whether David could stomach the naked realities of battle. David healed extremely quickly, although the manner in which his body did so was not like the others. He did not blink into existence at the front doors of the hall. Instead, a fallen field medic from the Korean War bandaged David's wound.

Mukhulai worked with David on the use of a bow for the remaining time until the horn took him away with its siren call. After returning, they removed the bandage and found it had nearly healed. Although the wound felt hot to the touch, no scarring was evident. Mukhulai sent word of this to Bulwyf, and they resumed training.

After some time, David found he was being pitted against more and more warriors from the hall. He also found he was getting the better of the exchanges more often. Once, while Mina and Boris were visiting, Boris asked if Mukhulai had ever had someone who was this quick of a study with the use of various arms. Mukhulai said, "There is nothing natural about the boy's progress. It is not the sprouting of a plant from a seed, but the awakening of a forest."

Mina and Boris were a welcome distraction and even trained David on how to clean and use firearms. A Finnish sniper named

Simo came at times to show David how to "long fire"—as he put it. There was a subtle art to aiming iron sights a few degrees above a target in order to score a hit at long range.

The boy drank it all and left no dregs. He soon lost the fear of being harmed in the rush of combat. "It's art," he said to Mukhulai after learning how to dual wield scimitars one day.

"It's the oldest art humans have," Mukhulai said.

Some time passed this way, but David had no way to mark its progress. It was a fevered dream. That is, until Jubei came and woke him. The samurai arrived and bowed deeply to Mukhulai. "May I meet David in the arena?" he asked.

"Yes," Mukhulai said, "but be aware you should not take him lightly. His legs have firmed."

Jubei nodded and bowed to David. "David, will you meet me?"

The boy, who had progressed so far so quickly, bowed to Jubei, and the samurai noted the difference in his countenance.

David hefted a miaodao long sword and aimed the slightly curved blade at Jubei. Mukhulai had sneered when he noted David choosing the Chinese sword increasingly often for duels, but he conceded that it was a fantastic weapon.

Jubei released his main tachi from its sheath and readied his stance with two hands on the hilt. David adjusted to match his hold and waited. Seconds hung long and heavy in the air before Jubei made his first strike. David felt the atmosphere move around and through him. He did not lose his center. Jubei advanced with fluidity and grace hiding the brutal strength behind his first blow, an overhead downward strike aimed at the center of David's skull, which David effectively parried while swiftly dodging to his right. He knew better than to try to counter without understanding Jubei's movements.

"If I didn't know better, I'd say you were aiming to kill me with that strike," David said.

"I will not dishonor you with less than my full strength," Jubei said.

Mukhulai, who stood at the front of a gathering group of spectators, said, "Every man you've fought since twenty horns ago has been striking to kill. You haven't noticed because their efforts were futile. To you, they appeared to be holding back."

"You've gained great strength," Jubei said, changing his stance to a wide legged crouch with his elbows high and the point of his sword aimed at David's head. "I will test it."

Jubei lunged, maintaining his impossible crouched position and leaned his torso forward. This, matched with the full extension of his arms and the length of his sword, gave him immense reach, and David had to rely on his feet to protect him by moving his torso out of the way of the sword thrusts rather than attempting to deflect them. They were too fast. He switched his sword to a single hand and stood upright on one leg with his other foot planted lightly on his shin, the sword poised above his head.

Jubei was intrigued by this, as it appeared to offer up David's entire midsection for impaling, but the seasoned warrior didn't get a chance to try. David's raised foot came down as he crouched low in liquid motion. His free hand joined the wrist of his left holding the sword and the momentum carried his strike into the base of Jubei's sword with the discordant sound of metal attempting to occupy the same space. Jubei was knocked off balance in his stance, his arm thrown wide. David stepped in and planted a straight kick into the samurai's midsection, sending him tumbling.

David advanced but did not chase. He rained a series of two-handed blows on Jubei, which kept the battle-hardened warrior off balance, and then swept his front foot with a light kick as Jubei's weight shifted from it. The result was a man full of openings. David did not hesitate. He struck for the midsection, his miaodao thirsting for climax.

David's sword did not find its desires fulfilled, however. It met with Jubei's wakizashi before it could bite flesh. Jubei had pulled it even while off balance and used it to stall a killing blow. He was now fighting with his full daisho. The samurai used the moment of stillness offered by his opponent contemplating two swords instead of one to regain his balance and advance.

At first, the crowd, now grown to hundreds, cheered the dual wielding onslaught of Jubei on David. The speed of the strikes was absurd, and David's adrenaline surged as he blocked them. Jubei's larger sword brought strength and the smaller struck with opportunity and stealth. The wakizashi flashed through the flesh on David's forearm as he artfully parried. They were formidable, perhaps more formidable than Mukhulai's dual scimitars, but David minded his breathing and matched Jubei's pace.

Soon, he was no longer falling back but standing his ground and circling as Jubei struck and countered David's ripostes. The pain in his arm made David feel alive. The stakes for him were life and death. David felt the ground beneath him lend power to his blows, he felt the wind following behind his strikes, he heard the arena becoming his ally.

Jubei changed his stances to try and knock David off balance, but the boy had taken his measure and was putting him on the defensive. The main tachi came down from above and to the right in an arc toward David's neck, a desperate move on Jubei's part, and David stepped forward in a seemingly reckless maneuver. His speed was perfection as he placed his hand on the hilt of Jubei's large sword and pushed it out to swing harmlessly over his head. Jubei made to stab with his smaller wakizashi, but David's long sword was already biting into the flesh of the man's bicep. Jubei's thrust only served to further impale it.

David freed the miaodao from Jubei's arm and saw the wakizashi fall to the arena floor. Stopping here would disrespect Jubei, and David knew this. He stepped back, swept left, and carried his blade across his friend's stomach. The contents spilled to the floor, and Jubei fell forward atop them, mercifully covering the gore. David stood tall and bowed deeply before him.

Gravity had once again taken hold as adrenaline waned. Now, he was merely looking down upon a felled man—and a friend, at that. Perhaps the glories of battle were enough to sate the desires of the men and women here, but David had begun to think that he was cut from a different cloth.

The crowd cheered and stomped so loudly that it felt as though the hall itself may collapse around them. David couldn't help but to survey them. Mukhulai clapped his hands together and smiled.

When David turned to see his fallen friend, Jubei was gone. Blood-stained earth where he'd rested was all that remained.

Sarena meandered her way through the crowd to David. "Don't worry, he will return after the next horn," she said. She turned toward the weapons rack and surveyed the armament. Her coverall and cowl falling into a heap next to the rack, she hefted a spear and turned to David. "How do you think you'll fare against someone who doesn't much care for honor?" she asked.

David was weighing the question when she hurled the spear at him. He knew he didn't have time to fully dodge the projectile, so he used the face of his blade to push the spearhead out and over his right shoulder. It sailed into the crowd and buried itself in the shoulder of one of the onlookers. The crowd roared.

The temporary distraction was all Sarena needed to close the distance to a frighteningly small space. She brandished a thin sword that was long enough to pose a danger. David instinctively stepped backward and realized he had just opened himself up to the ideal range for her attacks. The sword pistoned at him half a dozen times, once scoring a small gash on his bicep as he manipulated his more cumbersome weapon to block and feign attacks. She wasn't fooled.

"I see Mukhulai hasn't been focusing on the incidentals with you just yet," she sneered. "You're still green."

She lifted a cloud of sand and dust into his face with the toe of her worn boots. Succumbing to his temporary blindness, he gritted his eyes closed to try and clear the debris while delivering a wide and hard slash through the middle ground between them to dissuade her from moving in to finish him. The act of desperation may have worked, too. David didn't feel her block the slash, so he assumed she'd moved back.

Once one of his eyes cleared enough for him to chance a glance, he opened it partway to discover she was gone. The pommel of her sword connected with the back of his skull. Had she been stronger, this would have been enough to put his lights out, but he was able to fall to his knees and roll forward from her. His eyes were still cloudy, but he had his auditory sense. She was pursuing him this time, meaning to finish this quickly.

David abruptly stopped his forward momentum, flattened his chest to the ground with palms spread, scissor kicking his legs behind him. Sarena released a cry of surprise as her knees were locked together, and she doubled over from the purity of one of Jacob's favorite topics of discussion: inertia.

"I may be green, but I'm a quick study," he said as he gained his feet and stood to face her.

She stood and said, "It's not just that. You seem uniquely suited for learning how to battle. Considering six hundred years have passed in the living world while I honed my skills here, you should have been dead before I unsheathed my sword. Yet, here you are, standing to fight again. Your story is filled with questions, David Dolan." The remarkable woman slid her unremarkable sword into its scabbard. "You are special."

Ω

Not long after David fought with Jubei and Sarena, the horn called the warriors out of the hall. Their fervor upon departing was at a fever pitch, and David wondered if their adversaries would notice the wider vein of bloodlust running through the warriors of Valhalla on the field that day. Once the battle was done, the hall filled with banter and noise of joyous celebration. Fighting would take a backseat to reverie for some time, and today David meant to join them. It felt like ages since he'd seen and spoken with Boris and Mina. He also wanted to see Jubei.

Weaving through the Bacchanalia, hands clapped his back and cheers issued from those around him. David had gained a modicum of celebrity from his time in the arena and his duels. It showed as cups clashed in his honor and his name appeared in the whooping songs flaring within the crowd.

He soon arrived to find the trio where they'd supped with him at his first feast. Jubei stood, bowed, and then offered the seat to his left.

"Well, if it isn't the warrior prophet. Surprised to see you here since you've been spending all your time with Mukhulai," Boris said. "Starting to wonder if you may have a particular taste for far eastern morsels."

David laughed. "Mukhulai isn't my type. Too much fur, for one, and I'm already attached, for another."

"Ah, a pretty little thing waiting for you at home? Familiar story," Mina said as she reached for food from one of the trays.

"Her name is Rose," he said. "We've been together forever, and if it's all the same to those pulling the strings on me, I'd like to keep it that way."

"Lucky girl," Mina said, and turned her attention to filling her cup.

"Oh, don't be glum, my Yankee princess. Boris will warm your bed for you," the Russian said, answering any question as to how much he'd had to drink already.

Mina blushed but didn't admonish him. Jubei, quiet as he often was during their banter, turned to David. "You've become quite skilled with the Chinese sword, David. I was honored to have met you in the arena."

"The, um, honor was all mine. I never expected to harm one of the only people I've met since my accident who I consider a true friend, Jubei. I'm sorry," said David, and cast his eyes at the splintering wood on the table edge.

"Apologizing for honoring me? I won't stand for this. We keep our actions, David, and we do not apologize for our victories. You are a warrior now. It is time to put childish notions aside," Jubei said, and placed a firm hand on David's shoulder giving him a shake.

"Impostor syndrome," Mina said. "That's what they call it in the military when you don't feel you deserve what you've earned. Could be a new rank, or a slim victory where you lost friends, or whatever. Means you don't feel worthy or you feel bad about leaving others behind."

"Sounds as though it is humility," Jubei said. "Humility is good,

David, but recognition of your progress is not a direct route to vanity. Enjoy your success."

David surveyed those around him. His gaze returned to Jubei, whose eyes were still on him. "I came because I remembered, Jubei," David said.

"What did you remember?" Boris asked, surprisingly attentive despite the deep rouge on his cheeks.

"I remember what happened after the bridge collapsed, but before I woke up here," David said. He shook his head and clenched his fist. "There was a boy. I pulled him from his car as it sank in the river and tried to get us both to the shore. I don't think we made it, though. I don't know where he is. His name was Tim, Jubei. He was just a kid."

Jubei, Boris, and Mina were quiet.

David looked up to see they were giving one another knowing glances. "What's the inside dialogue here?" David asked.

"We think we know one of the prerequisites for being taken into Freja's fields or here," Mina said.

"Your story strengthens our combined thinking," Boris said. "I wasn't just caught in the sight of a skilled sniper. I was dragging a comrade out of the battlefield. He, Mikhail, was shot through the shoulder, but he had a good chance. I still don't know if he made it."

"I'd taken a voluntary mission to retrieve a girl who had been kidnapped by insurgent forces," Mina said. "We usually knew how that type of thing panned out, and I couldn't stomach the thought of what they'd do to her. Our unit had zeroed in on her location, and we were sweeping the building for more friendlies when I punched my ticket." Her chin pointed to the sky as she drank heavily from her cup.

"I met Sanada Masamune and his cohorts to dissuade them from charging the local shops and families for protection," Jubei said. "They'd wrung coins from people's pockets for far too long, and it needed to come to an end. All of our stories seem to have a commonality, as do others here."

"I can see that doing something good is a running theme, but then why is Sanada here? He was a crook, and he jumped you," David said.

"He met me in a duel knowing he was not my better," Jubei said. "It was his cohorts who joined after I'd slashed Sanada."

David rubbed his temples and then reached for his own cup to fill it with the concoction produced by the carafe. "Still seems a bit thin if you're comparing what he did to what you did."

"He honored me, David, and that may be enough," Jubei said.

David said, "Okay, I can buy it. I was eligible because I didn't leave Tim to die on his own."

"You risked your life, your future, and all the things you had laid out before you to make a play for him and his. The weight of that is heavy," Mina said.

David nodded. "Do you like it here, Mina?"

She didn't hesitate. "I like Boris and Jubei and you." Mina said. "I don't like being pitted against other fighters and monsters in some perverse version of *Groundhog Day*."

"Yeah, I had trouble seeing this as a reward for your endeavors too," David said. "Does anyone ever leave this place?"

Boris laughed. "Oh, now you've done it, little lapochka. You've stoked the flames of another of Jubei's theories."

"Not a theory, just an observation," Jubei said.

Mina interjected. "He saw something once on the field. A member of Freja's army cut down someone from here, but they didn't lay on the ground to be resurrected like usual."

"His name was Abdirahim. He wasn't much older than you are, David. I spoke to him when he first came here, as you did to Mina. We offered him a place with us, but he refused."

"Ran scared as a rabbit from a hawk," Boris said. "Mina's talons, I guess."

She hit him on the arm. "We think he was afraid of the uniform. Maybe it was that I was American."

"The boy was from the cradle of civilization, you see," Boris said. "Somalia, to be exact. Jubei managed to put that together before the kid ran off."

"Still, he heeded the call of the horn, and we saw him out there from time to time," Jubei said. "When he was cut down on the field, he simply disappeared. The man who felled him stood wide eyed, a look of terror on his face."

Mina said, "Jubei thinks they joined together. That somehow the kid and the other guy became one person."

"How did you jump to that specific conclusion, Jubei?" David asked.

"The man who felled the boy, his eyes changed color. They were a light blue before Abdirahim died. After, they were as dark as a starless night."

CHAPTER EIGHT
OUROBOROS

David needed to speak with Bulwyf about what he'd learned. He made his way to the oval room of doors off the main dining hall. He rapped on the door and stood waiting for a response. None came, so he tried the handle and found it to be open.

Can't be too mad if I show myself in when you don't lock the door, David thought, convincing himself of intruding into an area he knew required an escort. Quickly striding through the halls, David once again glanced at the statue of Achilles. The sheer beauty of the sculpture was remarkable enough on its own, but the weight of the story of this hero made it shimmer all the more. The greatest warrior the world had ever known wouldn't be here, not if Jubei's theory were true.

It didn't take long for David to reach the doors to Bulwyf's chambers, and he found these open as well. Out of respect, he didn't cross the threshold without announcing himself. Bulwyf called him inside expectantly. The Norseman sat cross legged on his ornate throne. There were no other guests.

"I've come because I have some questions for you," said David, hoping his directness wouldn't be taken for disrespect.

Bulwyf nodded solemnly. "It's been some time since you joined me in my chambers, though not as much as you may think. Time here moves differently than it does in the veiled world of mankind. I'm sure your angel friend spoke to you of this anomaly."

"We did touch on the subject. Still, there's no telling how much time has passed at home," David said.

"Yes, there is," Bulwyf said. "Less." He leaned forward, casting cruel shoulders toward David. "I first joined the raging horde of Valhalla around one thousand and one hundred years ago. That's more than many here, but not the most. Back then, we tried to understand this place from what we learned from newcomers. Instead of sunrise and sunset to guide us, we use the horn to set our days. You have probably noticed the time between horns is something you begin to feel in your nerves."

David nodded his understanding. "I could feel my hair begin to stand on edge in the arena. I was excited for it. I always knew when it was close."

"It appears to be a set amount of time, but there's no way to tell if that's true," Bulwyf said. "The world around us is too erratic to use as a tool to measure this. One of the first learnings we had was how time flies here compared to the world we left behind. We would feel decades transpire, yet newcomers would tell of a few years passing in the world of the living. You may find mere weeks have passed in your old life, even though it feels as though you've been here for—"

"—months or years," David finished.

"Aye, David. Aye," Bulwyf said. "This isn't what brings you to me, though. I know this. You came to ask if you can leave Valhalla."

"Something like that. But there's more to it," David said. "I've heard of people leaving here. Jubei saw one."

"Aye, Jubei spied the one from Africa. We have many from the continent. All warriors of Valhalla are known to me as I sit on this seat. That boy was killed by a man whose soul was missing something,

something the boy had." Bulwyf straightened his legs and put his feet on the floor.

"I'm not following," David said.

"You don't strike me much as the following type," Bulwyf said. David took it as a compliment rather than confusion from the phrase. Bulwyf had kept up with the idiosyncrasies of language by meeting and conversing with so many who had been born after him. Many of the warriors in the hall spoke without accents and understood phrases and terminology David would have used in daily conversation. "This place, do you think of it as a punishment or a reward?" Bulwyf asked him.

"I didn't know at first, but now it seems to be a punishment. There are plenty of people who appear bored or sad," David said.

"I believe it is neither," Bulwyf said. "Tell me, does your society push young men into the fields to work?"

The question threw David for a moment. "We aren't much of a farming culture anymore, but I don't think that's what you mean. We have mandatory school until we are around eighteen years old. After that, some go straight to work, some go for more school, and some become skilled in a craft."

"Aye, not much use in putting them to work before they are ready, is there?" Bulwyf posed.

"So, you're saying these people aren't ready?" David asked.

"Something to that effect," Bulwyf said. "What Jubei saw happen to Abdirahim and the man who struck him down has happened to me three times since I first awoke at the doors of this hall."

David said, "So you've known all along?"

"I was here for quite a spell before it happened, but the first time changed me," Bulwyf said. "I was not always this tall, David. The man Bulwyf cut down was a mountain moving across the field. The circumstances found me to be the better warrior that day, though he'd taken much of my arm with his spiked maul. After he vanished, I filled with him—his memory, his love, his hate. His thoughts invaded my own. The experience was maddening at first, but soon I came to know I was no longer Bulwyf, but also Arminius. Since then, we have also joined with Chandragupta and Sitting Bull."

David tried to imagine the inner discourse between all the men inside of Bulwyf. "Do they still talk to you from inside?"

"That is not how it is," Bulwyf said. "We are not separate, but one. All the lessons of our lives have melded into the man you see sitting on this chair crafted from the shorn branch of Yggdrasil. I am still Bulwyf, but much more besides. This is the secret of Valhalla."

"I think I understand now. Will everyone here eventually become one person, do you think?" David asked.

Bulwyf said, "That is what I believe the field is intended for, yes."

"Has anyone ever joined with one of the creatures from Helheim?" David asked.

"It is believed that they have been joined by those of this hall and the Folkvangr, as well," Bulwyf said. "They too are warriors, David. But they gave their lives at the whims of unjust cause. Their listless existence is not a punishment for that, but a projection of their understanding of what they have done. One might say they are our opposites."

"And what exactly do you believe brings people here? Sacrifice?" David asked. His questions rose as quickly as Bulwyf could knock them back down.

"Valor is what brings men and women to the halls of Valhalla. This and nothing else," Bulwyf said. "But valor alone is not enough to move on, it seems. What is enough will remain a mystery until the halls stop flooding with warriors faster than we can be joined together."

"I didn't think you would know what comes next," David said. "Jacob wouldn't tell me, either."

"My knowledge only reaches to what lies beyond the gates to the mountain at the perimeter of the field. It is my belief that your destiny will take you to the mountain," Bulwyf said. "It is also my belief that the mountain can bring you back to your reality."

David's eye's widened. "What is beyond the mountain?"

Bulwyf said, "Not beyond, but within. Within resides the embodiment of envy. Jormungandr, the world serpent."

"I haven't heard of it by that name, but I think I know the world serpent. It fights Thor at the end of the world," David said.

"You may know of it by a more Christian name," said Bulwyf,

as he pointed to a tapestry adorning the wall of his chamber. On it, there appeared many spheres arranged atop one another as they ascended to the apex of a tree. Wound around all the worlds was a massive serpent with its mouth agape as it endeavored to swallow the sphere at the top.

David's mind fell on the name of the creature, but before he could utter it, Bulwyf said, "The great Leviathan."

Ω

David left Bulwyf's chamber with an understanding of his situation. He returned to Mukhulai out of habit, but the Mongol warrior didn't seek to train him. "You have the look of a child who hears thunder," Mukhulai said.

"Bulwyf and I spoke. I think I have to go meet a giant snake," David said.

Mukhulai laughed loud enough for people training near to pause and glance. "You didn't hear thunder, son, you heard the hands of a god clap above your head!"

"I don't have the slightest idea what I'm supposed to do," David said.

"Have you since you awoke in the world beneath the veil?" Mukhulai asked.

"No," David said.

"Then you sail in familiar waters," said Mukhulai, clapping David on the shoulder. "Best not to overthink things. Tell me, which instrument have you found to be your favorite since learning the martial arts?"

"I like the miaodao, but the curved sword offers better movement for multiple opponents, and the long sword is so well balanced that I can't be easily moved while defending. Even the simple broadsword feels great when I use it. I don't think I can claim a favorite," David said as his eyes measured others fighting around them.

"Precisely. Each weapon has benefits for different situations," Mukhulai said. "Not one is perfect, because every instance of battle

213

will be different. The weapon that matters most is already known to you, David."

David's eyes flashed recognition. "The mind. It must be clean, and clear, and always at hand, and..."

"...always sharp," Mukhulai finished. "This is the only weapon which can be honed to perfection."

The horn sounded loud and deep through the hall, calling the men and women out to the field. Mukhulai began to walk to the exit of the arena, passing by the weapons rack, knowing his killing instruments would appear when he walked outside. "Don't worry, young David. Worry clouds the mind," he said and disappeared amidst the shadows of the tunnel.

David stood for a few moments before deciding on his next course. He walked to the tunnel, retrieving various pieces of middleweight armor on his way, and looked at the weapons rack. He left the arena without taking one.

Out in the main dining area, there were scant few people still making their way to the field. Platters sat empty on tables and the absence of a mess seemed inappropriate considering the reverie that had held court here just a few moments ago.

David walked past the long tables without doing much thinking. He simply felt compelled to go, so he did. The compulsion that carried him was different than what took hold of the righteous warriors of Valhalla before they took the field, for what propelled David was not the grip of bloodlust, but rather the need to survive. He must survive to return to his life and to Rose. She must be missing him just as much as he was missing her. He had committed himself. Through the madness and chaos, he would rise from this place and return home.

Having never attempted to exit the hall before, David was unsure if he would be able. He quickly found that there was no resistance crossing the threshold, and sunlight soon washed over him. The warriors were fighting in the fields of Valhalla for this horn. David glanced to where he'd first crossed to the hall and saw the earth beginning to fall away to allow for the sad souls of Helheim to join in the battle. The mountain, rising to impossible heights to kiss the sky, was in the opposite direction. David would be able to cross to it on foot easily enough, but there were plenty of men amassing between him and his goal. Still, he must chance it if he was going to get beyond the hall before too much time had passed in the world, where Rose and his mother were likely struggling.

David jogged toward the mountain, taking a wider arc to avoid the fighting. This tactic proved to be ineffective; the clashes of will and steel spilled further and further from the center of the field. He would have to pass through the dust ups, even if just some of them. Still, he didn't regret leaving weapons behind. The field wasn't for him. Bulwyf's information had all but proven it. He would have to make do with just his wits.

Increasing speed from a jog to a run, David vectored as far from the mass as he could. Drawing closer brought clarity to the scene, which was a blur in his mind. He'd never been this close to the massacring that took place on the field at the call of every horn, and he imagined the display would be something more familiar, like a scene from a movie.

It was nothing like that.

The warriors from Valhalla were throwing themselves into battle with complete abandon. Freja's troops stood out in that they fought with unity and restraint. The lost souls of Helheim were pure opportunists, dashing in to confront warriors who may be more easily caught unawares, and subsequently being chopped down in most cases. Marksmen were also at play here, and the slower-moving creatures were easy prey for them. Their bodies fell in near unison to the reports from rifles all around them.

David reached the scribbled battle line and dashed through groups of people fighting. He had made it nearly halfway through the tributary of violence before being confronted with any real danger. A whip-wielding woman wearing an iron mask and plate-studded leather armor had sighted him and moved to intercept, the range of her chosen weapon giving her an advantage that others wouldn't have had.

David paused, redirected toward the outside of the crowd, and tried to keep enough distance to avoid a strike. She mirrored his movements and followed with a whooping battle cry, flexing her wrist to keep life flowing through the cruel whip. David resigned himself to let her make the first move, and she did not take long to choose her moment. He hurdled two men wrestling on the ground, and she dashed in toward him, flicking the barbed fall at his midsection. David knew ducking would not help him to avoid her—the whip could cover too much vertical area for that—so he stepped toward her and the perceived danger. Taking the blow where the centrifugal force would be far less and would greatly reduce the lethality of her strike. Still, the attack drew blood from his upraised forearm, and he relished the right cross he delivered to her unprotected chin. He was in motion again before she hit the ground.

By his measure, he had another fifty yards to cover before reaching open ground once again. *Good.* He knew he had become faster since his fate brought here. He could cover the distance in two breaths.

Dodging and ducking, David advanced as a blur to most of those around him. He truly believed he was going to make it without further confrontation when reports from rifles coincided with the sounds of bullets meeting flesh nearby.

Chancing a glance behind him, he found that more than a few men and women, his whip wielding nemesis for one, had been picked off by a sharpshooter. Ducking slightly lower in his sprint, he advanced and saw more fall around and ahead as the volley of bullets continued. Sure that he was going to catch one of the rounds himself, David was surprised when he cleared the crowd and was running through the open field once more. Not a great feeling when you know sharp eyes are behind rifles.

He scanned the surrounding area to see if he could spot cover or the assailant, even turning around to run backward for a bit, when he saw the tan fatigues atop the pure green grass of a small hill nearby. The flickering light of a scope told him he was being sighted, and David dropped to the ground as flat as he was capable.

He was surprised when he thought he saw an upraised hand waving at him. "What the hell is going on?" he said to himself.

Another shooter, roughly fifty feet to the right of the first, chose to raise their head and wave as well.

When seeing them together, David realized it was Boris and Mina clearing the path for him. They'd known he was leaving or spotted him coming. He smiled at his fast friends and waved back. Standing and turning to continue his short journey, he was still facing the hill when he saw arrows rain down on it from above. Must have been fired from Folkvangr longbowmen. Boris and Mina had been felled for revealing themselves.

David imagined them joking about their rotten luck over warm vodka in the hall, and he smiled. He realized in that moment he would miss them more than he had expected.

Knowing their experience was probably less than pleasant, semi-immortal or no, he made sure not to waste their efforts and took off as fast as his legs could carry him. He moved still faster and drew close to the gates at the mountain base well before the fighting had ended behind. He stopped to look one last time at the macabre purgatory he'd taken part in. He decided that this place was not a gift to the warriors, but not a curse either. These people were being processed for something, as Bulwyf said.

For what, he did not know.

David approached the doors and realized he had not once asked Bulwyf if they were locked. Even if they weren't, how could he hope to move them? They were at least five stories tall, probably more.

"They will open for you if you're meant to enter, David," a soft voice uttered from the rocks of the mountain to the right of the door.

David looked and spied Mardoll sitting cross legged on a small natural seat of granite. Her eyes were on the field. "Don't fret, just approach and you will see if it is meant for you to enter," she said.

"I feel stupid for not having a plan," David said.

"My Folkvangr plan for every battle before each horn from the moment the last one ended, yet the outcome is always the same," Mardoll said. "Fate laughs at the most well-honed plans."

David began to walk to the doors to see if they would allow him to enter. He stopped once more and asked, "Freja?"

"Yes, David?" she said.

"Why did you tell me your name was Mardoll?" David asked.

"Because that is my name," she said. "I have many names, David. As will you," she said.

David did not know what she could mean by this, but before he could barrage her with questions, as is the way of the innocent, she said, "You do not belong here. You, one of fire, belong to the sky."

"Goodbye," said David, sensing the conversation was over.

"Good luck," Freja replied and dropped an animal skin of liquid into his hands. She gifted him with a smile he wouldn't soon forget and turned to leave her perch.

Ω

David walked to the doors as he sipped Heidrun's mead and they opened inward for him without pageantry. The cool wind from within smelled of decay as it wafted out and past him to become one with the open sky. The boy reached into his pocket to feel the coin he'd carried with him throughout his journey in this world. For some reason, the knowledge it was with him lent some form of comfort. He walked into the dark mountain against the breeze and all logic— sometimes destiny can carry people over thresholds they would never think to cross otherwise.

The doors closed behind David, and he found himself in the black, but not without vision. *Another interesting physical development.* David walked on, expecting there to be a series of tunnels to navigate, but found he was in what appeared as a yawning expanse. The mountain itself might have been completely hollow for all he could tell. No ceiling in sight, darkness without limit, and walls lined with dark green stone he could not identify.

As he continued to venture through the cave, he noted that other than the sheer size of the space, the primary characteristic the interior of the mountain held in abundance was uniformity. Smooth rock beneath his feet and deep emerald-green walls, receded away from beside and behind him as he advanced further.

Becoming increasingly concerned he would be unable to find what he sought, a way home, he began to trot inward, scanning the interior as far as his vision would pierce the abyssal surroundings. The idea of returning to the entrance and following the walls around seemed to scratch at his mind just before David saw a structure jutting from the ground ahead. He slowed to a stop as he tried to gain his bearings.

What he could discern looked to simply be more stone from the walls, but this lay behind the initial discordant structure he'd spotted. The anomalous shape outlined from amorphous dark was made from the same material as the mountain floor itself. Atop it jutted an object smaller still and far too symmetrical to be stone.

David eased forward, and movement from behind the structure shattered the calm. Unnerved, David looked for anything he could use as cover. Darkness broke to a soft green glow, emanating from sliding shapes he could now see were the same as those adorning the walls.

Detail flooded the space, and David could make out a massive body beginning to uncoil from around something at its center. The coils unwrapped in a stealthily quiet manner for their size and revealed the head of the creature that had been resting behind the structure, comprised of three large stones stacked atop one another as makeshift steps. A large sword nestled within the apex rock as though it was the oil soft leather of a sheath.

More of the beast illuminated, and David realized the source of light was its scales.

"What mouse has come to see me?"

"I knew you were going to talk, I just knew it," David said more to himself than to the creature Bulwyf had called Jormungandr. "I am no mouse, and I mean you no harm."

"What harm could you bring me, should you have meant any?"

"Fair point," David said. "I am David. For the time of one hundred and sixty-seven blasts of the horn on top of the hall of Valhalla, I have been here, though I don't belong to this place. I have come to leave and return to my home."

"None leave. I cannot leave. The souls cannot leave. Why should you be able to leave?"

"Because I need to leave. I shouldn't be here in the first place," David said.

"No, not a mouse at all. Nothing but a petulant child. I had hoped for more when I heard the doors opening. Tell me, do you feel this to be unfair, your imprisonment here?"

"I haven't thought of it as imprisonment before, but it would be unfair to keep me here against my will. I haven't done anything wrong. I also haven't died yet."

"Nor have I, yet here I am. My flesh is shorn daily to feed the embalmed souls around this mountain, an act they delight in time and time again." The light emanating from the scales brightened further to reveal more of the expansive space within the mountain. David could not tell where the body ended. Perhaps it didn't, and the coils of the world serpent were true to its name as they knotted deep within the crust of this land. "What do you strive to return to?"

"I have family, and a girl I love," David said. "Staying here isn't an option."

"Men do love to speak in absolutes," Leviathan said. "Women, when they come, they speak less in certainties and more in desires. David comes and speaks in both. You cannot leave, and I cannot leave."

"Why can't you leave?" David asked, hoping to find a way through the logical impasse.

The scales ebbed in their glow, but Leviathan's eyes radiated with ferocity. "We were all made. You were made, I was made, the earth was made, the heavens were made, the veiled worlds were made. All crafted from nothing by the most masterful hand you could possibly conceive with your limited view of what is and what is not. Others, like me, were made for specific purposes. Mammon houses avarice, Belphegor is the vessel for sloth, gluttony lives within the hide of Beelzebub, the shaitans of the desert are dervishes of rage, Lucifer became the container for pride, but I was crafted before them all. We have our places in the universe to test the sway of free will."

David ventured, "What do you preside over?"

"I am the embodiment of envy," the serpent said, and its head rose above the cavern floor as the entire interior of the mountain began to shine with the green glow from its scales. David realized that the coils from Leviathan's body lined the exterior walls of the mountain as far as the eye could see. Coils upon coils stacked to heights beyond his sight or ken. The glowing pulsed a beauty within the confined space, and he found himself feeling sorry for this bridled creature.

"Speak of your life, David," Leviathan said. "Tell me of what you have."

"Well, I have a girlfriend, a car—well, probably not a car anymore... I'm sorry, but you are massive," David said. "There's no end to you."

"One such as you will not perceive the scope of my expanse," Leviathan said. "My body spans worlds."

David noticed scales glowing a darker hue of green than the rest of the beast. "Is this your end, by the sword here?" he asked.

"The tip of my tail, yes," Leviathan whispered. "So, it is a sword you see atop this rock."

David snatched a long glance at the sword he'd seen before the serpent itself. "Yes," he said. "I see a beautifully crafted great sword in the rock there."

"How interesting. I did not expect you to see a weapon. A book, perhaps—many like you seek knowledge, so they see a tome of sorts. I could have guessed perhaps a woman, maybe your woman, but you already have her, so I see why that is not the case—"

"Everyone sees something different?" David asked.

"Yes. The top of this rock holds your one truest desire," Leviathan said and shined light down upon the rock to better David's view. "Many men desire power and see weapons their hearts assuredly believe will deliver such. You do not feel usual, though, and I had hoped you might see something unusual as well. Though the size of the sword is not often unwieldy. You said it is a great sword?"

"The portion visible from the rock is almost as tall as me," David said.

"Ah, this is unusual," it said, and the coils slid ever so slightly as the great snake vibrated with excitement. The effect wasn't slight to David, though, and the mountain moaned under the grinding strain of the coils. "For what purpose might the mighty David require such a powerful blade?" Leviathan asked.

"I'm not sure. I've never actually wanted much of anything except a simple life to share with those I love. I don't want money or power," he said. "Nothing that can be won with a blade."

Leviathan snorted. "You're honest?"

"I am," David said, crossing his heart and then feeling slightly embarrassed by the gesture.

Leviathan took a moment. "Then your brain doesn't understand what your heart knows to be true. You're young, even for a human. New. Too new to realize that which you really desire is not so easy for most to gain. Quiet solitude with those you love is what most everyone dreams. I am no exception."

"Who do you love?" David asked. He did not know where this conversation was taking him, but he did know he hadn't been killed yet. The giant snake must be lonely because it liked to talk.

"I love all of you, naive one," Leviathan said, as though reading his mind in a roundabout way. "I desire nothing more than to be with you all every waking moment of your lives. To feel what you feel and to see what you see. The things you must taste! Oh, that would be a delight. Far better than what I taste like."

David saw the tail had been gnawed upon and quickly returned his gaze to the creature's face. "What if I can take you with me?" David asked.

"From a prison made by the creator?" the world serpent asked.

"It's not an impossibility," said David smoothly advancing toward the rock sheath. "I've seen quite a bit since I came here, a lot of it I'd read about back home. The myths and legends that are true are innumerable. So, isn't it likely that the story about Pandora's Box holds some truth?" Leviathan narrowed its eyes on David but didn't say anything. He went on, "I'm betting there is a way to bust you out of this prison."

"Even if it were possible, I'd be struck down the instant I emerged into your world," Leviathan said. "No, my place is one of torment. It is here."

The agitation in the scales was growing, and David could tell by the moaning of the mountain that it was as fragile as he'd hoped. He just needed to get to that sword before it began to crumble around him, but when it did, it could bury the ancient entity and buy him time.

If Bulwyf's story was true, then the giant monster was meant to be released at the onset of the Apocalypse. Destroying its prison would probably have the effect of releasing them both from Valhalla and sending him to the real world. It was a gamble, especially considering he was risking taking Leviathan back with him, but he had to chance it. There was no other way.

"You can't give up like this, that's not what the avatar of one of the seven deadly sins would do. You are Leviathan! Jormungandr! Destined to wage epic battle with Thor himself." David had no idea if this part of the myth was true, but he was on a roll. "Are you really content to lay here quietly and be used as an endless buffet for cretins?" He paused. "I had no idea you would be so broken."

This struck a nerve, and David began to hear rocks falling in the gloom beyond where the glow touched.

"Do you see any links in my chain with cracks?" said Leviathan as it flexed its body outward to further strain the mountain. The scales surged so brightly that David could now see the damage being done to the rocks and feel the ground shaking under his legs as it It began to crack and fissure. "I am the swallower of worlds!" the great serpent screamed, pulling its coils inward and then smashing them out into the mountain again.

Light from outside began to shine in on them.

At this, David seized his moment. He leaped from where he had been standing and made a dash for the sheath. "I knew you had it in you," David said, as he continued to close the distance between himself and his goal. Leviathan hadn't yet looked down upon him. *I might make it*, he thought, while keeping his attention on the projectiles falling from above. He reached the base of the sheath and bounded up it by bouncing back and forth on the ascending steps until he reached the apex.

Before him stood the sword. David hadn't been wrong—the blade was at least as long as he was tall, and he had no idea how he might wield it, but he had to try. Gripping the pommel with both hands, he heaved his strength skyward, and the sword yielded to him without friction, nearly costing him his footing.

The mountain sighed as though he'd removed a splinter from its foot, but Leviathan roared. It felt him take possession of something precious, perhaps its sole possession.

David hefted the blade in front of him to make ready to defend himself. The handle, a foot and a half in length on its own, affixed to a butted base. That turned in a right angle to the flat back of the blade for five or more feet until ending in a surgically sharp point. Appearing as though it had just been forged and sharpened, it glinted sunlight from a crater left in the side of the mountain where Leviathan's rage had produced a landslide.

The weapon felt light to David, as though it barely weighed a thing, but before he could test its balance, he was struck by the shielded scales of one of Leviathan's coils and thrown back to the floor. David was wracked with pain. He didn't know how far he'd been thrown, but he guessed it was an impressive distance.

"You thought you could deceive me and take what is *mine?*" Leviathan asked. "I was naive to let you get this far, but your efforts will end here, mortal. I will take you inside of me and have you forever."

David stood as the face of doom lowered to within feet of him, its mouth agape. He hadn't paid much attention to the teeth inside until now. He'd have been scared shitless if he had, row after row of meters-long teeth perfectly lining a mouth equipped with two vicious fangs ten times as long. Venom slid slowly to the tips until their viscosity pulled together enough for droplets to fall free.

"Alright, I admit I was going for the sword, you got me there, but that doesn't mean we have to stop brainstorming," David said. "We can still try to get you out of this mountain." He raised the sword in front of him again, this time with the blade facing aloft.

"Fool. The mountain is not my prison. This *realm* is. I've been free to come and go as I please for eternity," Leviathan reared back. "There's no joy here, no reason to leave the mountain."

David assumed it was making room for the forward strike that would ultimately end him.

"What? There is plenty of joy out there," David said. "Why did you stay in here the whole time, dummy? There's a donkey out there that pisses mead." He tensed and waited.

Leviathan's eyes blazed. "To protect what was given to me and what I can never have. What you hold in your hands is not a sword."

David looked at the blade. "It looks a lot like a sword. The kind for killing huge snakes, too. I think you might be off-base on this one."

Leviathan did not bother with a retort. Its mouth flew open to the limits of its width and surged with speed that David was not expecting. Still, he had been anticipating the lunge and focusing on his breathing.

He was waiting for the perfect timing that he'd learned from the greatest sword masters who have ever lived. Steeled for this moment, David slashed the blade vertically an instant after the great maw was within range. He saw blood fly as he cleaved the tongue and extended its fork another few feet. Leviathan recoiled.

David didn't know how he could use this mountain to leave Valhalla and return to the world of the living. He had been improvising to this point, but the sound of three coins clinking in his pocket jarred understanding within him. The melded coin had once again become three.

Those coins you have will weigh you down. You should endeavor to lose them by any means you can, Kharon had said.

David reached into his pocket and pulled out the coins. Leviathan, stalled for a moment by incredulity from having been wounded, attacked again. The head came from the left and with more caution, but the strategy remained the same. Its mouth hung open in hopes of devouring David, and he freed himself of the three coins by tossing them down the gullet of the beast.

David made ready to dodge to the right, though he wasn't optimistic. The distance to clear the mouth was more than twenty feet. As he tensed and leaped, the sword disappeared. One instant it was in his hands, and the next it was gone.

Time slowed to an impossible pace. He heard the drawn-out sound Leviathan made in response to feeling the coins it swallowed, but it began to break apart in his ears. His vision fractalized as reality spun. David realized he'd experienced this before. This was like the dream he'd had before waking on the banks of the Styx. He was about to travel again, but this time he was conscious for the ride.

Leviathan's mouth became a twisted vortex, and David felt the world around him falling away. There was some force pulling him forward that he could not explain, but he willingly gave himself.

As he advanced into the tunnel, three simple words embraced him: *I need you.*

PART THREE

SKILJA

CHAPTER NINE
REUNION

Chelsea woke to the beeps of David's machines and the sound of gallons of air being pulled into Brendan's lungs as his chest heaved under her head. She lay thinking about Rose and hoping the girl could hold it together for a little bit longer.

They'd been confronted with a lot at this point, but David was on Rose's mind through it all, and his condition was breaking the girl. Chelsea couldn't see her on the other side of the mound of man between them, but she imagined Rose was curled into him in a deep sleep.

As if to intentionally dispel what Chelsea had just been picturing in her mind, she heard Rose say, "Something's happening."

Chelsea's head whipped up fast enough to startle Dodd awake and she nearly doubled back over from his arm instinctively pulling in on her.

"Easy there, galoot, you're going to squish me," she said.

Dodd pulled his arm back and rubbed his eyes with his other hand. "Sorry, sorry," he said. "You scared me awake."

Chelsea ignored him and pushed herself up on his chest, forcing a gush of breath from him. "Agh, hey, I said I was sorry."

"Hush, you," Chelsea said. "What's happening, Rose?"

Rose must have ventured away while Chelsea and Dodd were deeply asleep. She was at David's bedside.

"The monitors are all shifting," Rose said. "I don't know what that means, but he just moved his hand."

Chelsea finished her assault on Dodd, pushing herself off before lifting her hands from his chest and standing upright. This time he didn't protest, just rolled to his side and made his way to his feet with far less grace.

Scanning the monitors, Chelsea saw what Rose meant. The readings were Greek to her too, but they were shifting from what they had shown minutes before. Static lines were now dynamic. Numbers fluctuated. She looked and saw Rose holding David's hand. He was clenching her left, and she had laid her right atop the back of his.

"Rose, are you sure he moved? You didn't squeeze his hand, and it felt like it moved because you wanted it to?" Chelsea asked, trying not to be unkind as the mind may play insidious tricks on those filled with despair and exhaustion.

Rose simply looked at her. "He moved. His fingers curled around my hand."

Dodd saw Rose's expression and decided he had heard enough. "I'll get the on-call nurse," he said, leaving the room at a drowsy lumber.

Chelsea moved herself to the other side of the bed with Rose and looked down at David. His eyelids fluttered. "I think he is really waking up," she whispered. The bravado she'd been keeping up for Rose's sake fell away, and she cried the tears she'd been holding back for the last few days—tears reserved for one of two outcomes she'd been preparing for.

Joy glistened on the cheeks of David's mother.

Rose took her right hand off David's and placed it around Chelsea's waist. "I'm so happy he will be seeing our faces first," Rose said.

David's eyes finally cracked open and both Chelsea and Rose

gasped. David took them in and smiled, "Sorry I'm a little late. I would have called, but I didn't have good service where I was."

Rose collapsed onto him, wrapping his torso in her arms and planting kisses on his cheek.

"Guess I'm not in trouble, then," he said and gave his mother a wink.

Chelsea squeezed his arm in response. "No, you're definitely grounded for a while. I'm thinking house arrest forever with no eligibility for parole."

"Can I have a bunk mate?" he asked.

Rose pulled herself off him and gave his shoulder a smack. "Don't get fresh in front of your mother," she said and took up her spot on his bare chest again.

A short nurse blew into the room, checked the machines, and inserted herself between David and his family. "Sorry ladies, I need to borrow him for a minute," she said. "Good afternoon, young man. My name is Nurse Marrakech, but you can call me Marra. Can you say that name?"

"Marra," David said and rolled his Rs for flair.

"Very good. How about your name? Do you know that?" Marra asked.

"My name is David Michael Dolan," he said. "This is fun."

"Well, I'm glad you're having a good time," Marra said. "How do you feel?"

Before David could answer, Dodd entered the room with the duty doctor who rounded the bed and checked the monitor readouts after saluting a quick hello to the group.

"I feel good. Great, actually," David said.

"That is encouraging to hear, son," the doctor said, then turned to the nurse. "How is he?"

"Memory is good, cognitive function looks good, and his urinary catheter is already out," Marra said. "To say he's responsive is a little bit of an understatement. Though his jokes could use a bit of work."

"Jokes, huh? You *are* feeling great, David. Your EEG looks good, but according to your chart, it has since you arrived. I am Dr.

Morocco, but your treatment physician is Doctor Fannis. He is your specialist, and we've notified him. I'm sure he will be making his way here very shortly. Have you been informed of your newfound celebrity status among the medical community?"

"No, I only got back just recently," David said.

"Interesting choice of words. Nurse Marrakech, can you place a note about that. David, do you have memories of dreaming?" Doctor Morocco asked.

"You could say that," David said and turned his head to Dodd, who'd become a wallflower. "Who's the muscle over there? Does my celebrity status come with a bodyguard?"

"That's Detective Dodd from Homeland Security. I think he might be your new stepdad," Rose said.

"Oh, now you're the one getting fresh," Chelsea said.

"Okay, I can get behind that. But you have to come to all my little league games, Pop," David said.

Dodd smiled and saluted David before delivering an awe shucks grin to Chelsea—who looked like she wanted to hit him.

"Well, this is very nice," Morocco said, pulling the bedding off David's feet to begin performing reflex tests. David wiggled his toes and went along with it for a minute or two and then said, "I think we are starting at steps one through ten when we should be somewhere around step thirty, Doc." David quickly pulled the IV and stickies off himself, sat up from his position laying back on the pillows, and swung his legs to the edge of the bed. "I already told you guys, I feel great."

Rose asked, "Do you feel a cool breeze at all?" She gave him a coy smile.

David looked down and saw his quick move to the edge of the bed had caused the hospital gown to bunch up around his thighs. He was giving a show to a bunch of people who hadn't bought a ticket. "Whoops, sorry about that," he said and rolled to his side to pull the gown down. Before the doctor could stop him, he hopped off the bed and landed on his toes, bouncing like he was warming up for a morning jog.

"Still got a view from this side of the bed," Marra said. Rose and Chelsea laughed, and David threw his hands behind him to cover his backside as he squirreled his way around them to the bathroom. Doctor Morocco made chase. "David, you're overdoing it. You could become lightheaded and fall down, resulting in another head injury."

"Fit as a fiddle, Doc. Fit as a fiddle," David said and closed the bathroom door, barring the doctor. They heard the sink turn on, and David began to whistle the tune to "The Devil Went Down to Georgia."

"Alright, then. This is unusual," Morocco said. "Nurse, has he been this lively since he came out?"

"I arrived shortly after he awoke, but I'm going to say yes anyway," said Marra, unable to wipe the grin from her face.

"Yes," said Chelsea and Rose in unison as they began to hug one another. Dodd came over and joined in. The atmosphere in the room was too contagious not to.

"Right, well, I have to update my report for Fannis. Marra, can you keep a lid on him while I'm out of the room?" he said

"Oh, I'll give it a shot," she said, and the doctor left as briskly as he had arrived.

The door opened, and David reentered the hospital room. "I can't remember water tasting that good in my entire life," he said. He patted his body with his hands and took in a deep breath. "Pants."

The gang broke out of their huddle and looked to him. "Pants," David repeated. "Gonna need 'em."

"Oh no you're not, mister. Not yet, anyway," Marra said. "You get those bare cakes back over here and in this bed."

David sized her up. "Mom, think I can take her?"

Chelsea looked at the nurse and back to David. "I don't like your odds."

"Nurse Marrakech, I would like to barter with you for a moment," David said. She held his lighthearted gaze and waited for what he'd say next. Despite her hand-on-hip posture and serious look, her slight grin revealed how she'd become charmed by the boy. "I will concede to sitting in that chair there"—David nodded to the chair in the corner that pulled into a makeshift bed—"but I won't be getting back in that bed. Do we have a deal?"

"Might want to reconsider the chair, son," Dodd said. "It's pure hell."

"Seen the back door to hell," David said. "Not worried."

The nurse rounded the bed and walked up to him. "Deal," she said and stretched out her hand. David took it, gave it a firm pump, and then rounded the group, keeping his back to the wall as he sidled over to the chair and sat. "Ooof, that fake leather is cold."

"Well, that's because it isn't meant for bare bottoms, now isn't it?" Marra said. She took a section of tissue paper from a roll under the hospital bed and brought it to David, who inserted it beneath him.

"You know that you can tie the back of that gown, right?" Rose said.

David just smiled up at her. Rose broke away and skipped over to him, all but leaping into his lap and hugging him again.

Dodd and Chelsea closed the void her absence left between them and watched as the nurse scolded the young lovers. Their smiles whisked away the lines of worry that had creased their faces just hours before.

Ω

The hospital staff, namely Doctor Fannis, demanded that David stay overnight for observation despite his protests. Ultimately, Chelsea was the one to rein the boy in and put her foot down. A mother's *tone* was all it took.

During the time in the hospital, Chelsea, Dodd, and Rose filled David in on the aftermath of his accident from their perspectives, and what was transpiring in the tri-state area. Dodd left the room a few times to make calls and reported David's new status to the DHS. They informed him that the local police station had been unreachable for some time, and Dodd feared the implications of this were dire for the surrounding community.

Before Nurse Marra ended her shift, they managed to weasel some relevant information out of her and found out she was staying with friends because she didn't feel safe at home. The increasing oddities and volatility of the world had come upon them sharply, but society continued to lurch forward in a makeshift facsimile of its previous state. The onus of keeping up appearances fell upon the people deemed essential employees. Most all else were hunkered down with their stockpiles and refusing to leave their homes come hell or high water, both more distinct possibilities than some might realize.

While they spoke, Dodd and Chelsea played cards at the table, and David and Rose stayed close to one another. It was clear to Dodd just how in love the young couple was by how they had to strain to keep from becoming intertwined at any moment, like trying to hold two magnets from meeting once they'd been brought within the distance of irresistible attraction.

David's lack of surprise after he processed the information pinged Dodd's attention. The boy wasn't foggy minded in the least, but news of the world being overrun with the supernatural should have caused some reaction from him.

Dodd asked, "David, you said something when you'd just woken up that struck the doctor as odd. Me too. You said you'd just gotten back. Where did you think you were?"

David took a few moments to consider how to start and then told his tale, beginning from his drive onto the bridge to when he awoke in the hospital with them. There were instances of interjections, like when Rose was despairing the loss of Tim to the Hudson River, or when Chelsea asked specific questions about the cultural aspects of David's journey—mostly regarding his conversations with Jacob— but also about the people David had met in Valhalla.

David punctuated the story by saying, "It's not where I thought I was, but where we all end up after we are done here." When he finished, they sat in silence before turning in for a short spell to keep their internal clocks from being tuned to the wrong side of the Earth's rotation. David found himself unable to sleep, and was content to stroke Rose's hair as she rested next to him.

Dodd left to get coffee and breakfast for the band when day broke. His return with a pair of pants for David had received much fanfare; sweats from the gift shop paired with a matching hoodie.

"Thank you," David said, extending his hand to the man for the first time. Dodd took it and was surprised at the strength of the boy's grip. David flashed him a toothy smile and retreated to the bathroom sanctuary to get dressed.

Once he was finally able to be discharged, which took some leaning by Dodd due to Fannis's zeal and his desire to gather more information on David for whatever study he had concocted, the merry foursome departed the hospital near noontime.

Dodd took a look at the sitting area for Sam, but only saw the book keeping his seat. Across from it sat another, who stared at the book intently. This guy also pinged Dodd's memory from his first visit to the hospital. When the group was halfway through the lobby, Dodd noticed the man was watching them, but no further confrontation occurred.

They loaded into the car—adults in the front, kids in the back—before anyone broached the subject they had all been ignoring since they'd shared their stories back in the hospital room. "We are all together now, but what do we do about what's happening?" Rose asked.

"The important thing is to stick together," Chelsea said.

"Bingo," Dodd said. "The worst thing to do in times of unrest is to strike out alone."

"Cop thing?" Rose said.

"Survival thing," Dodd said.

"He's right," Chelsea added. "When we were on digs in rough areas, it was a known rule to stay together in larger groups. Dissuades the predators. To a degree, anyway."

"How about we celebrate a bit before getting serious?" David said.

"What do you have in mind?" Chelsea asked.

"Mom's home cooking," David said, beating a drum roll on his knees with his palms. "Nothing makes everything seem okay more than Sunday dinner."

"I thought you didn't get hungry anymore?" Rose said.

"Not hungry, but I'd like to test that against real food in the house I grew up in. We feasted in the hall often, but I never had the need to eat. It was more something to do to pass the time. It puts off my appetite even more now that I know where the food was coming from, but I'd like to try. Plus, a dinner together isn't just about the food. It's about the experience. I think we could all use a good amount of togetherness, right?"

"Can't argue that," Dodd said. "Can't turn down Chelsea's cooking either."

"Sounds to me like it's settled, then," David said.

David and Rose turned their attention on each other, and Dodd took the opportunity to ask Chelsea about David's story. "Does everything he said check out to you?" he asked.

"More or less, yes," Chelsea said. "The overlapping religions could all have been known to him. That much is easy for you to see based on what I do for a living, but David only took a periodic interest in my career. He never delved headlong into things like theology. There's the angle that he picked up most of it from his college classes, but that doesn't check out much."

"Why?" Dodd asked, keeping his eyes on the road.

"He was an engineering major, with a minor in sociology," Chelsea said. "Doesn't really line up."

"Nope. Also, a massive whiff by our investigation team to miss that the kid we thought could have something to do with the bridge collapse was an engineering pupil," Dodd said. He turned onto the last main road before the one that housed Chelsea's colonial. "If there wasn't so much going on, I'd have a hard time rationalizing this, but rational really doesn't hold water right now. Found upriver, kiln-like scorch marks where he was recovered, the in-coma total body makeover, and then his story."

"Don't forget that he knew about some of what we were up to here while he was out," Chelsea said.

"Yeah—"

When both noticed David and Rose were quiet, it was already

too late. Chelsea looked back and saw the pair holding hands and quietly observing them.

"So, you guys believe me?" David asked.

"Looks that way, kid," Dodd said. "If you're anything like your girlfriend, you are the trustworthy sort."

"Two peas in a pod," Chelsea said.

CHAPTER TEN
SPIRITED AWAY

Dinner was relegated solely to items from the freezer and pantry, but Chelsea wouldn't disappoint. While she and her large assistant put together a meal, David and Rose were able to slink away to David's room.

"I can't believe you're here. There was a part of me that thought you might never come back to us," Rose said, twirling her necklace between her thumb and fingers.

"Really?" David asked, admiring the amulet she fiddled. "You've never been much of a fatalist."

"Oh, I was going to be at your bedside reeling you back in one way or another, but it was just darker with you gone, Rose said. "I never thought it could happen."

"If I've learned anything from where I was, it's that bad things can happen to good people," David said as he stroked her hair. The two lay in silence for some time, enjoying the feel of each other's warmth. "Rose, I don't think whatever has been happening to me is over yet."

"I know. I don't think so either. I was half expecting your angel friend, Jake, to pop out of the sky and scoop you up while we were driving."

"He prefers Jacob—at least, he did. It's not even his actual name, but then again, I guess he has like twenty of those," David said.

"You're rambling," Rose teased.

"I'm a rambling man," David said, flicking her earlobe. "I know I haven't seen the last of him."

"Well if he tries to take you, he's taking me," Rose said. "Probably your mom and Dodd, too."

David said, "I don't believe he intends to take me, or us, anywhere. I feel like he was preparing me for something. After hearing what you've all been saying about the state of the world right now, I might be on to something."

"Oh? Now you think you have superpowers and can beat up demons and demigods?" said Rose, grabbing at the sweet spot on the inside of his thigh that always made him lurch and squirrel away.

David jumped and rolled her over, mock pinning her to steal a kiss.

"You'd better watch yourself, mister. We live in the age of consent," she said.

"Well, I'm sorry, madam, I didn't mean to offend your sensibilities or honor. I'll simply be on my way," he said and pushed himself into a full handstand on the bed rolling his hips to a beatific dismount. Rose gaped at him.

Knock, knock, knock came the old cue from the floorboards. "Hey, you two, no rough housing up there," Chelsea called through the floorboards.

"No funny business, either!" Dodd's voice boomed, followed by what sounded like a deep cry of pain from what David assumed was his mother beating on the man.

"Okay, that's new," Rose said. "You're a gymnast now?"

"I told you, I trained with some of the greatest fighters the world has ever known," David said.

Rose sat up. "Still, it's something to hear, and it's something else to witness. What else can you do?"

"Haven't really considered it," David said as he bounced on his toes. "My guess is that I can do everything I was capable of there."

"So, you're telling me you can *actually* sword fight?" Rose asked. "Do flippy flips? Make julienne fries?"

"I can," David said. "Maybe not the fries."

Rose stood and walked over to him, placing her hands on his chest. "Let's see what else you can do."

She pulled his head down so their lips could meet. David kept his hands at her waist and savored the moment before lifting her effortlessly from the ground, holding her above him, their lips joined throughout.

"This should be fun," Rose said through the veil of hair that had fallen over their faces.

The two laughed as "Dinner!" was called from below.

Ω

Chelsea had organized a meal with fare from a few different reaches of the globe, compliments of her travel experience. There was chicken tikka masala with jasmine rice and quinoa, jerk beef atop polenta, and sweet potato fries—a David Dolan favorite. Homemade hummus with an assortment of vegetables rounded out the feast.

Dodd made no bones about showing off his appetite. Chelsea and Rose also dug in. It didn't take long for Chelsea to notice that David was tasting, but not eating.

"Really not hungry at all yet?" she asked.

David took a long drink of water and said, "I'm not sure if I'll ever be hungry again, Mom. This might be the way of things now."

"It's hard to accept that you won't ever need to eat again. How do you fuel that body of yours, then?" Chelsea asked.

David smiled. "Not sure. Maybe I run on good vibrations now."

Dodd began humming the tune to the song. "Oh, great. You know he is cuing you in with these now, right?" Chelsea said.

"Doesn't matter. All that matters is *oh, my, my, what a sensation.*

Oh, my, my, what elation," he rumbled in a deep baritone, keeping beat by tapping the fork on his glass.

"Glad to see they are getting along so well," Rose said to Chelsea.

"Yes, it's just dandy," said Chelsea, and she laughed when Dodd switched to the song by the same name. "Alright, cut it out. We need to get serious here. What should we do?"

"I say we put a pin in that one until morning," David said. "Kind of feels good to just be normal again, even if it's just for tonight."

"I second the motion on the table," said Rose, tapping her spoon like a gavel. "Should we put it to a vote?"

"Well, we will only be getting a tie at best, so I'd rather just concede," Chelsea said.

"Shrewd," Dodd added.

"You were going to vote with them, weren't you?" Chelsea said, turning to Dodd with her steak knife in hand.

"You'll never know," he said and waved his napkin at her in surrender.

The night continued this way even after they retired to the living room to relax. There were moments where reality—and the odd dangers it now presented—came up, but one of them would quickly whisk it away into their back pocket for safe keeping until morning.

After one too many dad jokes, Chelsea decided to tap out and make her way upstairs with Dodd in tow. She made a bit of a show by outwardly describing the sleeping arrangements they should have, but Rose knew a front when she saw one. She also noted that Chelsea hadn't bothered to relegate her to the couch for the evening.

This suited Rose just fine.

Ω

An antiquated alarm clock ticked past three in the morning in David's room, and his eyes remained fixed on the ceiling. Rose, crooked neatly in the space between his arm and chest, breathed deeply and rhythmically. He was left to think of what his life would be like if he never slept again. Food he could eat, sure, but it was clear he didn't need to. So far he hadn't been able to push himself to sleep no matter how relaxed he tried to become. The thing that bothered him most was losing his dreams. He couldn't get past never again dreaming.

A shriek through the night jarred him from circumnavigating his thoughts. David cocked his head and listened. He felt the next cry before he heard it. Something outside, beyond the treeline, was approaching the house. Again, the cry carried through the walls of the home, rousing Rose.

"Could it be a fox?" Rose asked, rubbing sleep from her eyes.

"Not likely. It's too far away to carry here with that kind of volume," said David and he pulled her close to kiss her forehead. "I think it's one of the creepy crawlies you guys have been telling me about."

The cry repeated for a few more minutes without slipping into a pattern of rhyme or reason, and the two lay awake listening. It was Dodd who came knocking.

"Let's huddle up in the living room. Best not to take chances," Dodd said. He was in the doorway, wearing a sleeveless undershirt tucked into his slacks, and had one hand on the pants to keep them from falling as he retreated to get dressed. They all convened in the living room as planned, the shrieking having increased in volume and in tempo.

"They're targeting us," David said.

"How can you tell?" Chelsea asked. She had the guidebook Leonard had lent them with her.

"It's not something I can explain, but it's something I know," David said. "Might have to do with why I was spirited away by Jacob in the first place. Doesn't really matter. I'm going to handle it." He stood and surveyed his bed wear: a pair of navy mesh shorts and a black T-shirt. That should suit him fine for sneaking around in the dark.

"I don't think I can let you head out there alone," said Dodd, standing as well.

"Neither of you are going out there, period." Chelsea said. "What makes you think you can handle whatever trap they have in store for you? Based on this guidebook, it's a banshee. That means death, David."

David looked to his mother but decided to appeal to Dodd first. "I appreciate the sentiment, but I need you to stay here with my mom and Rose to help fortify the house. Mom, they're going to come in if I don't go out, and frankly, I'd rather take care of it out there. As far as going at it alone—"

David turned and walked to the china cabinet serving as the centerpiece for the room. He knelt and slid his hand into the two-inch gap between the wood bottom and the floor. With his hand placed as close to the middle of the base as the length of his arm would allow, David lifted the cabinet from the floor without moving from his crouch.

"I think I can handle whatever they have to throw at me," David finished.

The three gawked silently.

"That thing legit?" Dodd asked.

"It's not Ikea press board, if that's what you mean," Chelsea said. "That hutch is a family heirloom, solid desert ironwood."

Rose said, "You made your point. You can put it down."

David lowered the china cabinet without the slightest show of strain and stood up. His presence crowded the room.

"You see why I'm not being cocky? That isn't all, either. I gained more than a few traits while I was in the other world, and so far all of them have been with me since I've come back. I won't have to worry about you guys if I go out there alone. You'll be here with firearms, ready to put some holes in any would-be intruders. You've already established that these things don't really like being shot."

"I don't like this," Rose said. "It feels like they're baiting you. Let's say they already know about your abilities... What's their endgame? Why would they call you outside to kill them?"

"She's got a point," Dodd said. "But I'm with you, David. I don't think I can be more help to you than I can here. Especially after seeing you do that."

Chelsea stood and left the room. David's eyes followed her out and he hung his head. "I didn't think Mom would go for it," he said.

She returned in a minute with a shotgun that commanded attention and laid it on the couch with two boxes of shells. She swiftly went into the dining room and returned with her .38 and a box of ammunition that clinked as she dropped it on the table.

"Dodd, give Rose your service issue, and you take the Browning," said Chelsea, nodding to the shotgun now leaning on the couch with its polished walnut stock.

"Shit. Won't catch me arguing with a woman holding a gun," Dodd said, hefting the shotgun and inspecting it.

"David, you go out with the .38," Chelsea said holding the small pistol out to him.

"Don't need a gun. You're going to have to trust me on that. I will take the sawback, though, if we still have it."

Chelsea nodded and descended the basement stairs, her pace quickening as the sound of a shriek reverberated through the house. They were getting closer.

After some rustling, she returned with a dagger-like bayonet that was well maintained despite its age and handed it to David handle first.

He hefted it and balanced the weight in his palm before returning his attention to the others. Dodd had finished inspecting the shotgun and seemed satisfied as well.

"Here, take my cell," Chelsea said, handing her phone to David, who slipped it into his pocket. "Call Rose or Dodd if you run into anything that requires help, and we will do the same. Dodd, put my number in your favorites. Rose, you too."

"Your number is already in my favorites," Dodd said.

"Same," Rose said.

They stood on that moment for the better part of a minute, letting it punctuate the last dregs of reality they'd drunken in just hours before. A lasting shriek ripped through the house, pulling them toward action.

"I'm going," David said and wrapped Rose in a deep hug.

"Be careful, okay. I won't lose you again," Rose said.

David smiled at her and gave her a kiss before pulling away. He walked to Chelsea and kissed her cheek then rounded out the group by slapping Dodd on the shoulder, lurching him forward. "Keep an eye on them," David said.

"Think they'll be the ones keeping an eye on me, given what I've seen 'em do so far," Dodd said.

David turned and bounded up the stairs.

"Where are you going?" Chelsea asked.

"Out the second story window. Don't want them seeing me exit if I can help it," said David, and he was gone.

"Well, I guess that's par for the course," Dodd said. "I'll cover the back door."

"I'll cover the windows and the stairs," Rose said.

"I've got the front," Chelsea said.

By the time they'd finished their planning, David's bare feet had already hit dew-wet grass, and he was across the yard, sprinting down the tree line. His face was stone, his fire burning brightly.

He was going to make a statement tonight about what he would do to protect his family.

Ω

David had been gone for five minutes, and the shrieks continued. Dodd noted they had stopped coming closer as soon as David left, a sure sign that this was a coordinated effort. He kept the shotgun's safety off.

"How long do you think we should wait before going after him?" asked Chelsea, breaking the silence that hung in the room.

"We shouldn't follow him," Rose said. "He wanted to go alone so that he could act without worrying about us. As much as I hate that, I think he's right. He's on another level."

"She's right, Chelsea," Dodd said. "Being in a combat situation with friendlies involved is a totally different scenario. Couple that with David not knowing exactly what he is capable of, and it's easy to see why he wants to handle this alone."

Dodd was seated on the arm of the couch with the business end of the shotgun pointed at the door he'd been on the dark side of just a few days ago.

"I don't really care if he wants to skip around out there like John Wayne. I'm going if he doesn't call in ten minutes," Chelsea said.

"Do you really think you should be worried about anything other than yourselves right now?" a voice from the basement asked.

The three exchanged startled looks and then trained their weapons on the hallway where the basement stairs began their descent. The door was still open from Chelsea's trip to retrieve the bayonet for David. Her mind raced through the contents of the basement, but she couldn't think of any other dangerous weapons stored down there.

"Whoever you are, you'd better stay put because the instant you show yourself at the top of those stairs, we are going to unleash hell on you," Chelsea warned.

The sound of creaking wood announced the intruder's decision. Dodd raised his finger to his lips and moved to put his back to the dining room so that he could cover the basement door and maintain the ability to swing the barrel of the shotgun to the back door should the need arise.

Rose crouched on the floor and used the armrest of the couch to stabilize her arm as she aimed the sidearm at the basement door, anticipating it to be filled with someone or something in a few seconds. Not a single muscle in Chelsea Dolan's body had even so much as twitched since she aimed the .38.

"Now, that's no way to treat a guest you've invited into your home," the voice called.

"I'll be fucked if I invited you anywhere," Chelsea said. "Last warning."

The intruder didn't say anything further but continued to climb monotonously, stressing their nerves to the breaking point. The basement light that spilled on the adjacent wall filled with shadow just before a man emerged from the basement. He held a statue the size of a basketball in his left hand. Chelsea had time to note that he was well groomed, well dressed, and there was nothing to indicate that he was anything other than an ordinary person before she unloaded the .38 into him at center mass.

Her opening salvo was punctuated by Dodd releasing three rounds from the shotgun. He was pickier about where he aimed—one in the knee, one in the arm that held the statue, and one in the forehead.

The intruder hadn't lost his footing despite his comical stance, leaning backward with his head pitched so far that only his Adam's apple was visible.

"Dodd, I need more bullets! Do you have more?" Rose said, motioning her hand to him.

Dodd didn't think they would need to put more punishment on the guy, but he reached into his pocket, produced another loaded clip, and tossed it on the couch next to Rose. "Push the button on the side there and the spent one will slide out. That's the last one I have preloaded, so make it count," he said. The statue rolled to a stop on the floor as Rose's empty clip dropped from her gun. Chelsea finished pushing rounds into her revolver and snapped the cylinder back into place.

"Oh, you're fucked all right," the man said as he raised his head. There were scorch marks where the slug had slammed into his forehead, but no further damage. It was a safe bet that this was the story for the rest of the rounds, too. Rose looked and saw how many of them were shaking out of his clothes and onto the floor. None had penetrated. "You have been ever since you spread your legs in Syria twenty-three years ago."

"What are you?" Chelsea asked. Her voice weak.

The man leaned over and scooped the statue. "Why, I'd thought you already knew me," he said. "You even have an action figure of me in your home."

Chelsea hadn't paid much attention to the idol in his hands when he materialized at the top of the stairs. He was holding a find from the dig in Syria, the same dig where she had met David's father. The statue he held was of Asmodeus, with him depicted as The Devil of Two Sticks.

"You're claiming to be Asmodeus?" Chelsea asked.

"In the flesh, madame," said Asmodeus, bowing lavishly then stepping out of the hallway into the living room. He stopped there as Dodd shouldered the shotgun. "It always pleases me to meet humans who know of me."

"How'd you get in?" Rose asked. "There are no windows down there."

"Ah, the tender one has a point. I don't need windows when there is an idol. This is a beauty too—excellent job in restoring it. I think I'll hold onto this." Asmodeus made the statue look as though it was walking on the air by pitching it back and forth. "You two don't have to bother trying to fight anymore. It's futile. I'm only here to take her, and I'll be on my way." Asmodeus smiled at Rose and licked his lips with an inky tongue.

Dodd put another slug into the demon's forehead, advanced two steps, put one in his groin, and smashed the stock of the shotgun into the idol before taking a jab at his neck. Asmodeus reached up and wrapped his hand around the shotgun. He paused.

"I take it you've figured out that it still hurts. Bully for you," said Asmodeus, pulling the weapon to the side. Still, Dodd's size wasn't all for show, and he put forth a healthy amount of resistance, making the demon strain.

"Rose, run," said Dodd as he was lifted into the air.

Chelsea walked up to striking distance and unloaded six chambers into Asmodeus's face. He howled with rage and threw Dodd across the room, into the china cabinet David had lifted ten minutes before.

"You chicken shit," Chelsea said. "You waited for him to leave before you showed yourself!"

Asmodeus ignored her. "Rose, you'd better run. Can't you see how hard they're trying to distract me so you can get away? You might even make it all the way to the street before I take you. They'll be dead already, of course."

Rose read the subtext. She stood and let the gun drop to the cushion of the couch. "I'll go with you, but please don't kill them."

"Rose, no. Go!" Chelsea yelled but was choked off when

Asmodeus struck two fingers into her throat to silence her. He shoved her aside and walked over to where Dodd was rising, shattered pieces of teacups and plates raining down from his back.

"Don't hurt them," Rose pleaded. "Please don't."

"I'll stay true to my word," Asmodeus said. "I insinuated that I wouldn't kill them if you came willingly, and I won't, but no man should ever target another's groin." He stomped on Dodd's leg, a sickening crack issuing through the room. Dodd cried out in pain. "That's"—*stomp*—"just"—*stomp*—"not"—*stomp*—"right." A final *stomp* punctuated the act and Dodd passed out from the pain.

Rose began to cry.

Asmodeus looked up from Dodd, his eyes aflame. "Oh, don't waste your tears here, little girl. Save them for when you see the light leave your boyfriend's eyes."

Ω

David crossed the lawn parallel to the tree line of the shallow woods behind his childhood home before plunging into the shadows afforded to him by the conifers. He was positive his rough location was known and that he was walking directly into a trap, but he didn't think his adversaries knew just how far he'd come.

What he'd like to know is why he was being targeted in the first place. The mystery of the bridge collapse was all but solved in his mind. All those souls lost, just to try and extinguish his. Tim, too, had perished. David was certain of that now. His mind turned to the group of people resting on the banks of the Styx, fare in hand for Kharon but unwilling to accept the ride.

Whoever was out here had failed to kill him once, and David was betting they'd fail again. This time he'd have the opportunity to wring some answers from them.

The shrieks lessened after he'd leapt from his bedroom window into the night air. He'd counted on them hiding, and they wouldn't know how well versed he was with these woods. Never underestimate the knowledge a child holds of their first haunts. With the rough target area in mind, David made use of his speed and bare feet to stealthily move to flank them from behind. Sure enough, he heard quiet movement up ahead, and he advanced as a whisper.

The trees were thicker here, but the low hanging branches were not as prolific as they were nearer to his house. He could see a good distance ahead of him, and as soon as he made out the shape of a figure standing fifteen feet ahead, it let out another blood curdling shriek.

David resisted the urge to cover his ears or cry out. The sound was blistering at this distance, but he managed to mettle up to it, and when it died, he pounced. The figure had heard David leave the ground and made to turn, but it was far too slow to catch him as he landed just behind and leveled a straight kick into its back, his forward momentum adding to the effect.

The result was impressive. David watched the figure fly forward six or seven feet and ricochet off a wide-trunked oak before hitting the ground just about where it had been standing before. David looked down into the face of a woman as worn down as leather left to bake in the sun. She observed him from the flat of her back without speaking.

"Is that scream the only thing your mouth is capable of producing? Because if it is, your time here is up," David said. He was surprised at how much he meant to harm her despite her fragile appearance.

"I can speak, David Dolan," she said.

"Good, then you might live a little longer," David said. He crouched and filled his palm with a healthy volume of her gray-white hair. "Who sent you to pull me out of the house?"

"My mother, of course," the woman said.

"Your name?" David asked.

"Imogen," she answered.

"Your mother's name?" David asked.

"Lilith."

"Your goal?"

"Ultimately, we wish to kill you and destroy your vessel, lest it fall into the wrong hands," Imogen said. "The immediate goal is to waste your time and hope to kill you in the off chance you're dim witted enough for that." Her wrinkled face bunched all the more as her skin was pushed aside to make room for her insidious smile.

A large figure moved with ferocious intent from the woods to David's left. He saw it, dropped the sawback, and used Imogen the banshee to shield his front from the attacker while he quickly checked his rear. Nothing there, supernatural or otherwise. He felt confident of that.

By the time he focused his full attention on the attacker, it was already upon them. With the swift swipe of a rather large limb, Imogen's weight vanished from beneath his grip. He was left with only a handful of hair and a sizable portion of her scalp. David almost laughed when he noticed that she was flung into the same tree he'd kicked her into, but his adversary pulled the mirth from him by unleashing a flurry of swipes.

"Woah now, big fella. What's your hurry?" David asked. "Don't you think you should check on your friend there? She may be dead."

The figure had stopped its full offensive to gain its bearings, as David had easily dodged its wide arm swipes. David used the opportunity to take a longer look at his opponent and was not surprised to be standing in front of what was very clearly a bi-pedal wolf. It was an imposing creature, to be sure, and the growls it issued should have cowed him, but he felt very much in control.

"Do you have any speaking abilities, Sparky?" David asked. The wolf answered by dashing forward in an attempt to tackle him to the ground. David sidled this and used his right arm to gain an over-hook advantage on the beast's left arm.

Despite the clear size difference, and some very real strength on the part of the wolfman, David pressured his shoulder joint directly into the ground and heard it crack out of place upon impact. Imogen shrieked. The wolf howled in pain. David growled in anger.

He needed to finish this quickly.

Taking the beast's back, he reached his hand over the snout and into its top jaw. The wolf greedily snapped, but David's leverage pulled its neck backward, and the bite held little force. His neighbor's yappy Yorkshire Terrier had given him a worse bite.

With mercy far from his mind, David pulled backward and felt the spine of the creature snap before he heard it. The life fled from the muscles of the thing, and David let it fall face first into the dirt.

Remembering that this was no natural animal, David took the extra five seconds to twist its head off its hairy shoulders before leaving it to fertilize the forest floor.

Imogen was slumped on the tree, her midsection spilling a bloody bile from where Sparky had mauled her out of the way to get to his meal ticket. David retrieved the sawback and walked to within arm's reach, crouching down. "Can you die, Imogen?" David asked. "Because if you can't, I will spend the rest of eternity peeling pieces of you from your bones. Answer me quick and true, like you were before your buddy interrupted us. Am I clear?"

Imogen laughed. "It is not in my nature to lie, or to stall. It is in my nature to deliver the reaper's call."

"Why do they want my body gone?" David asked.

"It may provide the key to the old one's escape," she said.

"Who?" David asked.

"Azazel," Imogen said. "The great shaitan of the sands. Mother believes you are a good match for him. He means to use your body to escape his prison.".

David took a moment to think. This was believable, and it might explain why Jacob was preparing him, but something still didn't feel right. "Why would your very evil mother want to stop another evil entity from escaping?" he asked.

"This is a question which I cannot answer with any certainty. I speak true," Imogen said, punctuating the statement with a pathetic whimper and a smattering of black blood from her mouth.

"Any guesses?" David asked. He was impressed at how easily information flowed from her.

"Oh, a few, yes," Imogen offered. "I'd imagine she doesn't believe she can hold onto her station with a fallen angel as competition. Mother is human at her core, after all. At least what was human before Eve was pulled from Adam. She does not wield great power herself, but she wields great numbers of children."

"Why are you being so compliant? You are aware I am going to wipe you out as soon as I am satisfied," David said, thinking he'd wrung her dry.

"Oh, yes. Quite cold for such a young man. So sad, so sad. I know I will die tonight. But I have lived long and there are fates far worse than death. One way to answer your question is to tell you about myself. Quite important, this detail." Imogen smiled coldly before slipping into a heavy brogue. "Imogen is a banshee o' the ol' world. When I loose me wail, someone is destined to be dragged from this world that night. Someone who hears, that is. Who heard me wail tonight, young David? Ye... and who else?"

David's anger flared at her cruel intentions, but he resisted the urge to act out of malice. Instead, he reached forward and took her chin in hand. She stared back at him knowingly, and in the slight pause before he acted, her grin began to reappear. He slipped the sawback between her ribs and removed her head before she could don it completely.

He wouldn't suffer it twice.

After she was slumped over on the cold earth, David tried the cell phone. He called Dodd's first and his mother answered, but he couldn't make out what she was saying.

"I'm coming right now, hang on," David said and ran straight back to the house as quickly as his feet could carry him. He had known he was playing into their hands, after all, but his mistake was in assuming he was the target.

The forest passed as a blur until he was released back into the open air of his lawn. The house was in good shape. No sign of forced entry, at least not from his first glance. Ending his sprint a few strides early, he slowed enough to bound once and cover all the stairs leading to the entryway.

"It's David, don't shoot," he said, cursing himself for not covering how they would be able to tell it was him coming into the house. He tried the doorknob, but it was locked, so he checked the hiding place for the spare behind the lantern above. Bingo. He slid the key into its mate and turned the deadbolt, moving to the side of the door and swinging it open. He didn't think a slug from that shotgun could kill him, but he wasn't interested in finding out.

"Hey, you guys, I'm coming in," he said. "If you shoot me, I'm going to be really upset."

No answer.

Then a whisper. "David."

David rushed inside, rounded the small wall separating the foyer from the living room, and felt the weight of the world hit him in the chest. He saw his mother fussing over Dodd, who was strewn over the remains of the destroyed hutch. David knelt next to her and placed his hand on her shoulder.

"What happened? Where is Rose?" David asked.

Chelsea looked to him and the pain that shone through her eyes told David that Rose was no longer with them. "He took her, David," Chelsea said, straining. "He, a demon, came from the basement. He looked like a normal man—"

"Don't waste your words, Mom. Is Dodd's life in danger?" asked David, fearing Chelsea's voice would leave before he could learn enough to act.

"Maybe. He's had his leg shattered in at least three places. If a bone cut an artery..." Chelsea whispered. "I called 911."

"Good. You got an answer?" David asked, knowing the reliability of emergency response would be shaky at best right now.

Chelsea nodded to him.

"Did he hurt her?" David asked.

Chelsea shook her head no. Tears streamed down her cheeks.

David placed his palms on her cheeks and wiped them away with his thumbs. "I'm going to get her. Any idea where they went?"

Chelsea shook her head again and mimed placing a phone call.

"Got it," David said. "I'll come to the hospital when I get her back, Mom. Don't worry. I will find her."

Chelsea grabbed his shoulders, put her forehead on his, and squeezed him, sobbing out, "Love you."

"I love you too," he said, planting a kiss on her forehead. "He will be okay, Mom. We all will."

David hoped his words would fortify hope in his mother, but she crumpled onto Brendan Dodd's chest and continued to sob soundlessly, as though her grief was too heavy to ride upon the air.

CHAPTER ELEVEN
ANGELS CRY

David grabbed the keys to his mother's car from the hooks by the back door and dialed Rose's phone number.

"Well, that didn't take you long," Asmodeus answered.

"Where are you?" David asked flatly.

"Let's not rush through this so hastily," Asmodeus said. "By now, you've got the idea that you are not in control of your next few hours, yes?"

"Yes," David said and keyed the ignition.

"Good boy. Did your mother tell you who I am?" he asked.

"No. Don't care, either," David said. "Just tell me where to meet you."

"Oh, you're no fun at all, David Michael Dolan," he said.

David was aware that whoever abducted Rose was trying to get him angry. He wanted him to rush into the situation enraged, but David had been taught better than that.

"Sorry to disappoint," David said. "I'll tell you what... If you tell me where to go, I promise to ask your name and even pretend I'm impressed." David put the car in reverse and turned around in the driveway so he could quickly exit when prompted.

"For now, head north on Route 90 toward the Rip Van Winkle Bridge," Asmodeus said.

David threw the car in drive and turned out onto the road. There weren't many people out an hour and a half before dawn, and that made for easy travel. It was doubtful that any police were checking for speeders right now given what was going on, and even if one did prompt him to stop, he'd just lead them to wherever Rose was and hope to explain later.

"So, who are you, and what do you want with me?" David asked.

"I am Asmodeus, son of Lilith and Samael. I've been alive long enough to have seen your kind slither from the sea on your bellies." The disdain in his words dripped through the headset. "What I want is simple. You arrive here and turn yourself over to me, and I let Rose go."

"I pull up, get out of the car, and Rose comes to me," David said. "She gets in the car and drives away alone. That's the deal." David turned onto Route 90 and headed north along the Hudson River.

"If it makes you feel better, sure," Asmodeus said. "But you already know if I want her collected again, it will be as simple as plucking a chick from a hen house, so do behave yourself."

"Of course, David said. "We're all gentlemen here."

"I've been called that from time to time, yes. Tell me, do you think the large one I toppled in your house will lose his leg to gangrene?" David could tell Asmodeus was savoring the moment. "That was my hope when I destroyed it. Even if he doesn't, he will never be the same. Big men like that are never right after such an injury. He will probably choose to swallow a bullet rather than bear the pain of recovery."

"Rose. Put her on the phone for a second," David said.

"Why? We both know you will come anyway. No, I think I like the idea of you heading here not knowing if she is alive or dead," Asmodeus said. "The old Boy Scout cabin you used when you were younger. Meet me there."

The call abruptly terminated.

Ω

David drove to the limits of the vehicle and still felt as though time moved in slow motion. He took Route 90 to Route 9 and traveled north until he reached Rhinebeck. The woods crowded the road as he drove. He expected to be assaulted by more demons or monsters, but none manifested. There was only the road ahead, hiding everything beyond a few hundred feet in shadows.

Once he reached the preserve where the cabin was nestled, he slowed his speed and became more cautious of the surroundings. An ambush seemed inevitable, but none came. The car left the pavement and rolled over uneven stones and ditches pockmarking the dirt access road. When he was younger, they'd disembark from a van a few miles away and humped their way, carrying supplies to maintain the illusion of nature.

David began to smell campfire smoke as the headlights broke through the cascading abyss ahead. He was so busy searching the surroundings to see if he could spot the source of the smell that the man standing in the road barely registered in time for him to stop. Dust kicked up as the tires slid on the dirt, but the man didn't move from his path. David threw himself from the car with the engine still running.

"Asmodeus?" he said.

"In the flesh," Asmodeus said.

"Where is Rose?"

"You know, you would have done everyone a favor if you had just died in the river," he said. "It didn't have to come to this."

David studied him. He was very average looking with his business casual attire and well-organized black hair. He looked like he could be out for a night of drinks and dancing if there weren't bullet holes in his clothes. Then there were the eyes. They weren't brown; they were black.

"Did you destroy the bridge and kill all of those people just to get rid of me?" David asked. The smell of smoke grew in strength.

"Yes. I know it seems a bit lavish, destroying half of a bridge just for one boy, but I'm sure you've figured out by now that there's something more to you than just good luck. Have you ever wondered why things came easily to you? School was probably never hard, not with the building blocks of creation so heavily twined within you. Sports were likely so easy that you just chose not to participate. Am I ringing a bell here? You've always been a bit special compared to the others. Life must have been pretty boring."

David knew what he was saying was partly true. He *did* find the rat race of normal teenage endeavors to be boring, and that was partially due to there having been so little challenge. The only thing he ever found exciting was Rose.

"Why didn't you just finish me off then, if I was such an important target for you?" David asked.

"I would have, although hearing about how you tried to save that little boy and failed was a tasty bit of news. I can feel the regret from your inadequacy leaking from you. It's delicious, but even tasting it is not worth the cost of leaving you alive."

Asmodeus smiled, and for the first time since this nightmare began, David knew he wouldn't just kill him. He would annihilate this dark smear from all existence.

"Your little friends came and intervened on your behalf," Asmodeus said. "They even staked out the hospital to ensure none of ours could reach you. Heavy bodyguards. You must have done something right to earn that kind of service. None here now though, not since you woke up from your nap."

David walked toward him. "Where is Rose?" he asked. He didn't intend on asking again.

"A bright boy like you hasn't noticed the smell of acrid smoke yet?" Asmodeus asked. "Surely you can tell the difference between the sweet smoke from dried hardwood and the smell of, say, a cabin fire?"

Realization hit David's features, and Asmodeus only had an instant to savor it before David's body blurred into motion.

Asmodeus made to cut him off, but he underestimated the size of the fire he'd lit within the boy. David didn't feint or deviate from the path ahead. He barreled through Asmodeus before the demon could react and, had he been paying attention to such things, he'd have seen the very moment when doubt entered Asmodeus's psyche before he was cast to the side like a doll.

David cleared the hundred yards of winding and heavily forested path between him and the cabin and saw the small building jetting flames. The plumes of black smoke it belched into the sky were veiled against the devouring darkness of a moonless night.

David ran through the front door of the cabin and walked into the main mess room. Smoke was omnipresent, but he didn't yield. He felt no heat. The smoke didn't sting his eyes. His lungs didn't burn. Had he been thinking, he may have noticed he wasn't breathing.

He didn't have to.

Ω

Michael, Raphael, and Uriel arrived at the cabin just after David entered to search for Rose.

"Asmodeus is here," Raphael said.

"He won't be when he senses us," Michael said, not bothering to conceal his wings. There was little need to in such isolation. "Your plan to save the boy fails here, Uriel. He will leave that cabin and attempt to destroy Asmodeus using power he cannot control."

"He may," Uriel conceded. "If the girl is in the cabin and has already succumbed to the fire, it is all but a certainty. You speak true, but should we pass judgment on David here and now based on such an action, given the circumstances?"

"Annihilation is forbidden," Michael said. "Even the creator's silence does not give us the right to do such a thing."

"We do not have the authority, but who are we to speak for the creator? Surely you can see the boy is not bound by the same logic as we," Uriel said.

"Spare me your Socratic games," Michael said. "Even if the boy does have the right, it still proves he is not responsible enough to wield the power he now has. A power he has thanks to your intervention."

Raphael walked to stand between them, his golden wings

outlined by the crimson and sapphire of Michael and Uriel. "Let us watch and see how things transpire. There is no good to be had trying to divert lodestone, brothers. Arguing over an outcome that has not yet unfolded is unwise."

Uriel turned his eyeless gaze to Raphael. "Ever the peacekeeper."

The three archangels stood side by side and watched in silence as fire dismantled the cabin.

Ω

A quick scan didn't reveal Rose in the first room, and David began checking the others. As a kid, he would tell ghost stories and lies about kissing girls in these rooms.

Now, he frantically searched for the only girl whose lips his had ever met.

The first two bunks yielded nothing. David stepped through the flames consuming the floorboards and walked into the final room. There on the bottom bed, amidst a holocaust of fire, lay a small figure. The cedar wood of the bed was strong. It burned but held its shape as a funeral pyre for the lost soul laying upon it.

David knelt before the bed and took the huddled body into his arms. Denial invaded his mind, and he refused to accept this was Rose. His Rose could not be reduced to the charred shell he now held. The mind of the young man so in love refused to accept such finality. His eyes fell on the silver charm, which had fused with her skin as it melted in the kiln the cabin had become, and he could no longer lie to himself.

This was the necklace Rose had been given to protect her from evil. This was Rose.

Once upon a time, a boy fell in love with a young girl who was simplistic, beautiful, and unassuming. He'd stressed over broaching the subject of taking her out for the first time despite clear signs of her interest in him, and he'd blustered and fumbled at attempting their first kiss. The boy had been rescued when she pulled him into her lips by the collar of his shirt.

Their love would bud early but grow at a steady rate to produce a fine and lasting fruit. They were united in mind and soul far before they'd chosen to entangle their bodies in the act often described as an apex for lovers. The boy and the girl wanted for nothing more than the company of each other while apart, and they shared themselves wholly and unselfishly while together. It is true that the vast majority of first loves fizzle and dim as quickly as they are ignited, but there is a fraction of truth to the idea of being soul bound to another if the conditions are met.

David clutched the better part of himself atop the burning cedar bunk and was unable to accept the reality before him, he was stricken numb by the loss of his other.

What remained of Rose in the world of the living was lifted in the boy's arms from the pyre. The shift in weight caused the bunk to collapse. He paid the spectacle no mind. His feet moved without his will or consent, taking him outside onto the wooden porch where the flames had yet to reach.

Three angels watched him come and fall to his knees while holding what Uriel knew to be the boy's one and only desire. They watched as Asmodeus sauntered to the cabin with a smile. He made no play at hiding how he savored David's anguish. Uriel felt David's agony, and it pained him to see the last of the boy's innocence be consumed by the same flames dancing upon his perfect Rose.

"I'm sure you feel sadness," Asmodeus said. "Truly, I did not want things to come to this, but we had to break you. Sometimes it's best to cast a stone through the stained glass."

Hair hanging over downcast eyes, David's hand caressed Rose's fire ravaged cheek. He gave no indication he was listening.

"If it makes you feel better, you'll be with her soon. You already know there is a chapter after this one," Asmodeus said. The demon flourished his hands about, indicating the world around them. "She will be there. All you have to do is stand right there, and I will deliver you to her quickly. I can give you that mercy."

"Was she dead before she burned?" David asked.

Asmodeus shielded himself from the implication of this question with his smile. In truth, he'd been told to kill the girl at the house and finish David off in the woods with the help of some of his weaker brothers and sisters. His mother did not have faith that he possessed the necessary strength to finish the job alone, not after David had been through whatever trials Uriel had set for him.

Lilith was sure David had realized his strength, and she was doubly sure he was more of a threat than Asmodeus was willing to accept. Maybe more than even the archangels themselves. Why? This was the question Asmodeus continued to have for Lilith. Did he not have the blood of the divine coursing through his veins as well? What's more, his mother was the proto-feminine, not the facsimile of weakness Eve had been. By all accounts, Asmodeus was this boy's superior, though he found the ease with which David cast him aside on that path to the cabin to be somewhat rattling. But still, some walls take more than one blow to topple.

David raised his eyes to meet Asmodeus's smile. What the demon saw within that gaze told him he would not have the tidy execution he had been hoping for. What the demon saw was the reflection and amplification of his malice by magnitudes. What the demon saw were the flames of the cabin rising around David as he gently lifted Rose from his knees and laid her to rest on the weather-dried wood of the cabin's front patio. What the demon saw terrified him.

David rose, and Asmodeus was devoured by his intentions. Upturned fists framed a young face twisted by rage, all the while the flames spread rampantly about him consuming not just the cabin, but the wet grass around it. Dancing a flurry off the roof, the fire behaved without normal gluttonous intentions. Instead, it lifted, ebbed, and swirled about as though it were writhing in congress with the torrent of pain David was releasing from within. The spectacle was of the rawest quality and beautiful to Asmodeus, who reveled in the very emotion exuding from the darkness within David. Asmodeus learned something as he stood awestruck by the spectacle: David's vessel could overflow.

"What is happening, Uriel?" Michael asked. "I have never seen such from one who was not forged with fire."

"I cannot say I know the answer to your question," Uriel said. "However, I believe David has taken something within him that has allowed for him to easily bridge the gap between his mortal bonds and his divine potential."

"Such beauty," Raphael said, more to himself than his brothers. The archangel of spirit and healing had also become transfixed by the kabuki dance the conflagration performed as David's cries of agony raked the trees around them. "His pain," he said, "it is overwhelming."

Realization caused Michael's expression to turn from shock to anger. "Valhalla. Did you bring him there to meet the serpent, Uriel? Did he receive something from Leviathan?"

"I believe he found the manifestation of that which he has always had within himself, yes," Uriel said. "He will be quite difficult to destroy at this point, I'm afraid. Even for you, Michael."

Uriel removed his blindfold and turned his gaze on Michael. He saw his brother as a beautiful instrument for vanquishing evil and keeping the order they'd grown to rely upon for the entirety of their existence. Uriel knew his brother had come here to annihilate David, but Michael needed David to act first before he'd feel as though he would be justified within the bounds of the creator's wishes.

One must not destroy with wanton abandon. One must prove that the danger David posed to existence was real and present and threatened the very order they were created to keep. After all, the creator did promise to never purge Earth of life again via deluge or otherwise. However, Uriel did not know if Michael would continue to harbor ideas of destroying the boy who shared human and angelic blood, knowing David wielded the same power as archangels such as he. Perhaps more power.

"You have doomed them. You may have doomed us all," Michael said. "There will be punishment."

"The punishment has already been given, brother," Uriel said. "I will be leaving you soon, a price I pay to save him and maybe you. Perhaps it saves everything. Before I go, please hear me. The boy is no longer a boy."

The light cast from the spreading inferno danced on his face.

"The boy is no longer a boy," Raphael repeated.

Michael stood fast, his wings flexing as though they wished to take flight either to gain distance from the spectacle before them or charge forward toward it.

Uriel walked toward the cabin. Neither Raphael nor Michael moved to stop him.

Ω

Asmodeus watched as the flames continued to grow in size, casting colors from across spectra both visible to human eyes and those they were never meant to see. The inferno was nearly upon him, and the heat was unbearable. Asmodeus felt true fear for the first time since the days of Solomon as David's cries coursed outward with the force of hurricane winds. He began to step backward reflexively from the heat, though escape had not yet occurred to him.

The cacophony of sorrow ebbed, and David regained himself enough to register Asmodeus's retreat. In answer to this, he reached a hand toward the perverse demigod. Ropes of blue and red lassoed from the inferno and encircled Asmodeus. He wouldn't avoid these flames, flames he knew were of the same origin of the fiery swords that had brought to heel those much greater than he.

David stepped from the circle of wood where Rose lay. It remained untouched by his rage. He closed the gap between them with a deliberate approach, tearing what remained of the demon's resolve. The warden of lust cried out, "Mother! *Father*!"

His cries continued as he backed to the wall of flames, only to be stopped by heat that would consume him should his feet propel him further. David persisted forward.

"Wait," Asmodeus said. "We can change this. We can reverse it. There are ways to bring her back." Words spilled from his mouth. "Don't you want to see her again?"

David, whose movements had previously been maddeningly slow, appeared instantly before Asmodeus. A hand enveloped in flame reached out. Fingers curled around the neck of the monster masquerading as a human and Asmodeus screamed like a rabbit in the maw of a wolf.

No longer the boy or man he'd wished to be, but the avatar of agony, David began the process of ending Asmodeus's existence when, to the surprise of both, a stream of blue flames appeared in the center of the demon's chest. Asmodeus's face showed his shock at being devoured as blue flame spread throughout his body, reducing him to ash from within. David didn't understand until he let go of the limp neck in his grip, and the body of the demon fell to the side.

Before him, with eyes of pure enlightenment, stood Uriel. "I could not let you kill him out of malice, David."

The sapphire wings had been flexed outward during his attack, and they matched the color of his sword. David looked mutely upon the true form of his friend, Jacob the wanderer.

Vengeance had been snatched from the tips of his fingers, threatening to send David over the brink. He stared deep into Uriel's eyes, no longer worried about being pulled into knowledge too great for him to bear. Before he could act, Uriel stepped forward and wrapped David in an embrace. He held him, and in his touch, David knew Uriel shared his sorrow. His mind calmed.

They separated and Uriel's arms bore the marks of the flames he had met from touching David, flames which burned brighter than his own. He'd been hurt to calm the boy, and he'd known he would be. David remained in silence. Words were too heavy for his tongue to lift as grief overcame anger. He registered the other two angels as they came into the clearing, and though a nuanced recognition of danger told him they were both a threat, he did not move to attack or defend.

Uriel looked to Raphael and Michael and raised his hand. "This first," he said and walked around David toward where the cabin had stood.

The flames, now reduced to small dancing sprites amongst the cinders, no longer warded any of them from approaching. The sapphire angel walked to the small oval of untouched wood and the ashen pearl who lay atop it. He knelt before her with his back to the others.

David panicked and made his way toward Uriel. "What are you doing to her?" he cried.

"Please, David. Please trust in me," Uriel whispered. His wings flared outward to their full span and folded forward over Rose.

David paused, but the tension in him did not release. He felt the presence of the other angels as they approached him from behind and stood beside him, one on his right and one on his left. Neither spoke.

Light emitted from Uriel's enclosed wings and the sound that touched them was that of a flowing river in the spring. David finally eased his tension and no longer leaned forward defensively toward Rose's body. He could feel the benevolence emanating from Uriel.

Once finished, Uriel's wings moved from Rose's body, and he stood with her in his arms. When he turned to face them, they could see she was restored to the picture of beauty she had been before Asmodeus had smeared his evil upon her.

Tears wetted David's cheeks. Lesser emotions of anger and grief were outweighed by superior love. Uriel approached and held her before David, who took her in his arms and collapsed to the floor.

"She is not alive, David," Uriel said. "It is not our place to govern life and death. That is beyond us, but you may once again look upon her as she was meant to be seen."

Michael and Raphael moved to Uriel, who allowed them to approach.

"You've done what we have no right to do in destroying him," Michael said.

"What will happen?" Raphael asked.

"I do not know," Michael said. "I fear he is beyond our protection."

As Michael's words revealed his love for his brother-in-arms and friend, they witnessed Uriel lift into the air before them. No wind rushed under his wings to lift him aloft. He was being taken by another power.

Uriel looked down upon them and smiled. "I have no regrets," he said to Michael and Raphael, who watched in awe, two creatures witnessing something for the first time after eons of knowing an existence without mystery.

"David," Uriel called. "Flourish, my friend. You were brought into creation for a reason. This is what I believe." Higher and higher to the tops of the trees he rose. "Realize your potential as a creation born of both earth and flame, and you may see your Rose again when your journey is complete." Uriel's eyes flashed. "Remember, we all exist to push back the darkness."

At this, the archangel lifted his gaze skyward, and he smiled as his ascent quickened, taking him far beyond the meager forest. A heartbeat of time separated the routine retreat of stars and a great expanse of light to briefly outshine the rising sun.

Uriel was gone.

Raphael and Michael regarded one another and then took to the sky.

David held Rose and rocked gently on the scorched earth. Dawn's light ushered shadows away, and morning dew, heavy with the burden of its own weight, fell gently throughout the forest.

EPILOGUE

The bow of the great freight ship rose and fell on the swells of the Atlantic as the cargo liner coursed its way to the port of Ashdod in Israel. The chief mate called in his report to the captain and relayed that all was well as the second half of the night waned to make way for sunrise.

They were still ten days from port, but many of the crew were uneasy as they began the final leg. The tramp voyage, with their vessel taking cargo from various ports of call as needed, lacked occupancy by those who might have booked passage due to the lack of a set schedule. Despite this, a strange passenger had boarded the ship with payment in hand. He'd known their destination to Israel despite no advance notice having been delivered to travel agencies. Odd, to be sure, but the passenger produced all the necessary paperwork and paid in cash. The captain saw no need to refuse him.

"Spread your arms and embrace travelers to our ship, Emine," he'd said. "Especially when those travelers' fists are gripping coin they are intent on losing."

Emine had called for accommodations for the traveler whose

paperwork identified him as Alexander Scott of the United States. At first, things went as the well-wound gears of a stopwatch, but the rumors began soon after.

"The man doesn't eat, he doesn't sleep," members of the crew said.

"There's nights where heat is coming from his cabin. It burns the hand to touch the door," others said.

Emine was no stranger to the superstitious tales of sailors. As a younger man, he'd once witnessed strange lights in the sea at night, his tales of which had been ridiculed by his then chief mate when he was a younger man. Stories were told, some were true, others were steeped in the fledgling dregs of truth. And some were just that—stories. Still, he was wary of the young traveler, and kept his whereabouts close at hand at all times to ensure he was not a danger to the ship or crew—for his own peace of mind if nothing else.

Tonight, he spied the boy out on the deck of the Panamax freighter, a place where he shouldn't be. Donning the binoculars from a gilded hook on the bridge, he took a closer look and saw Mr. Scott standing there, looking out at the sea ahead. The tails of an overcoat whipped about in the wind behind him.

Emine called down to the sailors on the deck to go out and get the passenger back below or at least back to the safety of the covered crew areas, but he received no answer.

Cursing, he climbed down the stairs and made his way to the front of the ship. The night air was cool about his face as he walked the deck between the containers bound for the western edge of Asia's continent. The stars winked out one by one as the Earth rounded its way to point them back toward the sun.

As he approached the passenger, Emine was confronted by the odd sight that may have emboldened his crew to ignore his summons. Water splashing about the bow of the ship as it cut through the swells of the sea was turning to a fine steam around the passenger. It seemed a trick of the light at first, perhaps the gloaming having an effect on his old weary eyes, but, as he drew within a few tens of feet, surety of what he witnessed solidified.

Great heat was pouring from Mr. Scott as he stood at the front of the ship. Water was unable to reach him. The phenomenon affected the man's attire too, his clothes as neatly pressed and wrinkle free as if he had just removed them from beneath an iron. Emine spied salt falling to the deck in quantities great enough to congregate in sliding piles that pushed with the pitch of the bow and the will of the wind.

"You there, sir," the chief mate called. "Mr. Scott, sir!"

The passenger turned to regard him, and his expression gave Emine pause. There was an intensity on this young man's face that he'd seen before during his time in the Turkish-Iraqi conflict. Young men hardened too soon.

"Passengers are not allowed to ride the bow or be in the cargo area," he said. "I'll have to ask you to return to your cabin until first light. Thereafter, please remain in the crewed areas of the vessel until we reach port."

The passenger's face softened. "I am sorry. I've never had the pleasure of taking in the sea from the front of a ship underway," he said and walked to Emine, who was relieved by the change in Mr. Scott's visage. Something still nagged at him, though.

"What did you say your business was in Israel?" asked Emine as they made their way back.

The passenger paused at this and turned his head to look down into Emine's eyes. "I mean to holiday in Israel for a few days, and then travel to Syria to see my father."

Emine followed as the passenger continued on.

"Syria, you say? That is interesting," Emine said. "Take care in going to a place like Syria. Things are not well in the country these days, as I'm sure you know."

The passenger did not grace Emine's advice with a response.

"Your father, I hope he is safe from the conflict there," said Emine, trying to pull anything from Mr. Scott.

The man calling himself Alexander Scott stopped as waves of heat flowed over Emine, the seaborne chill being torn from his skin.

"He is safe and waiting," said the young man. "Death will not find him unless it travels with me."

March 16th, 2020 — August 20th, 2021

ACKNOWLEDGMENTS

I began writing this manuscript in March of 2020, but the seed was planted over a decade ago as I crossed the span of the Newburgh-Beacon Bridge on my way home from college. Some measure of credit should be given to the state of that bridge for conjuring the thought of plunging into the Hudson River upon driving over it, but more should be given to John Keel, author of *The Mothman Prophesies*, for branding that idea on my mind in a rather unsubtle way. Do read the book and watch the movie if you haven't already. It's a trip.

A debt is owed to all things horror despite this series being firmly embedded in the dark urban fantasy column. For those authors who charmed and terrified me at a too tender age—such as Dean Koontz, Peter Straub, and Stephen King—I give a great many thanks. I'll never forget the feeling of wonder I had while reading *Watchers*, or the sheer terror instilled by *Midnight*, but it was books like *Lightning*, with such charming premises as time-traveling Nazi's who have a change of heart, that truly sparked a flame of intrigue within my young mind. The baton was then passed to stories like *The Talisman*,

Floating Dragon, *Salem's Lot*, and many other tales penned within the last two decades of the twentieth century forming lasting bonds between many readers—myself among them.

I also owe a debt of gratitude to contemporary dark fantasy and horror authors but none more than Kealan Patrick Burke and Todd Keisling—both of whom took the time to guide a stranger through certain murky passages within this rapidly changing industry. I am forever thankful for their kindness, advice, and most of all, their wonderful and terrifying stories.

Editors are the lion tamers of the publishing process and I can't thank Erin Al-Mehairi enough for all the nights she dedicated to helping me develop the manuscript and tighten the writing. I owe my thanks to Angela Traficante, the world's most efficient line editor, Maurice Mosqua for the incredible cover art on short notice, as well as Todd Keisling for taking up formatting this book for multiple platforms.

To all others who touched this project in one way or another, thank you. It's been a dream come true bringing this story to light.

Martin Kearns
Putnam County, New York
August 20th, 2021

Martin Kearns is the author of The Valor of Valhalla series and select short fiction. He is a special education and English teacher and lives with his wife and children in the woods of New York.

"Stories were my first love and during rare moments of quiet my mind turns toward those I've watched, read, and lived. They bring to mind possibilities, which are really where the seeds of a story begin. I truly hope to bring creative tales to readers who, like me, enjoy finding themselves lost somewhere in a world of endless possibilities."

www.readkearns.com

If you are able, please head to your preferred retailer and leave a review for this book. It helps!

Thank You